Praise for *COLOUR*

'Obinna Udenwe's *Colours of Hatred* is a daring novel that spans decades in its examination of how the effects of violence, political upheaval and revenge can alter the lives of individuals irrevocably.'

—Karen Jennings, author of *Crooked Seeds*

'A densely textured novel that produces a fresh view of the diverse ethnicities and impressive cultures of two countries, Nigeria and Sudan, with its deeper currents that work beneath the surface to reveal the otherness that hasn't been comprehensibly perceived. Socio-cultural fusions and clashes are deftly sketched and explored through a bi-cultural perspective, where one can see the variables on both sides of the equation. The wonderfully evocative narrative shines a bold light on the darkest corners of ethnic tensions, wars that leave unmistakable scars on both people and homes, where the worst fears are painfully confirmed.'

—Lemya Shammat
Assistant professor and former head of the languages and cultural studies department at King Saud Bin Abdul Aziz University in Jeddah.

'Udenwe's *Colours of Hatred* is both a commentary on contemporary Nigeria and an exploration of the power of love. He writes passionately about innocence and the loss of it, loyalty and betrayal, love and lust.'

—Chika Unigwe,
author of *On Black Sisters Street*

'Obinna Udenwe paints vivid pictures of life and family complexities in this novel. *Colours of Hatred* is a contemporary tale of malice, of mental health, of parenting, and of posterity.'

—Amara Chimeka
Editor and Publisher at *Purple Shelves*

COLOURS

OF

HATRED

Obinna Udenwe

JACARANDA

This edition first published in Great Britain 2024
Jacaranda Books Art Music Ltd
27 Old Gloucester Street,
London WC1N 3AX
www.jacarandabooksartmusic.co.uk

A CIP catalogue record for this book is available from the British
Library

ISBN: 9781914344329
eISBN: 9781914344312

Cover Design: Rodney Dive
Typeset by: Kamillah Brandes

...to siblings who walked the path of childhood with me,
Adaora Udenwe-Achi and Oketa Udenwe

PROLOGUE

— I have sinned against God and against man.

— What is your confession, my daughter?

— It is a long one, Father.

— Let me hear it.

Prolonged silence.

— Father, do you understand the meaning of beauty?

— What?

— I do not mean the beauty possessed by many, which everyone admires, and many men sell whatever they have acquired in their lives to lure into their beds. I do not talk of the gorgeousness of many who, from childhood, were made to believe they are beautiful and who occasionally stand in front of mirrors in the secret of their rooms and in the absence of the watchful eyes of their mothers to appraise their beauty. It is not the prettiness of those who when they walk down the streets in the sunny noon or on

1

chilly mornings, many turn their heads and strain their necks to appreciate.

I talk about profound beauty; the splendour of few, just a few who were created with the sacredness of beauty, the exquisiteness of some who the Almighty—even before creation—summoned other gods and the angels and a decision was reached on how they would be created or what their features would be. It is the beauty of a few who walk down the streets, even in the darkness of the nights, and all men born of women stare with mouths agape, drooling. They radiate and illuminate such that men neither dream of luring them into bed nor making them their wives. Men wish—just wish—they could feel the texture of their skin, perceive the overpowering smell of their bodies, and imagine angels waving them goodbye.

This confession is also about my beauty, Father.

— Now tell me, what are your sins, my daughter?

— My name is Leona. My mother is from the Dinka tribe in Southern Sudan, and this is my first confession in eighteen years.

SECTION I

ONE

APRIL 2005
ABUJA, CENTRAL NIGERIA

There are some things a human ear should not hear, like a young bride hearing that her groom was just brutally murdered by his own brother. Such things could make the ear bleed.

I flew to Abuja to visit Dad. He was the serving Minister of Commerce, and we were in his palatial sitting room with high stucco-finished ceilings and gold-coated chandeliers. Dad was dressed in white babaringa, just the way Olusegun Obasanjo, his principal, dressed. The white material of his heavy cloth matched the brilliant white colour of the walls that sparkled to the golden light flickering from the chandeliers in the room. Several imported cushions were scattered about and a massive television stood on the ground, almost reaching half the height of the wall behind it, making the images on it seem human.

I sat facing him, alone in the room. What he just said made the quiet of the room seem eerie, but for the almost mute sound coming from the massive television. He swallowed hard, his Adam's apple bobbing up and down, while tears issued from my eyes, streaming down my face and neck and dampening my shirt. Dad came and sat beside me on the cushion, but I drew away, repulsed.

'Look, you have to listen to me, Leo,' His rich baritone was imploring and subdued. He was a smooth diplomat used to getting what he wanted, always. It was the problem he had had with my mother, and why it did not work out between them soon after we returned from Sudan.

'What you propose, Dad, is evil.' I raised my head to look at him. 'I cannot for the life of me marry the son of the man who killed my mother.'

'Look Leona. Listen, please.' He shifted closer.

I moved away, raising my left palm before him.

'First, you should want to know why.'

'Why? No. I don't want to hear anything. There should be no reason for this kind of thing, none at all. None sensible enough to—'

'That's why you are a child, Leo. Look, I have been here for long. I have seen and passed through a lot. I cannot do anything rash. Before talking to you about this, I thought long and hard about it.'

'I have always known you,' I said. *You have always been egotistical and over-ambitious,* I thought but did not say. I stared him down instead.

'Whatever I have done, I did for you. Look, I don't have another child that—'

'Yes, Daddy. You do not have another child with my mother. You have four sons from two other women.'

That shut him up.

He stood and sat on another cushion.

'I loved your mother.'

'Oh, you did!' I snickered.

'I did. We went through hell together. Look, If not for her father's... your grandpa's wealth, I wouldn't be where I am today.'

'You never valued that. You never showed gratitude to my mother. You made her suffer. Even after you were released from detention and saw that she had sustained your business, you didn't treat her right. Women are objects to you, just like I am an object of vengeance to you.'

His mouth hung open. 'You are my daughter, Leona, my beloved child. Whatever I have belongs to you.'

'And not to your boys? Your boys that you wanted so desperately? Your quest for male children made you treat my mother like a rag!'

He looked down. Not that I cared about what he had; my mother left enough for me.

'Boys or not. I value you. You have always been my world,' he went on.

I snickered again. He used the word 'value', each time we argued, as if I was some merchandise he wished to acquire, like a new fast car or a new building in Dubai or New York.

He softened his voice some more; now, it sounded like the meowing of a cat.

'Look, you should want to know why I want you married into the family that killed your mother.'

9

'Why would I do that? Why would I marry Akinola Wale?' I asked.

I wanted to get the discussion done with. I could hear the noise of crockery hitting the sink as they were being washed in the kitchen. It could be Smart, Mum's housekeeper of many years whom Dad inherited and had move to Abuja as soon as Mum died. I made a mental note to discuss the matter with Smart. She would know something.

Dad came back to the couch. I guess it was his routine, every time he had business deals with some foreign diplomats or his business partners—this act of moving to the sofa to sit with you when he wanted to make a point. The way he tilted his head, blinked several times, and made his face innocent and calm could make anyone think he was God's son or the best thing after Azikiwe.

'Your grandpa… remember back then in Sudan when you were little, and he would come to the house in the evening to drink and talk about the war?'

I said nothing and just stared at him. He shook his head in resignation. I remembered everything that happened around that time but did not want to humour him with an answer.

'Once, when they were looking for him, on one of those days when we talked on the phone, he told me that if anything happened to him, I should make sure *you* and your mother were safe. Look, he made me promise him that nothing would happen to any of you and that if anyone harmed your mother, or you, I should retaliate.' He allowed that sink. 'See, my girl. I admit that things didn't work out perfectly between me and your mother. Things didn't go the way we planned or the way we hoped it would, but I loved her. I still love and miss her.' He removed his wristwatch and gold bracelet and placed them beside him. That was usually his way of making me take him seriously. 'Your mother was killed by the man who convinced Sani Abacha to incarcerate me for three years; after all I did for that motherfucking general.' He paused to cough. 'Pardon my words, but when I remember Sani Abacha, my blood boils. Look, your mother was killed by the man who wanted to run my business down. The same man who lusted after my wife while I was away.' He swallowed hard and fast.

'And this is the man whose son you now want me to marry?' I asked, looking straight into his eyes.

'Yes.'

'Why?'

He smiled wickedly, his lips barely moving.

'Because to know your enemy, you have to get close to him.' He sat up, leaned towards me, and said, 'To get back at your enemy, you have to be closer. You are the most beautiful woman I've ever seen. With you around him, he is going to be helpless.'

'How?' My mouth quivered.

'Leona, nullum magnum ingenium sine mixtura dementiae fuit. There has been no great wisdom without an element of madness. Listen, we are going to invoke the old long tradition—an eye for an eye.'

'What!'

11

'A tooth for a tooth.' My eyes widened. The lights in the sitting room flickered, dimming a little. 'Nothing more. Nothing less.' We stared at each other. The silence between us felt tangible. The lights flickered again, and the voltage increased. He looked around. 'We are going to *kill* his son.'

My mouth fell open. Then, the memory hit me, and all that happened to us in Sudan, years ago, came running through my mind.

TWO

1988
KHARTOUM, NORTHERN SUDAN

Do you remember how when you were young, you did things that made no sense and now that you are older, you think about them, reminisce, and laugh like one who is insane? When we lived in Khartoum, I used to count light rays at night. The first night Grandpa and Dad discussed the war was the day Mum caught me on top of Dad's car bonnet counting rays of light, and she reported me to him.

'Leona!' Mum called several times from the sitting room. 'Leona! Leona! Get into the house. Bad things could be lurking about!'

I ignored her. In Khartoum, there were so many lights twinkling at night that you could get caught up for hours, counting or staring at them. I wondered where they came from. I stood on the threshold of the house, staring at the sparkles of lights that illuminated the night from far away buildings and cars. It was a cold night, but after a hot day in Khartoum, one needed a reprieve from the chilly breeze snaking through the night. With my fingers, I counted the lights I could see.

'One, two, three, four,' I spinned my head to count.

Sometimes, flashes of light poured out from vehicles I could not see, and when that happened, I stopped for some time and continued. 'Fifty-five, fifty-six, fifty-seven…' I stepped down the five stairs attached to our house and climbed on Dad's car bonnet. I could see the lights now.

'Leona! Get inside! Now!' Mum poked her head out of the French window and called again. It was then that she saw me.

Our street, Menna Avenue, was not always busy. It was close to Al Qasr Street if I took the turn by the left and walked as if I was going to the madrasa where children sat on rugs spread on the ground and lights flickered like stars. I always wondered if the lights were from the Masjid al-Kabir Mosque. At afternoons, I never saw the mosque, but I was sure that the balls of lights twinkling before my eyes were from the mosque's dome.

'…Ninety-one, ninety-two, ninety-three…'

'Leona!' It was Dad now. I stopped.

'Come inside for supper. Inugo? You hear?'

I climbed down from the bonnet and ran up the flight of stairs.

'I didn't believe it when your mother told me you climbed on my car.' He held me away from him. 'Don't climb up my bonnet again, girl. Are we clear?' He smiled broadly.

'Yes, Dad.'

He escorted me into the living room. It was a two-bedroom apartment built with earth-coloured bricks and roofed with asbestos.

'Look, it is cold out there. I don't know what this girl was looking for outside,' he said to Mum who was in the living room putting down plates of food on the centre-table.

'What were you doing out there, Miss? Counting the stars?'

'I was counting the lights, Mum. They're so beautiful.'

I was standing in front of the table, peering at the large bowls containing grounded maize made into fufu, and egusi soup, made the way Dad taught Mum. He said it was what they ate in Nigeria.

'Imagine her jumping up and down on my car.'

'Leona?' Mum's eyes lit up, but she winked at me.

'I was able to see some lights sparkling from the Great Mosque Kabir!'

A kettle of boiling water whistled in the kitchen, and Mum rushed to turn off the stove. When she returned, she began dishing the food.

I sat on the couch, and Dad sat on the opposite cushion, watching Mum as she served the food. I brought the stools closer to the table so we could sit on them to eat. The aroma of the food permeated the night, and I salivated. I could see through the window, the darkness of the night lit here and there by the light from electric bulbs. I could also hear the cries of our neighbour's baby. Halima was delivered of her baby some days back, and the baby cried a lot. Since Halima returned from the hospital, I had not seen the baby because Mum forbade me from entering Halima's apartment ever. Halima's husband was fighting in the government's army against the Sudanese People Liberation Army, and she did not like us because we were from the south. Mum was not happy with her too. She said there was no need trying to be friends with someone who abhorred everything you did.

I once tried to sneak into Halima's apartment when she was pregnant. I wanted to play with Jemima, but she told me Jemima was not around, even though I could hear her voice in their living room. I told Mum later on, and she said Halima was an Arab witch.

'Tsk-tsk. What woman forbids a child from playing with another child, huh?'

Since Mum called Halima an Arab witch, I swore never to enter her house again because I always listened in when Mum discussed with her friends—all of them from Dinka, who spoke Thuongjang, which I did not understand much—and talked about witches and wizards.

Once, Mum said, 'There are witches everywhere. In villages, they attack people returning late at nights from streams. Sometimes, people wake up in the morning to find razor marks criss-crossed on their bodies. True!'

She was in the sitting room with her friends, it was late in the afternoon, and it was hot outside.

'Aaah! I know. It happens here. A Muslim woman close to my house is one. See. See. Yeah, here. That is the mark. She gave it to me, I am sure.' One of Mum's friends lifted her blouse so that the three of them could see the marks beneath her breasts. Her breasts looked slacken and dark. I looked away so Mum would not catch me gawking at her friend's breasts.

'Eh? Muslim woman? I thought there were no Muslim witches?' the other woman asked.

Mum clapped her hands. 'Tsk. Everywhere, there are witches. James said even in Nigeria, they have witches. Oh! And there, he said, it is quite terrible what the witches do. Terrible!' she spat.

'Aawh! Aawwh!' her friends exclaimed.

As soon as we began to eat, the door was thrown open, and Grandpa stepped in, carrying a huge nylon bag.

'Hallo! Hallo!' he greeted boisterously.

I dropped my fufu and ran into his arms. He carried me up even though I was eight years old and quite tall. Grandpa was tall like Mum, but he had broad chest and shoulders. He also had a full moustache and a short beard, with little hair on his head.

'Welcome, Grandpa! I saw the lights from the Great Mosque! I stood on top of Dad's car!'

'Good evening, sir!' Dad greeted.

'Good evening, James!'

'My queen. My Nubian queen. How many lights did you see?'

'Plenty, Grandpa.'

Mum hugged Grandpa. She drew a stool close to the table, and Grandpa sat down. Then, she brought a bowl of water, and he washed his hands and joined her to eat from her plate.

Dad licked his fingers and asked, 'How was your day, sir?'

'Fine, James. How are the experiments with gum-Arabic going?'

Dad laughed at his joke. Grandpa always asked him about his work with gum-Arabic.

'Business is crumbling. Look, the company may fold and move back to England. The unrest is killing everything. The economy is in shambles, there is corruption everywhere imaginable, and people are dying.'

'I agree. Now let me tell you,' Grandpa lowered his voice. 'This war will last a long, long time, very long time. The army generals in the forests out there in the south are strong and resilient. Most of them do not understand the grammar of a crumbling economy and all.' He belched.

'People like you should help in brokering a truce. You are a respected statesman; you were in the Sudanese Army before you joined SPLM. The rebels in the forest, in the south, and across the Nile respect you; and the government listens to you. Look, that is why we are still here in Khartoum, because we belong to General Joseph Akuei.'

'Yes. That is what we are doing. It is not easy, but we try. We try.'

Mum's stereo played silently in Dad's room, while Grandpa caressed his stomach with his left palm.

'Now, can we eat? You are teaching Leona to talk while eating,' Mum said. 'And please, both of you should stop talking about the war when she is here.'

She threw a glance at me. 'Eat your food, Leona. And stop paying attention to elderly people's talk.'

THREE

When we had eaten, I began to write my homework on a side table close to the door that led to the kitchen, while munching one of the chocolates Grandpa brought. Dad brought two Amstel Beer bottles and uncorked one for Grandpa.

'Oh, James, you know what I need now, a lot of beer in my system after the hot weather today and walking from one government ministry to the other.' He put the bottle in his mouth and took a long drink. Then, he exhaled and smirked.

'It was forty-one degrees Celsius today. I heard it on the transistor at the office. It was so hot,' Dad said.

'You once said it is always this hot in Nigeria,' Grandpa said.

'Not exactly. Look, Nigeria is sometimes thirty, thirty-one, or twenty-nine degrees Celsius. It is never so hot, unless in the north, but I have never been to the northern part of Nigeria.' Dad left Nigeria when he was young, to study in England. 'You said you don't know how long this war is going to last?'

For starting up the war talk, Mum gave him the eye and shook her head.

Dad placed his two legs on the table before him. There was no television in the room, but there was a big radio, into which he had to put twelve batteries before it worked. There were framed photographs on the wall. Several were photos of Grandpa and me at the Nile River and one we took at a shrine at Nubia. There was one of us with Mum and Dad, and pictures of Mum and Dad's wedding in Nigeria. In another, they were in wedding outfits and surrounded by Dad's relatives. Then there was an enlarged medium-sized photo of Mum and Dad with grandpa and mum's sister, Yaya, who was killed at the beginning of the war.

'I know how long it is going to last; a very long time, I must tell you, James. The South doesn't want the North. We are tired of being merged with people who have suppressed us for god-knows-how-long, even before the coming of the white man. We have nothing in common with the North... with the bloody Arabs.'

'If they hear that from your mouth,' Dad laughed and drank from his bottle.

'But they are Arabs.'

Several times, I listened as Grandpa lectured Dad on the history of Sudan and why we were at war. Grandpa believed that the Arabs of northern Sudan are not Africans. 'We are the real Africans.' He would say, proudly.

Once, while Grandpa was arguing with Dad and Mum, he said that in the late eighteenth and nineteenth century, the Northern Arabs came into our lands, riding on horse-back; raiding our people, our farms, and cattle; stealing from us; and taking slaves along with them. And when the British came and made us their colony, it was not a colony of one nation but two; the south, which was tropical and popu-lated by blacks—Dinkas, Nuers, Azandes, and many other hundreds of minority ethnic groups of African descent—and the north, a dry land, a Saharan world with origin and links to the Muslim Middle East.

I brought my homework and showed it to Grandpa.

'Good girl. You are getting it. Now, sum up what you've done. Okay?'

'Thank you, Grandpa.'

Grandpa told Dad that Britain administered the south and the north as separate provinces and discouraged trade between them. He said that Northern Arabs were not allowed to hold positions in the south, but with increased pressure from the north, the two colonies were shackled together as one country in the year 1946. This always infu-riated Grandpa.

'…mostly for the benefit of the North.' He had slapped the table while saying this.

Grandpa said that the worst thing was that they made Arabic the official language, even though the south was predominantly Catholic, and northerners began to hold positions in the south because southerners, our people, were trained in English and were not able to hold positions in their own territory.

Mum came in carrying a large bowl filled with maize. She sat down quietly, pretending to be engrossed in picking out stones from the maize.

Grandpa stood up and went to the window. 'There have always been deliberate efforts to provoke the South. You know what led to the first civil war?'

'The Anyanya Rebellion?'

'Missionary schools in the South were closed, and the government's attack on southern protesters resulted in sporadic fighting and mutinies, leading to a full-scale civil war.'

Mum always told me about the civil war, saying I needed to learn about our history, and when Dad protested, which was always, she would tell him to also teach me about Nigeria's history if he wanted to raise a responsible and patriotic daughter. The Sudanese civil war ended in 1972, helped by what Mum called the Addis Ababa Agreement with a single southern administrative region with various defined powers. She would say that it was the Addis Ababa Agreement that caused this second civil war because it did not address the plight of our people in the south. She said it is why we are continuously made to suffer.

Then, I heard Grandpa say silently from the window, 'I tell you again, James, this war will last longer than the first.'

'Tsk. I wonder why there hasn't been any sort of work-able agreement,' Mum interjected, for the first time, her eyes resting on the medium-sized photo on the wall. A few times, I had caught mum crying in front of the photo, but she always embraced me and said she was not crying, though I did not ask if she was. Then, she wiped her eyes with her sleeve or the edge of her wrapper. The last time, mum was holding the photo like Jemima's mother held her baby while breastfeeding her. That day, she did not wipe her tears, she did not stop crying; she fell on the floor and cried some more, while I watched, sobbing, until Dad returned from work and took the photo from her before taking her into the room, leaving me alone in the sitting room.

Dad fell back on his sit, watching Mum pick the maize.

'Look, agreements never work in Africa. Did you not have the Addis Ababa Agreement during the first civil war?'

'But—'

'You know it reminds me of the Aburi Accord of 1967, reached to prevent war between Biafra and Nigeria. But the war came anyway. Then, there was the Ahiara Declaration that didn't stop the war. Most times, these declarations, accords, and agreements, or whatever name they choose to call it, just become another wartime document. Instead of better, things get worse.'

'The greater part of our problems, in fact, Africa's problems, were caused by Britain,' Grandpa said heavily and sat back on his seat.

'Not greater part, all the problems. Look, same thing they did in Nigeria. In Nigeria, we Southerners are quite different from the people of the north. We have oil, we have rich agricultural fields, and we have water bodies. Yet, they merged us with the North because with the southern and northern protectorate as the same country, it was easier for them to transport farm produce from the north through the water bodies in the South. Now, there is no trust between the two regions. In fact, things are worse than it was before the independence and the war.

'Can I get you more beer?'

'Yes, please, James.'

Dad entered his room and returned with three more bottles, placed two in front of Grandpa, and uncorked one for himself. Mum gave him the side eye and said nothing. When Grandpa left, she would argue with him.

'Why don't you go to bed, woman? I can see you are tired. You're nodding like a lizard,' Grandpa said.

'Tsk. Nodding? Come on, leave me, Pa.'

Outside, it was getting colder. Halima's baby had stopped crying, and the lights from passing vehicles were no longer filtering into the living room. I was done with my assignment, so I crawled into one of the cushions just as Mum checked on the door bolts.

'Are you scared, Jang woman?' Grandpa teased.

'There is war. I am here because my father is a great man in Sudan and my husband works for the white man, and I live in their quarters. Otherwise, I should be with my people, running from one village to the other. Now, let me tell you, Pa, I am scared. I don't sleep at night.'

'You never told me that, Sweet,' Dad said.

'Oh, I don't want you to whisk me away to your faraway country.'

Grandpa laughed.

I used to dream of going to Dad's country. I wanted to see Dad's parents and play with them as I played with Grandpa, but I was afraid of the witches.

'The government is bad, generally. Even the North is not spared.'

'You know this policy of taking land from farmers and transferring it to government officials and merchants, it is awful,' Grandpa said to no one in particular. He beckoned to me, and I sat on his laps. 'You want to sleep, my gazelle?'

'No, Grandpa.'

'They also take land from their own people, from Muslims too,' Mum contributed.

'Yes, that's what I am saying. And it makes me laugh at them because they are turning their brothers against themselves. Soon, it won't be just the South they will be dealing with. The North will turn against Khartoum too.'

A dog barked again; then, two others took their cue and followed suit.

FOUR

There were women dressed in jilbab, selling fresh produce of sidir and baobab by the side of Al-Jamhoriyah Street. There were others selling kisra. Mum and I stopped and paid for five of the popular thin fermented bread. Another woman sitting beside big containers of doum palm fruit-dates and baobab and some traditional handcrafts beckoned to us, telling Mum how one of her trinkets would look good on me. Mum smiled at her and led me away, nearly bumping into a man hawking milk in a cart.

The street was lined by government buildings and other exquisite structures, housing private businesses and banks. Mum held my hand as we walked down the street. There were a few southerners and a handful of white people being driven in Peugeot and Volkswagen Beetle cars. Men selling doum palm milk mixed up with beggars in the streets and road corners, as if standing guard for people selling dates and cabbages. We walked down the side of an Islamic school and entered a shop owned by a young Nubian woman.

'Salaam, everyone!'

'As-salaam alaykum, Madam!'

'Waalaykum salaam!'

'You have brought your daughter like you said yesterday?' the young woman asked.

She was tall like Mum, Her neck had rings and her body was deep brown like the doors in our house. Young women were weaving hairs of ladies clad in long skirts and blouses. One tiny white woman sat on a short stool. She had freckles on her cheeks and nose, and dimples showed when she smiled, which was often. She was drinking Coca-Cola from a bottle while having her hair weaved.

'Yes. Can you make her a new hairstyle this time?'

'Yes, of course... of course, it will be different from the last one.' She brought a stool. 'Now sit, please, little one. Beautiful girl...' the woman said.

The white woman turned to look at me. Our eyes met, and she looked away. People always look away when my eyes met theirs. After some time, the white woman's hair was done. She came to Mum and said to her just as she was leaving, beaming, 'Your daughter is beautiful.'

'Thank you.'

'You are Dinka?'

'Yes, ma'am.'

'Oh! You're good-looking people. And just as well, I am researching on the Dinka tribe.' Grinning, she said, 'I wonder if I could talk to you.' Mum said nothing. 'Do you mind?' the white woman asked.

'Okay.'

They sat by the door, on a long bench.

'What part of Dinka do you come from?'

'I am from Biem.'

Excited, she asked, 'Oh, how do you pronounce that?' The white woman giggled loudly as if someone just gave her some sweets.

Mum taught her. She laughed some more and dusted the edges of her blouse.

'Dinka people are cattle keepers. They are the tallest people in the world,' Mum said with pride.

'Oh! That is awesome. I did not know that.'

I liked the way the woman exclaimed. I made my lips form an 'O' like hers did when she said, 'Oh!'

'You are educated?'

'Yes, of course. Tsk.' Mum rolled her eyes. 'We are partly nomadic people because during the dry season, we move our cattle to the riversides. Now the war is here, things have turned upside down. People are losing their cattle.'

The Nubian woman looked at Mum and shook her head. 'Things are bad,' She added to the conversation.

When we left, Mum would soliloquise about how women who owned shops, especially shops where hair was woven, were gossips, listening in on people's conversations and adding their voices uninvited.

'I was scared to come here. In London, people warned me not to come.'

'Tsk. I wonder why you people love to come here,' Mum said, her face looking serious. 'My husband studied in England, University of Plymouth. He said it is a great

28

country. Splendid, eh?' Mum liked using the word 'splendid'. I also liked the sound. One of the women gave me two confectionaries. Mum asked me to thank her, and I did.

'She is a beautiful little girl,' the woman said. The others agreed and talked about me—how long my legs were, how my neck stood elegantly, and one of them, the oldest, said my eyes were like the stars in the sky at night in the deserts. Everyone nodded in agreement. Mum rolled her eyes. 'England is beautiful. But here, it is natural; everything here is in tune with nature. We have a lot to learn from you. I have been here for four days. It's a great place, but the Sudanese don't value their country.'

'What is there to value in a country torn by war? The first civil war claimed half a million people. Now, the second one. How do we make progress? Now tell me?' another woman who was having her hair plaited asked. She wore a short skirt and a red top, matching her red painted lips.

'Aww! Half a million people? That's too bad,' the white woman said.

The woman with the red lipstick said, 'I studied in Cambridge. I spent four lovely years over there. I never locked my doors. Here, I sleep every night not knowing if I would see the next morning.'

'You are Dinka too?'

The rest of the women laughed.

'No, she is from the north,' Mum corrected.

The women discussed and argued about Dinka, Kordofan, and Omdurman. Someone gave out some dates to those who wanted to eat. In there, in that shop, everyone was Sudanese—Nubians, Dinkans, Arabians—it did not matter. They were one; though they had their personal differences. They all took time explaining things to the white woman. By then, she had ordered Coca-Cola for everyone.

'So Kordofan is in the north, right?'

'Kordofan is in the west, but Dinka also occupies part of Southern Kordofan. They occupy the Bahr el Ghazal region of the Nile basin, Jonglei and the Upper Nile,' Mum explained.

The woman wrote in her small book. She smiled each time someone explained something she found interesting. When she was done, after a long time, and my hair was almost completed, she said, 'I am Margaret. And it was wonderful talking with all of you. One never knows what she learns in ordinary places.'

'And what research are you engaged in?' the woman who studied at Cambridge asked. 'Your thesis?'

'Yes. I am studying for a PhD. Focusing on life in tropical Africa—culture, religion, history, with a special attention on Dinka as the largest clan in Southern Sudan.'

'I wish you luck. Perhaps you could write a book on our people, Margaret,' Mum said.

'I will, my dear. I will. And I will like to meet you again. Is it possible?'

And so, it happened that the white woman became a regular visitor in our house. She would sit in the threshold on an easy-chair with Mum, and they would talk until late in the evening when Dad returned from work. Mum usually served her cooked corn, sometimes rice or fruits. She was always smiling. Once, while they discussed, I heard the white woman ask, 'Do you people believe in God?'

'Ha! Margaret, yes. Tsk. Why not? We do. Oh my God, eh? Margaret!'

They laughed aloud. Then, I saw Halima carrying her baby. She, too, sat in front of her threshold rocking the baby from side to side. I wondered if she was a witch, and if she was, I wondered why her baby was still alive. I had heard that witches killed humans and ate their babies.

'We have only one God. We call Him Nhialic.' Mum made Margaret repeat 'Nhialic' several times. Each time, she mispronounced the name. They both giggled. 'Nhialic speaks through spirits. The spirits take temporary possession of people they chose in order to speak through them.'

'Serious?'

'Oh, I am serious. Tsk-tsk. Not joking, it is real.'

They talked more about magic, about herbalists, and about politics in Dinka. Mum said that they had no central-ised authority but that different clans were governed by Beny Bith, Master of the Fishing Spear. She said that Grandpa's father was one, and Grandpa too, since it was inherited—even though he was now a big man in the city.

'So, what is the duty of this Beny... Bith?'

'He is the traditional chief, the leader of the people. He commands the people to go to war or to fight a neighbour-ing clan—he settles land disputes or quarrels that regularly arise from shepherds or farmers. Sometimes, neighbours quarrel and fight because of cattle.'

'How serious?'

'Cattle are a huge part of our life.'

'That's interesting.'

Halima's baby began to cry.

'The day after tomorrow, I will be travelling to the south.'

'You should be careful. Tsk. There is war.'

'Yes, but the danger is not much yet. There is a lot I need to do. I need to take pictures too.'

'How will you understand Dinka—and any of the Thuongjang dialects?'

'The language? Oh, I am going with a guide who is from your tribe.'

'Splendid.'

They sat back, each to her thoughts. The baby's cries pierced the silence.

FIVE

JANUARY 1989
KHARTOUM

Grandpa and his friend, Thomas Makhar, were seated in the sitting room, talking. There was no breeze that night. I was with Mum in the kitchen, washing some corn. She was whistling loudly; the sound of her whistles always angered Dad. Dad returned home from where he went to meet with his boss, a British woman.

Grandpa and Thomas Makhar stopped talking when they saw Dad.

'What is it, James? Why is your face sullen like that?'

'Your daughter didn't tell you? Look, My company is planning to pack up, sometime this year. Things are not getting better. Prime Minister Sadiq al-Mahdi is not making any effort to end the war.'

'That's it, exactly what I was saying. How would he want the war to end when he is benefiting? Our people are being displaced in the South. In Darfur, things are beginning to turn awry.'

'I am worried.' Dad sat down.

'Why are you worried?' Grandpa asked.

Mum said loudly from the kitchen, 'The Koka Dam Declaration will put an end to the strife soon!'

'Oh, Mary! Your words hurt me. You talk as if you do not know that the prime minister and his cohorts have little regard for that declaration,' Thomas Makhar responded.

Dad said, 'Look, remember I told you about the Ahiara Declaration, didn't I?'

'The parties that met in Ethiopia and negotiated for peace between the government and SPLA should talk sense into this man, Al-Mahdi, eh!' Mum said.

Dad rubbed his eyes. 'I am worried. Look, my wife finds it difficult to leave this neighbourhood every day. My child cannot go to school. We are still alive because we live in this quarters, because you are General Joseph Akuei and they know that we belong to you.'

'See, James. Not to worry. Nothing will happen to any of you. You see, if they touch you, there will be trouble,' Thomas Makhar said.

'Come on, James and Thomas. Let me tell you why Prime Minister Sadiq will not carry out the peace plan. One, he cannot abolish Sharia law. Two, he is afraid of calling a constitutional conference. Egypt and Libya are his allies; so, he cannot cancel the pact between them. All these are what the Koka Dam papers stipulate. He is afraid of them. He is a man afraid of making peace. He enriches himself from this war. Some people do. As soon as peace returns, they cannot benefit. So, what do they do? They make sure that anarchy and violence reign supreme.'

Sitting up, Dad said, 'Look, in Igboland, where I come from, we have a saying, ani adi mma b'uru ndi nze.'

'What does that mean?'

Smiling, Dad said, 'When there is chaos in the land, the leaders benefit.'

'Exactly my point,' Grandpa said cheerfully.

'Your people are wise.' Pa Thomas nodded at Dad. Then, he coughed and said, 'Listen, Prime Minister Sadiq cannot end the state of emergency and call a ceasefire. He is egocentric.'

Dad sat down heavily.

'Do you have a beer, James?'

Dad nodded.

'So, what do the SPLA do then?' Dad asked.

'We continue to fight.'

Dad stood and with his jacket held across the shoulder with the left hand, he went inside. When he returned, he brought three bottles of Abu Jamal Beer from the refrigerator.

'Camel?' Thomas Makhar asked, 'Good beer,' he said as Dad handed him one. Abu Jamal Beer was popularly called Camel by Dad and others because of the photo of a camel on the label.

'Yes, it is. Better than the Amstel Beer you always give me, James,' Grandpa joked. Dad laughed.

'The Blue Nile Brewery will soon suffer some loss due to this war. The war will kill off everything good this country has, I am sure, Abu Jamal Beer inclusive,' Pa Thomas Makhar said, regretfully.

'I doubt that. War or not, folks will continue to drink beer.'

'I wonder how you managed to enter Khartoum, Thomas?'

'Oh, because of the meeting. Now, they cannot do anything to me. But I fear that if things get worse, this might be the last time I will set my foot in this hot desert called Khartoum. I will also travel to Omdurman, using this opportunity to see my wife's people.'

'Your wife is from Omdurman, eh?' Mum called from the kitchen, a hint of surprise in her voice.

'Oh, yes,' he responded.

'This war has eaten deep into the fabric that binds us together. Tsk-tsk; a southerner marrying a northerner, a Nubian marrying a woman from Khartoum-North. Tsk. It is a pity now that all that has to stop!' Mum called again from the kitchen.

'And a Nigerian, a man from a distant country across the distant sea marrying a Dinka woman, isn't that the height of it all?'

'Ah, General!'

Dad laughed.

Mum entered the sitting room, saying, 'Okay, because of this war, I divorce him, and hereby solemnly announce that from now on, all Sudanese women should marry only men from their ethnic group, hmm.'

Mum's right palm was on her breasts as she talked.

'You would make a good sergeant, woman.'

'As soon as they grant the south autonomy, I will join the army.'

'Look, why not join now, Sweet?'

'Ha, James! Now there is a lot of bloodshed, huh. I cannot join now. Tsk. You will die if you woke up one morning and found that I had left Khartoum to join the Liberation Forces.'

'Die? Look, I will go to the broadcasting station and proudly announce it,' Dad said. Everyone laughed. He sat down on the cushion and stretched himself on it. 'Then, you would take a photo of yourself after you have been there for one week and send to Leona and me.'

'Oh, your husband would want to see you in rags, looking so thin,' Pa Thomas added. 'I thought he loved you?' he laughed.

'True. True. Life in the Liberation Army is difficult,' Grandpa said. His face had lines of regret.

'The rebels are at a disadvantage. That was how it was in Biafra in sixty-seven.'

'We don't call them rebels. They are liberationists.'

Dad nodded, and then said to Grandpa, 'You know, Sudan reminds me of Nigeria. Look, Britain has caused so much hardship in Africa, and now they pretend they are doing us good, pacifying us with the Commonwealth stuff—Commonwealth Foundation, Commonwealth of Nations, this, and that. Look, it is all bullshit. It amazes me that they watch all that is happening, knowing it was their fault. And they still have the temerity to call us barbaric. All these ethnic cleansing and war wouldn't have happened if peoples with distinct history, religion, and culture weren't nailed together with a British hammer.'

Some vehicles hooted in the street. They paused for some seconds and continued.

Grandpa sat up. He told Dad that we have a similar political and colonial history with Nigeria. He informed Dad that on decolonisation, Britain ceded most of the powers to the northern elites, causing unrest in the South, and that during the transitional periods in 1950, when Britain was granting Sudan independence, the southern leaders were not even invited to the negotiation table. Grandpa hit the side of his head hard and continued, saying that out of the over eight hundred administrative positions available during the post-colonial period, only six southern leaders were included in the Sudanisation Committee.

Thomas Makhar broke in, 'I have always referred to that as nonsense Sudanisation Committee.'

The men laughed.

A dog barked in the silence as if to agree with them. A military vehicle passed our gate with speed, soldiers chanting.

'The government enacted a lot of damn fucked-up laws.'

'Hey!' Mum called and pointed in my direction. They ignored her.

They talked for some time. Then, Grandpa stood up from his seat and came to sit close to Pa Thomas. Dad noticed he wanted to share information that must not be whispered aloud, for the night had long ears.

'Let me get some more beer.'

But Dad had hardly turned when Grandpa said, 'There is trouble looming. If it happens, my prediction that this war will last forever will become true.'

Dad was silent. He was thinking of the safety of Mum and me. He hated it anytime there were rumours of the war lasting longer.

'There is a man in the government's army, Colonel Omar Hassan al-Bashir. He is dangerous.'

'I know him,' Dad and Pa Thomas said at the same time. There was silence. 'I fear that a coup might be in the offing.' The silence lengthened.

'I would love a coup. They should kill themselves. You never can tell; that could lead to the disintegration we yearn for—'

'Not when Colonel Al-Bashir takes over. He is as cruel as Cardinal Cesar Borgia.'

'This coup you talk about, how true is it?' Pa Thomas asked low-toned. We barely heard him.

'There are many chances that it is going to take place. Worse is, if it happens, things will change badly for us. The colonel and I are not the best of friends. He hates me as much as I loathe him.'

SIX

It was towards the end of May. There had just been a sand-storm, and Dad's car was covered in dust. He was washing it, and I was playing with Jemima at the front yard. Her mother went to the market where she sold the mats she wove in their house. Jemima's hair was braided to the front of her forehead. I liked the style of her braids. She wore a trouser and a long blouse. As we rolled the used tyre Dad changed from his car up and down the yard, two men walked into our compound and stood before Dad. They were men who looked as tall as Grandpa, but their bodies were lean.

I rolled the tyre in their direction. Then, I ran towards Dad's car to pick it and heard what they said.

'Tell him to return to the camp. Tell him the comman-dants of the SPLA want to see him.'

'I hope... all is well?'

'He knows why he's avoiding us. But tell him that he cannot run forever. He cannot. We loved him; we trusted him. His fathers before him championed the Dinka cause, he even lost a daughter to this war, but he betrayed his people.'

I heard the tall, lanky man clearly. I raised my head and

watched as he approached Dad, so close that his nose was almost touching Dad's.

'Look—'

'Tell the general that if we could risk everything to travel to Khartoum to deliver this message, it means we can get him if we want. He needs to come back and clear himself.'

Dad was silent. They walked away. When Dad turned and saw me, he asked me to go inside the house. I dropped the tyre and went in. Dad followed and we got to the living room; Mum was standing by the door. She was looking tired and afraid. There were beads of sweat on her forehead. She was holding a table towel and her hands were trembling slightly.

'I know one of them, eh. The one who spoke last,' she said.

'Oh! You saw them?'

'Yes, from the window. He is a devil. What's wrong, eh?'

'It is your father's issue with the SPLA. Look, I don't know what is wrong. But whatever it is, I think it is huge. They said he cannot run away forever, whatever that means. And that I should tell him that if they could risk their lives to enter Khartoum, they can find him.'

Balls of tears escaped Mum's eyes, and Dad caught her in his embrace and led her to the couch.

'Shhh! Shhh! All is well. All is well. They'll sort themselves out. Look, your father is a survivor. He is a warrior. He is their lord.' That night, Dad called Grandpa's friend, Doctor Malik Al-Jazrula, and they talked briefly. When the call ended, he told Mum that Doctor Malik promised to contact Grandpa. In the morning, the phone rang several times before Dad reached the sitting room. It was early in the morning, at about half past five, and the cocks were crowing occasionally. The breeze was not much, but it had not been a hot night. I was on my bed dreaming of Grandpa when the telephone sounded and woke me. I could hear Dad saying, 'Okay, sir. Okay, sir. Look, I will come right away.'

Dad entered his room and talked with Mum. After some minutes he drove out.

When Mum came to my room, she said to me, 'Your father has gone to see Grandpa in Atbarah, hmm.'

I once went to Atbarah before with Grandpa. It is in the north-east. One of Grandpa's rich friends who always argued with him was from that place. The last time he hosted us alongside Doctor Malik Al-Jazrula, he said the war would teach the South not to mess with the North, but he became angry when Grandpa said that it was people like him who caused us not to live in peace in Sudan.

'Because of the likes of you, I wonder if there is a time when we will live in peace in this country unless Sudan is divided. Now let me tell you, what caused this war is the North, because you people have nothing. This whole place is a desert. You see how hot it is, and this is May. In the South, there are oil fields, and the revenue from the oil gives Sudan over seventy percent of her GDP. In the South, we have a lot of tributaries to the Nile, a lot of water bodies. So, our land is more fertile, for we have more rainfall. Take Khartoum for instance, they have rainfall for only a few months in the year. The rains are never as enough as in the South. The North is sitting on the edge of the Sahara Desert, literally.'

When Doctor Malik and another friend tried to interrupt, Grandpa said, 'The North is greedy. And it is this greed to control our oil that will make this war to continue.'

'Your oil or Sudan's oil, James?'

'Here we go again!'

SEVEN

JUNE 1989
KHARTOUM, NORTHERN SUDAN

The radio had just announced a coup, and people were running helter-skelter. Everyone was talking about it. It was said that Colonel Omar Hassan al-Bashir had become the president, prime minister, chief of state, and chief of the armed forces of Sudan. In the midnight, a car stopped in front of our house. I peeped from my window and saw some soldiers come out of the car and stand by it. Grandpa came out too and glanced about. He came to the door. Dad opened it even before he knocked. It was the last day of June.

As soon as he entered the living room, I ran out and hugged him. He kissed me on the forehead.

'How are you, Goddess?'

'Fine, Grandpa.'

'How do you do? Did you miss me, my Nubian queen?'

'Oh yeah, I did, Grandpa.'

He dipped his hand into his pocket and fished out a necklace. The pendant had Pharaoh's face carved into it. It looked like a mask. Mum came out, rubbing at her eyes. He hugged her and kissed her chin.

'Dear. Dear.'

'Pa. How are you? I have been scared.'

A police siren could be heard in the distance. Some crickets chirped at the backyard. Grandpa was silent. Then, he turned and said to me.

'My goddess. It is night. Run to your room and sleep.'

'Okay, Grandpa. Will I see you in the morning?'

'Yes, of course, my goddess. I will be sleeping over.'

'What of those soldiers? They are waiting for you?'

He hesitated and looked away from me.

'Yes. They will wait until morning. Now go, my goddess.'

I went to the room but did not get into bed. I eavesdropped.

'We have food in the house. Should I get food, Pa, eh?'

'Don't worry. I can't even sit.' His voice changed.

My heart was thudding against its walls. I wondered if they could hear the sound.

'Pa, I am scared.'

Grandpa ignored Mum and said, 'Now. Listen, James,' he addressed Dad.

'Sir?'

'Did you make travel arrangements as I asked you to when you came to Atbarah?'

'Yes, I did. Our documents are ready too.'

'Documents? I didn't know… James?'

'I am trying to get things fast-tracked, sir.' Dad ignored Mum.

Grandpa looked at Mum and said, 'Calm down, Mary.

I asked James not to tell you.' He took in a deep breath and sighed. An owl cried loudly somewhere close by.

'I may not have much time. Some treacherous people are after my life.' Then, he lowered his voice; it was shaky. 'I am going to leave for Egypt within the next few days. From there I will travel to London. I have saved enough money in a bank in Britain, if anything happens to me. Take this.'

He gave Dad a bulky envelope. 'It will be of help to you when you get to Nigeria. Your company in England can help you process it. It is a lot of money. I have made you next-of-kin. You hear?'

There was a long silence. 'Tsk. Nothing will happen to you, Pa.'

'Nothing will happen to me, my child. Listen, if I get to Egypt, I will travel to London, and you and Leona can visit. Perhaps you may all relocate. Understand?'

'Yes.'

'Now, I have to go.'

There was silence. I could hear Mum sobbing. Then, I opened the door and ran out.

'Grandpa!'

He turned, and I ran to him. That moment, the room became so cold and sent shivers down my body like I had never experienced—not even on those nights that I stood on Dad's car in the cold, counting rays of light. The frogs at the drainage outside the house became silent. Grandpa held me for some time. It seemed as if he held me for one hour, but it was less than a minute. Mum was on the sofa, holding the helm of her nightwear over her mouth.

'Would you like to come to London, Goddess?'

'Yes, Grandpa. But don't leave now.'

'Don't worry.' He held me so I could look at him. 'Hey, listen.

Listen. I am travelling to London. Now turn.' I did.

'You see what your father is holding? Yeah. You see, I have given him some papers that he will use to bring you to London soon. Okay?'

I recalled that Margaret came from London. I liked Margaret. 'Okay, Grandpa. Are you sick, Grandpa?'

'I am fine.' He looked at me and asked with conviction, 'How old are you?'

'I am nine, Grandpa.'

'Good. Now you are a big girl. Big girls don't cry, you know?' I smiled and cleaned the tears from my eyes. 'Now, go,' he said. 'James!' Grandpa called.

Dad came and held me. Grandpa kissed my cheeks and left.

After a few seconds, the car roared to life and went into the night.

The new president had just established the Revolutionary Command Council for National Salvation and had banned all non-religious institutions including the trade unions and political parties. There was panic on the streets. Women sat in front of their thresholds, gossiping quietly; but men were silent because one did not know whom to trust and whom not to talk to.

It was late evening, exactly six days after Grandpa came. Mum was reading Margaret's letter, which arrived from London that afternoon. She had been busy and could not read it immediately it came. We had not heard from Grandpa again. Then, Pa Thomas Makhar opened the back door of our house and came in. Dad who was coming out of his room was startled.

'Pa Thomas? Oh! What is wrong that you come in from the back door?'

'Where is your wife?'

'Mary?'

'Who else? How many wives do you have, man?'

'She's in the sitting room.'

They entered the sitting room. Mum stood immediately. Alert. 'What is wrong? Has anything happened to Pa, eh?' Mum asked in trepidation.

'No. Sit down.' Dad and Mum sat.

He came and touched my head. 'There is trouble. I have not heard from the general. But you need to leave here as soon as you can… this night.'

'Okay!' Dad said. Mum began to sob.

'The SPLA is searching for the general—'

'SPLA?'

'Did he not tell you what is happening, James?'

'No, he didn't. But I understand there is trouble.'

Pa Thomas sighed heavily. 'Listen. Your father-in-law. He accepted a lot of money from the government and established a rebel group. He got some soldiers who were loyal to him to form another group, outside of the SPLA. The idea was to sabotage the SPLA and cripple the cause—'

'Oh, my God! Oh, my God! Oh, my God!' Mum cried. 'Why would he do that?'

'I am talking, James. I don't have much time. Your in-law believes that the civil war will go on for eternity. He thinks that the people of Southern Sudan will lose so much if it continues. He once told me that if we must secede from the North, it must be a gradual process, evolutional. He said our people need to acquire education, enter into trades, invest, travel out, and become influential. Then, we can do it. He believes that the military process is difficult and deadly—' Mum began to sob more. My eyes filled with tears and wandered between her and Dad. 'This new faction is led by a man called Nasiru, a young man, ruthless and strong. He's educated, but he was also trained in Somalia. Your in-law knows what he is doing, but he may have made mistakes. The SPLA is full of war-hungry and bloodthirsty people, full of people who are tired of what the North is doing to us and they know that, or rather, they fear that a democratic process will never work or will take hundreds of years. They have to take their destiny by force. The kingdom suffereth violence and only the strong taketh it by force. Do you remember that part of the Bible? I am old; I can't remember,' he asked no one in particular and managed to smile.

'Now, the SPLA have declared him a saboteur, a traitor.'

The ceiling fan swirled slowly, producing little comfort and some discomforting sounds.

'Haaaa!' Mum cried aloud yet again.

A baby's cry shrieked from our neighbour's house. Jemima ran out, calling someone's name. Some cars sped past. Then, everywhere became calm again.

Pa Thomas stood. He was wearing baggy trousers and a brown shirt. He wore a bowler hat and spectacles, but he looked strong even for his fifty-ish age.

'When should we leave?'

He stood, 'Immediately.'

He walked out the way he came.

EIGHT

1989
OMDURMAN, NORTHERN SUDAN

That night, around seven o'clock, a white Peugeot 404 wagon, driven by a short Arabian, stopped in front of our apartment in Khartoum. That night would open the door to the event that would change our lives forever.

'You have to hurry. Be quick,' the Arabian said in a whisper, all the time looking over his shoulder as Mum and Dad hurriedly threw a few bags into the boot. 'You have to hurry.'

Dad pushed me into the car. We were smuggled to Omdurman.

Omdurman is the largest city in Sudan. As we were driven through the streets, there were shops open for business, cars speeding past in large numbers, and people walking about. Men and women held hands as if the tension in the country had no meaning in Omdurman. There were others, dressed in quftan, rushing to the mosques for the solat. In some shops, music blared and lights radiated like kaleidoscopes in the air. I could not stop staring at the lights.

Finally, a gate opened, and the car drove through a gravelled driveway and stopped in front of a mansion built in the style of ancient Egyptian architectural design.

'Look, Doctor Malik Al-Jazrula's house,' Dad said to no one in particular. 'Remember him?'

It was an intimidating structure. At the back of the mansion was an orchard that stretched out to either side of the building and was visible from the entrance. The driver led us into the sitting room. It was a large room that led to a spacious courtyard of green lawns, made more beautiful by a water fountain and from there into several rooms whose doors opened into the courtyard. There were no couches, rather, there was an exquisite Persian rug and small pillows, and there were men sitting on the rug, papers spread in front of them. They were drinking milk from breakable china plates.

'As-salamu alaykum!' the men greeted.

'As-salamu alaykum!'

'Walaykum salam!' Doctor Malik Al-Jazrula stood.

He stretched his hands and hugged my dad, to my greatest surprise and relief, Grandpa stepped into the room. He took me into his outstretched arms as I fired questions at him. Then, Mum and I were taken to greet Doctor Malik's first wife and her six children. Thereafter, we were taken to the left chamber of the building to greet his second wife, a Nubian woman who had borne four children. One of them, Lemya, who recently moved in from her grandmother's place, was my age.

Lemya and I shared her room that night, and she told me about her school and about her half-sisters, whom she said were Muslims and ate with their hands and prayed all the time. She said she wondered why one would pray many times a day as if God was stubborn and needed to hear the prayers often enough to answer them. Lemya told me that the first wife always covered her face and, at first, she wondered what she looked like but she had finally seen her face and the woman had scary eyes. I had never met someone who could talk so fast and so much at the same time—like a bird.

In the morning, after breakfast, a Volkswagen beetle came for us. It idled by the gate. We were to be taken to the airport so we could leave for Nigeria. Grandpa said he had arranged with Doctor Malik Al-Jazrula's secretary to auction everything in our apartment in Khartoum. I had left many of my things, and I was unsettled about this. I was also not happy with the idea of travelling to Dad's country where Mum and her friends said there were lots of witches.

Grandpa stood by the chocolate-coloured gate, just close to the car, waving at me. Then, Mum forgot something and came out of the car.

'Woman, hurry up! It is not safe here!' Grandpa called.

Mum ran along the driveway towards the mansion. As soon as Mum disappeared into the large house, a new red coloured Peugeot 504 sped towards the Volkswagen, screeching, causing a cloud of dust to rise to the air such that we were blinded. Grandpa made to run back to the mansion but halted—perhaps he recalled that we were in the car. He spun around and drew out a shiny pistol from his belt and aimed at the Peugeot. He shot once but missed, for the car had skidded past and stopped beside him. Four men rushed out, carrying machine guns. He shot the first man on the forehead; but his bullet missed the second man who swooped on him and knocked him down with the butt of his heavy gun.

Doctor Malik Al-Jazrula's driver, who had been in the Volkswagen, ran down the street, screaming and flapping his hands, while we rushed out of the car. By then, three men had grabbed Grandpa. They stabbed him several times in the chest with three long daggers, and blood spurted and poured on their faces and their hands. I was screaming. Dad jumped over the Volkswagen, grabbed me, and tried to run towards the building opposite us, but someone rushed out of the Peugeot. He was pointing a gun at Dad.

'No move, Mister!'

He grabbed Dad by the wrist and spun him around.

'Please, in God's name. Please!'

His blow sent Dad to the ground. Another man came out of the Peugeot. He was their driver. He stood watching as the man who had grabbed Dad looked at me and asked, 'Where your mother?'

I was screaming, because of Grandpa and because the man who was staring at me had one of his eye sockets empty. A long scar ran from his forehead down to his chin. He was as tall as Grandpa; his head was shaven. His cloth looked worn-out.

'Where your mother?' he asked again.

I screamed.

'Please! Please, don't hurt my daughter. She is also, she is also your daughter. She has Dinka blood in her. Please,' Dad begged.

The driver said, 'I do not kill someone who does not look for my trouble. You are not from here, so I cannot hurt you, but your wife?'

Dad's eyes met mine briefly. I understood and ran. I hid behind the hedge in front of the other building opposite Doctor Malik Al-Jazrula's. The men did not give chase. The man with the hollow socket hit Dad and he fell. He forced Dad on his feet to face him. I watched as the others made sure Grandpa was dead. It was then that I noticed that people who were passing by had run back and were watching from a distance. No one came out of Doctor Malik's house. I wondered if they heard the gunshots and the screams.

Then, the one-eyed man said to Dad, 'We know your wife is in there.'

SECTION II

NINE

The walls of the sitting room—the paintings and artworks on them, the television, and the cushions were all blurry before me. My eyes were misty. The mist clogged my mind. I could not think clearly just as I could not walk straight until I got into Smart's room. My father wanted me to kill a man. He wanted me to live with this man, love, and cherish him for a few years, and just when I had made him trust me enough as his wife to leave everything for me in the case of his death, I would poison him. Me who could never hurt a fly; me, who even if I was at the scene of my mum's death and was face to face with the assailant, a gun in my hand, the assassin defenceless, I would not hurt him.

Smart sat up when she saw me. She had been reading from a prayer-book. I could see the confusion in her eyes. We were not on speaking terms. Sometime ago, when I was twelve and she had just come to live in the house, she noticed that for about two days, I was walking crookedly like a cat that was just hit on the fore-legs with a stick—

59

a young university undergraduate had just deflowered me. Without hinting directly, she asked me to massage my private part with hot water; so, I stayed away from her after that. Sometimes I wondered if by her knowing or guessing what happened to me and daring to give advice, I should have been close to her. She had tried several times in the beginning to court my friendship, but I always ignored her, ashamed, afraid of exposure.

Now, I was in her room, all teary-eyed and I was sure she did not know how to react. She said nothing until I sat on the bed beside her.

'Smart.'

'Leona.' She looked at me sceptically.

It was a blue-painted room; the embroidered curtains swept the floor. Her clothes were scattered about on the arms of a chair by her wardrobe. I could see some underwear here, a hair net there, a brassiere on the floor.

'Smart, I need to talk to you.'

She said nothing. She closed the book she was holding and brought her legs to the floor, her back raised. I could see some grey hairs on her head. When the incident happened at Enugu, she was in her late twenties. Now she was getting older—in her forties, I guessed. I wondered if she would feel comfortable discussing my predicament, discussing marriage with me when she was not married, when most of her life had been dedicated to serving my mother, and now my father.

I changed my mind and instead of telling her about my

dilemma regarding getting married, I asked her, 'Tell me, Smart. Did Mum ever mention anything about Chief Fegun Wale to you?'

She looked at me and said nothing.

'I want to know if you believe, if you believe the Wales have a hand in her death.'

'Leona… not many people think that.' She looked at me. 'Aside from your father and his close friends.' She shifted away. 'Why are you crying?'

I lied. 'My father believes strongly they did. I don't believe that. I don't want to believe that.'

'Then, don't.'

We said nothing then, and I pondered if I should tell her about my father's suggestion. But how could I tell anyone that I had been asked by my father to marry a man who had not even asked for my hand in marriage and poison him afterwards, a man I was not quite sure knew a thing about the death of my mother? I changed the story. 'Did Mum ever tell you anything about Chief Fegun Wale or his family?'

'Madam always mentioned that Chief Wale had a hand in chief's imprisonment. Chief Wale was Sani Abacha's friend. Everyone knows that. She never mentioned anything else.'

I looked at her. The way she sounded made me think she was not telling me the entire truth.

'I think you do not need to worry your head about who killed Madam, your mother. All I know is that whoever did, God will not allow the person to *rest*.'

'Not that I am interested in looking for whoever killed

her if—after all—she was killed, but when someone begins to point my mind to a certain direction, it makes me bitter. I hope this direction does not end up being a reality.'

'I think we should pray for Madam's soul to rest in peace, eh. That's all. It's been over two years since she died. God knows best.'

I took a deep breath. 'Good night, Smart.'

She watched as I walked out the door.

I could not sleep that night. I tossed and tossed over and over. When sleep eventually came, I had a nightmare. There were lots of wolves in the forest. They surrounded my mum, but she never seemed to be aware of their presence. I watched from a corner, unable to reach out and save her. I woke up and wondered if her soul was not at rest, if she wanted to be avenged. I wondered if the best way of avenging her was to kill the people who killed her; but who killed her? Why was she killed? One thing was certain; if she was murdered, whoever killed her did that to get at Dad, one way or the other. And if it was Chief Fegun Wale, would it be right to retaliate? If Dad had reasons or evidence to believe that he killed Mum, he had the wherewithal to make it public and seek justice. Why was he asking me to do it for him, for us? Why was he dragging me into darkness?

I showered and called Onyinye Ilo in London. She was studying at a university there. Whenever anything bothered me, I discussed it with Onyinye. We grew up together in Enugu and attended the same primary and secondary schools as classmates. It was her sister who arranged for her friends to have sex with us after she convinced us that it was the best thing in the world. I shook my head, trying hard to send the memory away but it was the sort that never left you, no matter how hard you tried.

Onyinye complained so much about the weather—she always did. Then, she told me about boys, how they were experimental. She never stopped talking about this.

'And you?' she asked. 'Are you still with that Kosisochukwu?'

'Of course, we are still together.' I rolled my eyes, antici-pating where this discussion was headed.

'Your people won't approve.'

'I don't need their approval, Onyinye. How many times will I tell you that?'

'You should look further. Cast your net wide. You never can tell what you will catch now that your father is a minis-ter. There are better opportunities, girl.'

'I don't want those opportunities. I love what I have. I am not complaining.'

'The boy is a seminarian for Christ's sakes!'

'Ah! Don't remind me. You break my heart—'

'Sorry,' she pleaded. 'Just that, as your friend, I thought it would be wise if I don't tell you lies. I can't deceive you. Soon, he will be a priest. Will you keep fucking him?'

'We make love. We don't fuck.'

'Spare me that bullshit. What's the difference? Okay. The difference is in the doing, huh. Okay,' she giggled. She had not changed a bit. 'You should try both, and to do so, you need to cast your net wide.'

'Try some other time, babes.'

'Well, what happens when he becomes a priest?'

'I don't know.' Instantly, I developed a headache. It always happened when someone mentioned the lunacy of my behaviour, hinting that Kosi and I had no chance together. I wished I could talk to Kosi. How I missed him! Thinking about him gave me headache and caused me to sweat more. I yearned to speak to him, to pour myself out to him, but I could not call him. It was going to be difficult to explain, even to Kosi whom I loved so much, the plans my dad had, the things he wanted me to do. 'I guess it's complicated.'

'And you sef, what are you even doing with a semi-narian? It is complicated, yes, but uncomplicate yourself na, sweetheart.'

'I think I should go back to sleep.'

'Hey. Have I vexed you?'

'Yes.'

Silence.

'I am sorry.'

'I know. Don't worry. But I need to sleep. I will call tomorrow or next.'

I thought of telling her about my father's suggestion.

'Babes, is something the matter?'

'I will tell you later.'

I ended the call before she could probe further. The clock ticked away. It was three o'clock, already. The dogs barked several times. The air conditioner hummed. Beside it hung the big rosary Kosi gave me from his pilgrimage to Jerusalem. I did not know how to say the rosary; I never said the rosary all my life, but I cherished this one and took it to Abuja from my room in Enugu. Now, whenever I remembered Kosi or someone—mostly Onyinye—mentioned him, my eyes went to the rosary.

It was funny how the rosary, instead of making me hunger for his touch and yearn for his tongue playing with mine, reminded me of his chosen career. It sort of served as a constant reminder that I was sleeping with one who would soon become a Catholic priest, not that it bothered me. Sometimes, I thought about what would happen when he became a priest, and I concluded that it depended on him if he wanted us to continue making love. I did not care. Whoever made the rule that priests were to be celibate did not have me in mind and they would rot in hell, as far as I was concerned. It was as if they intentionally set out to punish me. Whenever I thought of this, I wondered if I would have agreed to marry him, if Catholic priests were to be allowed to get married. I used to picture myself standing beside him in the altar, as his wife. Often, I wondered what I would look like, how I would dress as the priest's wife—in skirts too long they swept the floor, in blouses too big with shoulder pads puffing out like feathers. This made me laugh most times. Would I be required to lead some prayers, and counsel young people and couples and all sorts. I shook my head at this.

I lay down and covered myself, remembering things.

When we moved to Enugu, I was nine going on ten. Enugu is a city on a hill, and this accounts for its cold early mornings. When it rains in the evenings, it comes with so much force that vehicles have to park on roadsides, and in the dry season, vehicles and heavy winds raise dust, covering people's windscreens. At home, we dusted our furniture and crockery regularly. In several ways, Enugu is different from Khartoum. There are lots of open markets where women sell everything you can imagine; oranges, pineapples, bananas, pears as big as people's heads, and ugu vegetable for soups. Children play on the street until late at night, and women who live in apartment buildings with several other families gossip and fight regularly. It is in this ancient city—that was once the capital of the East Central State and of the lost nation of Biafra—that we bought a house as soon as we arrived from Sudan.

Every morning, when I awoke to the sound of cars speeding past our gates and honking, I would go downstairs to say, 'Good morning,' to my parents and eat a breakfast of bread and tea that tasted unlike what we ate in Sudan. I was adored and worshipped by everyone in the house; my parents, the gateman, the cook, and the gardener; even relations who visited told me how beautiful I was—I was taller than most of them.

Dad had established a business in Nigeria. He imported pharmaceuticals, and with Grandpa's money, he had created a niche for us in the social class of the town. After school, I received lessons from an elderly woman who served as my home teacher. She often stared at me more than she stared at the blackboard. When the afternoons were hot, we stayed inside Dad's large and spacious library and turned on the air conditioner. In school, I did excellently because my home teacher was always ahead of our school calendar. Plus, the food was superb. Things were good, and we were rich.

Dad built a huge business with Grandpa's money—part of the money he took that day at Omdurman. The school was great. I had good friends, but things were no longer smooth between Mum and Dad. They had turned into strangers living together. Mum would threaten to leave for Sudan, and Dad would say nothing. She would threaten to leave with me, and he would scream at her. But he knew—we knew—that Mum would never leave for Sudan. Her father and her sister, Yaya, were all dead and her extended family scattered across Southern Sudan, running from the war they had no idea when it would end. Dad knew that Mum would die if she visited Sudan. Perhaps this spurred him to behave badly towards her, knowing that she was trapped. Now that I think of her death, the sacrifices she made, and what her father went through to protect us in Sudan and to save up for our future, it made me mad.

I recalled when Dad's mother visited from the village. Before then, I had seen her only once since we returned to Nigeria. The day she visited was a Friday, and I did not go to school because Dad took me to a dentist after Mum suggested I see one to extract a tooth that was giving me trouble. I remember that I wondered about the wisdom in removing my tooth and if it would grow back after a dentist forced it out.

That morning, as we drove to the hospital, I was frightened, not because I hated injections, but because I wondered how the doctor would pull out the tooth. Would he use pliers? When I asked Dad, he grunted, said nothing, and set his gaze on the road. Since we returned from Sudan, he was always like that—quiet, cold. I had overheard him arguing several times with Mum. One word that kept popping up was 'ambitious'.

'You are becoming too ambitious!' Mum would scream at him.

By the time we returned home from the hospital, Dad's mother was there, seated like a cow on one of the cushions in the sitting room. She was a teacher in a primary school in the village. She spoke simple English and talked slowly as if searching for words to use all the time. When Dad and I stepped into the sitting room—me first, Dad following behind, his hand on my shoulder—she was resting her head on a throw pillow. I was surprised to see her. A piece of cotton wool soaked with some medication was in my mouth and it made me mute like a dumb. Dad was also surprised to see her.

He hurried to her. 'Ah! Ah! Mama,' he said. 'Look, you should have informed us you were coming. We would have sent the driver to pick you up. How did you find here?'

Both of them hugged, the kind of hug you give with your hands widely outstretched, and your chest meeting the other's, then your hands circling them round the neck or the waist, like Dad and Mum used to do when we were still in Sudan. They rarely hugged since we returned to Nigeria. These days, Dad was cold and silent mostly. He was going to become a politician, he would always say. He talked mostly when some big men visited the house, driven in luxury cars, men who wore long dashiki and whose cologne lingered in the sitting room, hours after they had left.

'Mama, look at you. You look young every day.'

Grandma was a fat woman, gigantic and tall and bent by the waist, but not as tall as Mum. She wore a milky-coloured blouse and wrapper; the blouse had shoulder pads that puffed up like the ears of an elephant and the wrapper was blue in colour with hundreds of yellow twinkling stars on every part of it. There was a bulge by the right side of her waist, where the wrapper was tightly secured. Her shoulders were large and her arms huge and thick with a lot of flesh.

She stared at me. I stared back.

'Come on, Leona, say good afternoon to Grandma.'

I touched my mouth with my index finger, signalling to Dad that I could not talk.

'Oh, that. Mama, ewe n' iwe, don't be angry. Look, Leona and I just got back from the hospital where she went to have a tooth taken out.'

'Come, Ada m, come.' She beckoned me to come forward, and I did. She hugged me. Then, she sat and placed me in between her spread out laps.

'Good afternoon, Grandma,' I muttered between clenched teeth.

'Mama, she's been having toothache since we returned to Nigeria.'

'How are you now, Ada m?' She caressed my cheeks.

I nodded. She smelled of sweat. But it was the kind of smell that was not awful, it was welcoming. It was motherly, like how Mum smelt when she returned from the market in Khartoum. Now, Smart did all the grocery shopping.

'Chizorom, itoka, you are so tall and beautiful too,' she said.

When we returned from Sudan and visited Dad's village, Grandma had asked Dad the meaning of my name, Leona, and he had shrugged. She said it sounded like the name of a dog.

'How can your child's name sound like that of our neighbour's dog, eh James?'

So, she named me Chizorom, meaning 'God saved me,' after Dad narrated to his family the story of our escape from Sudan. Then, she insisted everyone called me Chizorom.

'Gini bu Leona, biko nu? What is Leona? It is only white people that bear names that have no meaning. My child cannot bear a dog's name. No, nwam, your name is Chizorom. Inugo? Have you heard?' Grandma touched my cheeks, my eyes, and my hair. She touched my neck and checked the skin on my flesh. Then, she turned me around and gauged my height.

'Nwa nke a eto ya! This child is so tall!' she said, repeatedly.

Dad smiled and said, 'Now, Mum, why are your things in the sitting room? Are you just coming?'

'No! I came an hour ago—'

'And why are you here? Why did you not change your clothes? Did they not show you to a room?'

She was silent. She began to ask me questions about school and about my tooth. She wanted to know if it was painful. She wanted to know what I ate that made me grow so tall. She said that during vacations she would come and take me to the village so that other women would see how tall her granddaughter was. She was smiling and her eyes were twinkling like that of a little child.

Mum came out then. She sat on the couch closest to the door. Her face looked unhappy.

'Welcome, James. How did it go?'

'Fine. They pulled out the tooth. It was rotting already. The doctor said since Leona is still a child, she will grow another.'

We could hear clatters from the kitchen as plates were being washed.

'I am not a child, Dad.'

They laughed.

'Okay. Is it painful, Leona?' Mum asked.

I shook my head.

'But there is another one that is about to fall off. The doctor said it will fall off on its own, soon.'

Dad beheld Grandma's things beside her.

'Look, why did you not take Mama's things inside? Why was she not shown to the guest room?' he asked Mum.

'Tsk. Did she tell you that I did not? Your mother refused me touching her things. Perhaps she will now that you are here. Tsk-tsk.'

Grandma had refused to go into the guest room or to allow her bags be taken inside. When Smart tried to carry them, she refused. When Mum pleaded with her to allow her take her bags in, she refused. She just sat there, staring at the television.

Mum went to take the bag, which was close to Grandma, but she made me sit beside her on the chair. She brought the bag close to her, unzipped it, and brought out some huge flasks containing a big mound of fufu and another flask containing soup.

'I cooked for you, my son. I wonder if she cooks good food for you,' she said in Igbo.

I understood a little of what she said. Immediately, I left her seat and went to sit with Mum.

Mum did not understand what she said, but when Dad talked, she knew.

He said, 'Oh, Mama, you are so kind, but my wife can prepare all Igbo meals. I taught her back there in Sudan.'

Mum backed off then. She called Smart to come take the food to the kitchen and instructed her to warm it. Later the food was served to Dad and to Grandma, but Mum and I did not eat of it.

TEN

That night, my tooth fell off. I sat on one of the chairs by the dining table, working on my assignments, while Grandma and Dad discussed how difficult things were getting in the village. She told Dad everything that happened in the village since he was away; even the stories she told him when we just returned to Nigeria, she was repeating now, including how Mazi Amah's son, the one in Canada married an oyibo woman and refused to return, even to bury his mother. It was the worst thing that could happen to any mother, she said, to die and not be laid to rest by your own son and your first son for that matter. She asked Dad if he would have returned if she died when we were still living in Sudan. Dad said yes, he would have, but that she was not dying anytime soon; not with her health still strong and her bones as strong as those of a lion. She laughed, and her laughter hit the ceilings.

Grandma told Dad about his father's arthritis and that he could not visit the farms again. That was why she was in Enugu, she said, to remind him that he would need to send money often, as the government no longer paid pension, and things were hard. She told Dad about her friend, Mummy Ego, who was also suffering from arthritis, and said that everyone was suffering from arthritis now. Then, she remarked that it was like God was angry with the world and was going to use arthritis to wipe away all elderly people. She said her own was coming, and she could feel it in her joints because when the bus stopped at Ogbete and she alighted, it took her some minutes to stand on her feet. And she knew then that her arthritis was on the way. She reminded Dad to take her to the best hospitals now that he had money so that they could stop it and that Grandpa would need to go to the hospital too so that he could regain his strength and visit his farms again. They needed to feed too, she said.

'Look, I understand all these things are about money, Mama. Don't worry you will get enough money to sort yourself out before leaving.'

I wanted to open my mouth to ask Dad some questions about my homework when the tooth fell into my mouth. I spat it into my hand.

'Dad, my tooth is out.'

Dad rose on his feet. 'Seriously?'

'Yes! See!' I showed it to him. He took it and turned it on his hands.

'Let me see.' Grandma took it and stared at it, squinting. 'Now you will have to throw it to the roof, Chizorom.'

'Why?'

She laughed. 'Oh, oyibo girl. You don't know that when

a tooth falls out you throw it to the rooftop, to the lizards so that they could take the old rotten tooth and give you a new one. If you don't do that, you may not get any tooth at all, or the one you get may not be all that white.'

I was stunned. Few times, my teeth fell off in Khartoum, and I did not throw them to the rooftop. I could not recall what happened to them.

'Mama! That's superstitious. You used to make me do those things when I was little. Everyone did it then. Do people still do it?'

'Of course. Now, Chizorom, keep the tooth, you hear? In the morning, we'll throw it to the rooftop and ask the lizards for a whiter one.'

'Yes, Grandma,' I agreed, but I was stunned.

I climbed the stairs to Mum's room and told her what Grandma said.

Mum stood from the bed instantly and began to tremble.

'Where is the tooth now?' she asked.

I could see fear in her eyes.

'Here. Here,' I said. I opened my palm and showed it to her. She took it and went to the bathroom. She threw it into the toilet and flushed.

'Tsk. Don't worry, Leona. You will get a new one soon, tsk. And a white one too, okay?'

'I was scared.'

'You don't need to be scared. Teeth grow, naturally. If one falls off, another grows in its place. This happens until you become older.'

'But why would Grandma ask me to throw it to the lizards?'

'I don't know. She is superstitious.'

Remembering the discussion Mum had with her friends in Khartoum about witches, I asked, 'Is she a witch, Mum?'

'Tsk, don't be silly, Leona, eh!' she said, but without conviction.

I stood by the door of the toilet, watching her until she left the toilet, took me to the bed, and sat on it.

'I don't understand Grandma,' I said.

'Me too.'

'Do you think Grandma is a witch?' I repeated.

She stared at me for long. 'Now, go to your room and sleep. She is not a witch.'

'I am scared.' I sat on the bed, and she drew me close to herself.

'Scared of what? Scared of your grandmother?'

'Yes.'

'She is not a witch. Now, go to your room and sleep, tsk.'

ELEVEN

 I came out of my reverie, weary; and a short while later, I slept off, dreaming of Mum. I saw her in the company of Margaret, the Briton who was her friend in Khartoum. They were dancing in circles and, suddenly, it began to rain. It was in front of our house in Khartoum. I saw that their feet were not muddy like when Onyinye, Sandra, and I danced in the rain in Enugu. Anytime it rained, Onyinye and I danced and screamed and opened our mouths wide, while raising our heads for some rain water to enter. In this dream, there was no muddy dirt on their legs. Then, we were in front of the gate of our primary school and Sandra was chasing Margaret and Mum about while Onyinye and I watched from a distance.

I woke up with a little headache. There was a knock on the door. Smart was dressed in an over-sized polo shirt that was dirty on the neck and faded blue jean trousers. She looked so tiny inside the shirt.

'Oga said to tell you he had to leave early and didn't want to disturb you. But he said to give you this.'

I could not help but notice again the tufts of grey already mixing up with her dark woolly hair. She handed me a piece of paper and left.

Inscribed in what appeared to be hurried writing were the words,

'Think Over What We Talked About'

I squeezed the paper and threw it into the trash bin under the reading table in my room. Then, I yawned and went into the bathroom to prepare for the day.

Downstairs, Smart came to tell me that Dad's other children were coming into town and would be staying in the house. I wondered why he did not mention that last night or in the note.

I found a key to one of the cars in the compound, a dark sleek Toyota Corolla, and drove into town to find my friend, Adulike, who lived in Maitama with her family.

Adulike's father worked with the telecommunications company, MTN, which came into the country a few years before and was doing great. Adulike's family moved from Enugu as soon as the company got into Nigeria and her father was recruited to work as a Regional Director. Their house in Maitama was a small but well-furnished duplex, painted bright grey with four narrow columns in front. The last time we saw, she was a bit slimmer. I met her, dressed in her pyjamas and stockings, and sprawled on a couch in the parlour watching a Hindi film. She said I looked as if I had been crying all night.

'My father has been getting on my nerves.'

'He's always been getting on your nerves, Leo. What's up this time?'

'Fashy am, dear. Forget it.' I waved my hand to show it was not a subject I was willing to discuss. 'He is just an old man.'

'Your father is not an old man. He still looks hot o. I see him on television, every other day.' Her eyes twinkled.

'You talk as if you are beginning to like my father, eh, this girl.'

'I have always liked your father—'

'Hold it there.' I kept a straight face, but she could see I was holding myself not to be amused.

'Are you going to marry your father, girl?'

'And you, are you going to marry a widower?'

'I can marry a sexy widower.'

'And rich too.'

'Exactly o!' She curled her legs under her buttocks. 'Besides, your dad isn't exactly a widower. He has other wives.'

'You never cease to amaze me,' I told her.

She laughed and stood. I watched her wiggle her small waist away, and I recalled that when we were in primary school, Adulike was the shortest of us all. Now she had grown reasonably and looked quite beautiful. She never ceased talking about the men she had affairs with, mostly older men. Once when we were in Primary Five, Sandra caught Adulike in the classroom store, touching herself.

While I listened to the noise coming from the kitchen area, the memory came to me in all its clarity. Sandra had sighted Adulike through the classroom window and ran to call Onyinye and me from where we were playing oga. We had rushed in, thrown the door to the storeroom open, and caught her off guard. Adulike was leaning on the wall with her right foot on top of a stacked carton of books, and her left fingers holding her pant to a side, while slowly thrusting her right index finger into her vagina, with her eyes closed and her mouth open. She seemed far away. Something heavy got caught in my throat as we watched her, and no matter how hard I tried that day, I could not cough it out. Adulike pleaded that we should not tell anyone, and we agreed. Of course, we would not tell anyone because we all had our own secrets, lots of secrets.

Onyinye's secret was the worst of them all. We caught her with our class teacher, Anya Four Taati, when others had gone home after school. I was waiting for our driver, and I thought Onyinye had gone home, but when I went into the classroom to get my school bag, I heard sounds from the classroom store. I peeped through the window and saw our class teacher leaning over my friend, squeezing her breasts. His trousers were down, along with his inner shorts, while Onyinye was holding his penis in her right hand and her left hand was on the cheeks of our teacher's buttocks.

My eyes swooned. 'Onyinye?' I cried out. 'What are you doing?'

They quickly separated.

It was a bad day for me. I did not talk to Onyinye for almost two weeks, and I told our gateman not to allow her into our residence. The whole of that term, our class teacher, Anya Four Taati, did not ask me questions during lessons, and I suddenly began to do better in my tests and homework. He gave me good grades even in the subjects I failed, but this neither changed the way I felt about him nor made me and the rest of the pupils stop calling him Anya Four Taati. We christened him the moniker because of how his eyes constantly appeared to be looking in the direction of the east when he was looking towards the north, making those beside him think he was addressing them, when he was looking at someone in front of him.

Then, there was Sandra. We called her Sandy; she was tall, lanky, and talkative. People said we looked alike, but she was light-skinned. Her mother called her Queen Sandy, and it made her strut like a peacock. Sandy was stubborn and arrogant, but when she was asked questions, she never answered. Instead, she insulted the teacher and no one could do anything. She came from a family where there was always trouble. I used to think that her father went to a school where he learnt to beat up women because of the way he hit her mother and the maids and their gardener.

Once, we visited Sandy's house and their gardener served us some udara fruits. As we were talking in the sitting room, her parents returned from an outing, and we overheard the sound of their fighting because it entered into the house before them. They were surprised to see us; so, they kept calm, went upstairs, and continued their fight. We could still hear them from downstairs. Sandy was so embarrassed. We never told anyone in class that Sandy's parents fought each other like touts in a motor park, so long as she never revealed our secrets.

Mine was about Sudan. Mum wanted me to keep it secret that we were wanted dead by some people in Sudan. She never stopped believing that some people were tracking us and would eventually kill her. It made her nervous all the time. Her windows were always locked at nights, even though sometimes the nights were hot and there was no electricity. She always held my ears and warned me sternly against telling my friends or any of Dad's relatives and servants that we were running from assassination, and about Grandpa.

However, Onyinye told everyone the day I quarrelled with her. Earlier, I divulged the secret to her after I showed her my grandfather's pictures. First, she inquired about him, and I refused to tell her.

'We agreed to share secrets, Leo,' she said.

'But not this one.'

'Aw! Aw!' she exclaimed. 'But I told you all of mine. All.' She sulked. 'I told you about my mother when she got that infection, yeast infection, and she quarrelled with my dad; and I heard about it. I told you my sisters' secrets, and I told you about my elder brother who smokes hemp. So, why hide yours?' She was furious.

Then, I told her. 'Promise me you won't tell anyone, not even Adulike and Sandra.'

A week later, when we quarrelled in school, she told all my friends.

'You suck! You stupid Sudanese!'

'I am not Sudanese!' I yelled back at her. 'I am Nigerian. My father is Nigerian. Didn't Anya Four Taati say that citizenship is determined from the father's side?'

'But she is Nigerian, Onyinye,' Adulike defended.

'Oh? Oh? Do you know that she will die anytime soon? Do you know they're looking for her and her mother in Sudan? In fact, they ran away from Sudan because her grandfather, a greedy army man, was a traitor and he got himself killed. They are looking for her mother to kill too.' She turned around to face me and pointed. 'Even you.'

'Onyinye!'

'Deny it?' she asked and walked away.

Others looked at me with surprise. When school was dismissed, Sandra, Ezinne, and Adulike dragged me to a corner and asked if it was true. I nodded. They said it did not matter, that they would bury it in the secret places of their hearts if I did not want people to know about it and get myself and Mum killed.

We had our secrets, except for Ezinne who had no secrets we knew of, perhaps because she was rarely with us.

Now Adulike was serving me some bananas and

groundnuts and telling me how profitable it was to date older men.

'There was this man I met in my dad's office. He works with them. Somehow, he knew I liked him, and he gave me his card. We saw a few times, and I got some real cash. I am not talking about small money o, babes.'

I threw some groundnuts into my mouth and stared at her as she talked. I remembered what happened after we caught Adulike touching herself. I had been curious to know how it felt like; it must have felt good for Adulike to have that faraway look on her face like someone enjoying the after taste of sour-sop, but I lacked the courage to do it barefaced. So, I touched myself when I went to have a bath, inside the bathtub full of foam.

TWELVE

Adulike and I hung out until late at night. I had managed to get her to change and go with me to another friend's house where we gossiped, ate lunch, went to hang out in a mall, then went to other places afterwards. Adulike had said she wanted to take me round Abuja and see if she could hook me up with some guy.

'Come, Leo, girl. You should leave that your seminarian. Haba! Wetin dat boy dey give you chop, sef?'

I got back just after twilight and there were two boys playing ball inside the compound. They ran to me, calling me 'Aunty'. I stooped to their height.

'You are so tall,' one of them said.

'I want to be this tall when I grow up,' the other said.

'When you grow up, you will be taller. What are your names again?' I asked.

'Johnson. Aunty, what did you buy for us?' one of them asked. I totally forgot they were coming. The truth was that I did not care much about them. When Mum was still alive, she warned that none of them was to come to the house in

Enugu or Abuja. They lived with their mother in the house in Lagos. The other woman had two sons for Dad too, and they lived in Abuja but in a different apartment. But now that Mum was dead, they visited the house, and I always forgot their names.

'My name is Okwudili,' the second boy answered.

'Nice name.'

'What is the meaning of your name, Aunty?' Okwudili was older. He was six years old, I guessed.

I raised my eyebrow.

'Forget the meaning of my name. Come inside, let me see if I can find you both some gifts.'

'Mum said every name has a meaning.'

'Yeah.'

'So, what about yours? Mine is Okwudilichukwu—'

'And you know what it means?'

'Oh, yeah. It's like saying "leave judgement to God".'

He turned and beamed. They ran in before me.

'Wow!' I said to myself and pondered at the meaning of his name. I never thought of its meaning that way, for its literal meaning could be interpreted as 'Words are for God'. Now I understood.

Inside the house, Smart was watching television. She yelled at them not to knock anything down. As I passed, not caring to greet her, she said, 'Your mother... your mother asked me to tell you something.'

'Huh?'

'I will tell you tonight.'

I stopped abruptly. I could see creases appear on her forehead. Someone was laughing out loud on television. The curtains twirled to the sound of the powerful standing fan by the corner of the sitting room.

'She asked you to tell me what? When?'

'Shortly before she died.'

'Oh!'

'Yes.'

'And you never did?'

'We will talk tonight, by God's grace.' She looked remorseful.

I stuttered, 'Oh... Okay.'

She sat carefully, her eyes on me. My handbag was on the crook of my hand. My gown swept the floor as I hurried upstairs to my room. That was why I hated Smart. The children were already calling me to hurry.

They were standing by the room and while I unlocked the door one of them said, 'Aunty, what do you want to give to us?'

'I don't know yet. Let's see when we get in.'

I threw open the door, and they rushed in and dived to the bed. The younger one was five. Dad, eager to have more sons, had got their mother pregnant soon after she gave birth to the first one. Mum never forgave him, but the sight of the children, ruffling my bed sheet, and dirtying it as they jumped up and down made me smile.

Why worry about what has happened and what you cannot change, when tomorrow is uncertain. I thought.

I searched my drawers and found nothing. So, I opened my refrigerator and took out three small nylon bags.

'This is ukwa. You children will love it.'

'Yeah. We know, Aunty.'

'Aki n'ukwa.'

I smiled. 'That is when you have ukwa and palm kennel nuts mixed together.'

They were already opening them up.

'Aunty, do you have any toys?' Johnson asked.

'I will see what I can do tomorrow. Okay?'

'Okay.'

'Me I want a train.'

'I want an aeroplane.'

I turned on the air conditioner. 'Now, don't call me 'Aunty' anymore.' I held their gaze. 'I am your sister, you know?'

They seemed to look at me for some seconds. 'We know,' Okwudili responded.

'So, what do you call your elder sister?'

'Sister.'

'Sis.'

I grinned.

'Mummy said you are our sister but that she didn't give birth to you.'

'Yes. My mother is different. In English, I am your half-sister, but in Igbo, there is nothing like half when you come to family. Nwanne bu nwanne, eh?'

'Yes.'

'Good. So, if you need anything, always let me know, eh?'

'Yes.'

'Now go and ask Aunty Smart for your dinner. I want to rest.'

They hurried away.

At the door, I heard one of them call, 'Can we bring our dinner into your room? Aunty? Sister?'

'No! I want to sleep!' I smiled.

THIRTEEN

I was reading *The Kite Runner,* which I borrowed from Adulike when Dad came into my room. He had changed his clothes and now smelt of some mild body spray.

'The boys told me you asked them to call you 'Sister'.'

I looked up and dropped the book. I was surprised they told him that. I made a mental note to be careful what I discussed with those two. They were obviously closer to him than I thought.

'Oh, they did?'

'Yes.' He smiled, pulled out a plastic chair and sat down. 'That's so good of you. Look, we are family and we should be close. Look, there is nothing greater than a happy family. What affects one of us affects all. We make mistakes but sometimes what we think as mistakes turn out to be of great advantage. If the boys were much older, they would have been a great company to you.'

'You regret not impregnating some woman early enough?'

'Hai. No, Leona.' He was silent. 'Look, we should move on.'

I nodded. 'I want to sleep.'

'Your mother is not happy wherever she is.'

'Did she tell you that?'

'What your mother wanted most before she died was for her death to be avenged.'

'Huh?'

I knew Mum changed as soon as we arrived in Nigeria. What happened in Sudan changed her. It was like we came to live in Nigeria—to live in Enugu—and the colour of the city, the dusty brownish colour, clouded her senses and her imagination. She became hungry for privacy and became a little hard-hearted. It was like there were different colours for different places, and they affected one wherever they were. Whenever I thought of this, I imagined that Sudan had the colour of orange or yellow—bright and lively. Perhaps it was the fun trips I had with Grandpa, the visits to the markets with Mum, the gossips and the anxiety about the war that made it so. When we got to Nigeria, it was the colour brown or the colour of the earth—muddy, dark, and dusty. I could not wrap my mind around what it was.

Nigeria's colour affected Mum and changed her so deeply. When Grandma was hard on her, she hit back, hating her as much as Grandma hated her for being a foreigner. Mum ignored her and refused to visit Dad's village except the time Dad was arrested, and we were driven to the village before we travelled to Cameroon. When we returned from Cameroon and she took over Dad's business, she became more ruthless, running it with all her strength, as if her survival in this country that had been unfair to her depended on the survival of that business. She wanted to prove to everyone, her friends, Dad's friends, and his family that she could survive on her own, that she was worth something, and that she could run a business even more successfully than Dad. And when the government began to swoop down on her to strangle life out of the business, she began to repatriate most of it to Sudan. She was no longer as scared of Sudan as she used to be, and she began to spend more time in Omdurman than she did in Nigeria—Dad hated that.

'Look, my girl, you remember when I was in jail, that second year when your mother was growing the business so fast and refused to come visit? She opened a pharmaceutical company in Omdurman against my wish.'

'Yes. It was the right thing, Dad.' I raised my hands to shut him up. 'Abacha was stifling the business here.'

'It wasn't Abacha. Your mother was blackmailed by Chief Fegun Wale. He was trying to run the business down. She was a threat to his continuous success.'

My eyes widened. 'What kind of blackmail?'

'It seemed your mother imported some ammunition to oust the Head of State.' My jaw dropped. I swallowed back some saliva that would have dropped. My eyes popped out of their sockets. What was he talking about? 'As I said, it was blackmail. It didn't happen, but they planted the arms and all in her shipping containers. She was arrested and spent a few days in Dodan Barrack.'

'I never heard this.'

'She didn't want to tell you.'

That made sense. I was away in boarding school, having a difficult time. Dad was in jail and we feared every day that he was going to be killed. News of another execution of a political prisoner brought his own death closer.

'Oh! Why did I never hear of this? Why wasn't it in the news?'

I had followed the news every day for those three years.

'Because it was a high conspiracy against your mother, against our family, spearheaded by Chief Fegun Wale and his cohorts.'

'And what happened?'

He drew his chair closer. 'Look, I don't want you to hate your mother for what I am about to tell you.'

I nodded slowly. *What fallacy was he going to weave that could possibly make me hate Mum?* I thought. I nodded several times.

'He… this man began to sleep with your mother.'

My mouth threw open. 'No, Dad.'

'Well, Leona.'

'No.'

'See—'

'Please, don't insult my mother!'

He came closer and sat on the bed, placing his hand on my lap. 'Look, many families suffered during the dictatorship, in many ways.'

'This can't be true.'

'It is. I am sorry.'

'No.'

He looked at me.

'But why would he do that?'

'To spite me.'

'But you didn't know?'

'Look, I didn't know, then. If a man is a sadist, he could sleep with a fellow's wife to get back at him, whether the fellow knows or not. It is a show of power.'

'It would be a show of power if the man knew.'

'It is a show of power whichever way, whichever way you look at it, my girl.'

A generator in the next compound came on, and it took a moment for the sound to normalise.

'So, what happened?'

'That explains why your mother diverted the business to Sudan, but I didn't know then. They had little control over her business if the bulk of it was done outside the country, and General Omar Al-Bashir was sympathetic. Your grand-father had worked for him, after all.'

I took a deep breath. Why was I learning of all these now? I wondered what Smart was going to tell me—she said she wanted us to talk.

'There are many reasons why I suspect Chief Fegun Wale masterminded the killing of your mother. Perhaps she stopped seeing him. She grew the business, and I came and took over, and we got Obasanjo in with some of the money. He could not take that. He thought he would run us down.

Again, it seems your mother stole some business documents from him to start the steel factory, yet the government came and took over the factory, breaking your mum's heart.'

I swallowed hard.

'But whatever is the reason, the man that killed your mother is Chief Fegun Wale. He...' He looked away, gazing out the window. 'He slept with her against her wish throughout the time General Sani Abacha was alive. They made her believe they had the powers to get Abacha to order her death or imprison her. Look, they tried to wreck her business, our business. They pushed her out of this country. They pushed her away from you. They imprisoned me.'

'Dad?' My forehead was aching.

'Yes. So, you see, now this same man has asked me for your hand in marriage to his son.'

'And you want me to accept.'

'Look, it's a spite on us.'

'And you want me to lick the spittle from their mouth?'

'For a greater cause, Leona; to avenge your mother; she would want you to.'

'I can't kill, Dad.'

'Even if you saw someone point a gun at your mother's head, and you are in a position to defend her, to kill the person?'

'I don't know. I... I don't have the strength.'

'Don't worry, my dear. Agree to the marriage first.' He stood. 'A lot happens in this world that you do not know.

Do you not know that if you kill Wale's son, we will take over their business and pay them back for all they did to our family?'

'And you want to sacrifice me?'

'No.' He sat again and looked me closely in the eyes. 'No. Look, my girl, I can never do that. We have passed through a lot together; Sudan, the years of imprisonment, your mother's absence, and now her death.' He sounded as if he loved her. As if he still loved her. My heart beat rapidly. 'Everywhere in the world, power, fame, and wealth are built on the shoulders of risk and sacrifice. If you want to own the world, take this risk. Ad astra per aspera, but it is less of owning the world than avenging your mother. She died early, Leo.'

'I have no need for wealth, Dad.'

'Look, everyone needs wealth. I wonder what those in penury do, how they survive. You see, child, poverty is a curse to those who have it.'

'And to gain wealth, I go about it the wrong way; marry our perceived enemy, kill them, and inherit their wealth?'

'All wealth are from what you call the wrong way. Look, it is difficult to find a family's fortune built on good-will and innocence. One way or the other, toes are stepped on, people are made away with, and others' wealth is taken from them.' He held my gaze. 'Have you forgotten what is written in the Bible? What you have will be collected from you and be given to those who have more. Look, Leo, even the Bible understands, Leona, that sometimes, others' wealth and fortune is acquired by their adversaries.'

I was not quite sure what the Bible said, but I did not want to take him up on that.

'If a family has messed our life up and God provides us with an opportunity to deal them a heavy blow, shying away from the opportunity is like refusing to breathe while you are being strangled. Think about it. What is life if not a continuous effort to prey on its elements to live?'

I inhaled again and without breathing out said, 'You are messing with my head.'

He took my hands. 'Think with your head.'

'I will… think about it.'

He gently released my hands, caressing them as he did so. Then, he stood, nodded, and left.

FOURTEEN

I lay on my bed and tears came down my eyes. My heart was beating rapidly. I recalled now, those early days after Mum started to take charge of Dad's business, and she would not come home until late in the morning. I would creep to her door, place my ears on it, and hear her sob and slap herself. I wondered now what was going on at that time; I used to think she was missing Dad and was tired from trying to revive his business. I used to think she was tired of this country, that she missed Sudan—the weather, the food, the simple life with her friends, Margaret, and the others, and the gossip. Again, among the things Mum brought from Khartoum was the medium-sized photo which she hung on the wall in her room. I thought that made her sad most times, especially looking at her sister, who died alongside her two children at the same time. While in Sudan, Mum had heard that Yaya's husband had joined the Liberation Army to fight in the war.

I wondered now what was happening then.

My mind always went back to the time at Enugu when everything was torn to shreds in my family's life. I remembered that during vacations, I trekked through the streets of

Enugu. Mum was away all day, Dad was in jail, and Smart hardly talked to me. Enugu was a dusty town; its streets, tarred over twenty years earlier, was characterised by lots of potholes and clouds of dust. When it rained, water filled those potholes, and I usually watched as children played in the muddy waters and splashed them on vehicles and sometimes on passers-by. In dry seasons, the mud in the potholes caked and turned into brown-coloured dust that rose to the heavens when vehicles sped past. When people trekked back from schools or churches or markets, their shoes got covered with dust, the hem of their skirts and trousers too.

The only time I had some fun was in primary school. There were girls from wealthy families, and we easily became friends. There was a big gap between wealthy children and those from average homes in my school, and we noticed that the poor children had a certain calmness around them that both attracted and repelled; they were mostly conscious of their background and the burden of poverty on their shoulders. They walked with their eyes cast down and were always conscious, alert, easy to offend, and quick to attack. When crossed, their words were venom; the poor children were not many in my school because it was too expensive, but those around left an impression.

I had a group of rascally friends; we gossiped with the name of anyone we chose—our teachers were not left out. We classified the teachers and gave them names. One was called 'Hanger' because his arm was like a cloth hanger. The other was called 'Anthill' because his head protruded at the back. Our own teacher was Anya Four Taati because if he was looking at you, you would think he was looking at someone else by your side. Our clique played our own games and sat on the same seats and rows. After school, we waited for our drivers to come and pick us; then, we sat close to the doors of the cars, thrust our heads out of the windows, and waved at other children as they trekked home. From Primary Five, we started discussing boys.

It was during the first term of Primary Five that Onyinye and her family came to live in Enugu and bought a house in the avenue where we stayed. Onyinye's father was a close friend of Dad's. So, she was allowed to visit me, and we played inside the fenced compound of my residence. Every day, we met in school and continued those discussions we could not finish at home.

Each time she visited, she told me stories of how her elder sisters kissed their boyfriends in their sitting room. She was close to Rosa, her immediate elder sister, who shared some intimate stories with her; she shared the same with me in exchange for my stories about Sudan. It was Onyinye who first told me about a woman's private parts and the different funny names that they were called.

I thought of Smart and what she was going to tell me. I wondered if she was going to tell me that Mum wanted me to have nothing to do with the Wales or if she wanted me to kill them. But how would she know they were planning to kill her or to warn that I avenge her if they did? I thought of Smart and about Onyinye and how they both shaped my childhood in different ways; Onyinye, always present to teach me the things she was learning from her elder sisters; Smart, always quiet, watching and keeping an eye on me.

I recalled when Onyinye came to the house around five-thirty, one evening. I was in Mum's garden, watering vegetables. Some boys were playing football in a nearby field and their shouts could be heard faintly from where I was. Onyinye wore a long skirt and a cashmere top that showed her back. I was sure she got them from one of her sisters. We talked about school and discussed all our friends and teachers; then, she said, 'I caught Dave fucking Rosa!'

Onyinye had a slim voice that always sounded like that of a gong—long and high-pitched, yet slim. It was the kind of voice that rang a bell for a long time in your ears, and if she placed her mouth on one of your ears and screamed, it might even pierce your eardrum.

'Uhm?' My response was sudden because I did not understand what she said. 'What is *forking*?' I asked, shifting from the piece of block I was sitting on.

'It's fucking. F U C K I N G,' she corrected and spelt the words so I could pronounce it correctly. I reluctantly did.

'What does that word mean?' I asked, thoughts already running through my mind.

She quietly said, 'It means a man having sex with a woman. My sister was doing it with Dave, and I caught them.'

'Rosa? Your sister?'

'Who else? Yes.'

'Aw! Dave, her boyfriend?'

'Yes.'

I rolled my eyes, and Onyinye laughed.

'Where did you catch them?'

'Inside her room. They forgot to lock the door.'

'You did not knock?' I asked. The breeze was blowing up my flowery gown.

'I wanted to catch them. I wanted to see—'

'Ah?' I exclaimed, and she laughed some more. 'That's a bad habit.'

She giggled. 'Rosa was pleading with me not to tell anyone.' She was enjoying the look of surprise in my eyes. I hit her lightly on her shoulder. Onyinye announced proudly but in a lowered voice, 'See, Leo, she said if we are ready, she can arrange for us to do *it*.'

My mouth closed instantly.

'Who?'

'Rosa.'

'Do what?'

'Do *eet*.'

'I can never do that. It's not good. Mum will deal with me if she caught me doing anything silly with boys.'

The breeze was light, and it swirled the tiny leaves from the vegetables. I could hear the noise of our gate as it opened.

Onyinye was quiet; then, a light sparkled in her eyes and she said aloud, 'Rosa can arrange for boys to do it *to* us, at our place. No one would ever know.' I saw her lips quiver, she stuttered, 'She said it… is sweet and… it feels good. She said… it will be… fun.'

FIFTEEN

The boys were set to go back to Lagos, and Aunty Agii came to take them. She arrived Abuja that morning and the driver went to pick her from Nnamdi Azikiwe Airport. I was doing some laundry when she got in. I could hear her talking with Smart, and they seemed to blend well. Aunty Agii was on good terms with everyone. She was the kind of woman who gave one no reason whatsoever to be angry with her. She was like a cat; hit it, starve it, do to it whatever you want, it would still cling to you, pawing and rubbing itself on your legs and all. She talked smoothly and calmly, so that no matter how sad you were, she would make you listen to her.

When Mum was with us, the first and only time Aunty Agii came to the house in Enugu, Mum had calmly asked her to leave, calling her a gold-digger who came to reap the fruits she did not sow. Aunty Agii had stood up, raised her hand to stop Dad when he tried to protest, and walked out to the car to wait for him. Inside the house, Mum had fumed and said she could not understand why a man would bring another woman into his home without divorcing his other wife. She could not comprehend why men fancied polygamy.

Dad had argued that as an Igbo man, he was allowed to marry as many women as he could afford to marry and cater for.

'Even one hundred women, as long as I can cater for them and raise their children not to be a nuisance to the society.'

Mum had stood and stared him down, saying, 'To hell with your being Ibo, tsk.' She pronounced 'Ibo' no matter how much Grandma corrected her to say 'Igbo'. 'To hell with your fucked-up culture. The rest of the world has moved on.'

'And the rest of the world are Americans? Britons? Those fools who marry today and divorce tomorrow, and by the time they are forty, fifty, would have married and divorced three to four women? Spare me! Look, they are worse than polygamists. They leave children here and there outside the care of their fathers. Our people say, "Nkita nwanyi zuru n'akpa akwa."' Mum had looked at him, askance. She had not understood the proverb; so, he explained. 'A dog trained by a woman pilfers eggs.'

Mum grunted, 'Tsk! You chauvinist.'

'Call me whatever you like.'

'I thought men like you who studied in civilised nations would be at least modest and civil, huh? You feed the fire of patriarchy.'

Aunty Agii pressed Dad's car horn as he made to walk to the door.

'Don't ever bring that girl into this house, James. You hear me?'

'She is going to be my wife, woman.'

'Don't ever bring her here, and if you marry her, don't bring her children here. I don't want to ever set my eyes on them.'

'My children, all of them, should stay under one roof to imbibe my principles. I am not a damn American. I can't have my child living with her mother in another city and visit me only during the holidays.'

'She is carrying your baby, right? You should divorce me and go live with her and the children in her womb that she will bear for you.'

'I can't, Mary. Well, if you want to leave, go talk to your daughter; but as long as you choose to remain my wife, you will stay under my roof, with my other wife, Agnes, because I am going to marry her. And bring her to live in this house. And your daughter with my other children will live together and learn that they are siblings. Excuse me, woman,' he had said and stomped out.

Tears had ran down Mum's face, and I had gone to her.

'Let's go to the room.'

Aunty Agii came to me in the lobby.

'Hello, Leona!' she greeted.

She was dressed in a long flowery skirt. She looked

elegant. I stood up and stretched my hand, but she hugged me instead. I had forgotten how way taller than her that I was. She was a pretty woman; fair, broad, and comely. Her dimples looked magnificent and they always showed because she seemed to always be in a cheerful mood. She looked me up and down when she released me.

'Look at you, Nne. You are so tall. I wish my boys will be this tall.'

The way she said it, I knew she meant no harm. Her eyes were sparkling. She wore her hair natural. It was kinky.

'They won't. The gene runs in my mother's side of the family. Dinka people are tall people.'

'Oh! Well, Aunty was a tall woman,' she was referring to my mum. 'But you, Nne? You are so tall, taller than all women I know.'

'I am not a woman yet.'

'You are. Well, soon you will be in that sense you are thinking. I heard you'd soon be getting engaged.'

'Oh. Dad?' I wondered why Dad would discuss with her that a certain man I had not even met had asked him for my hand in marriage when he was not sure I was going to accept.

She smiled. 'Kedu? How have you been, woman?'

'Cool. I am washing.'

'I can see. Hope the boys haven't been giving you troubles?'

'No, not at all. I must confess, they've been great. Dad now returns quite early.'

'Hmmn!' Her eyes sparkled again. Her dimples were more prominent. 'I am happy to learn that.'

I smiled at her. She turned to leave.

At the stairs, she turned back. 'Leona?'

'Yes?'

'Thank you.'

I raised my brows.

As she climbed up, her well-endowed hips swung this way and that and her stilettos made *koi-koi* sound on the tiles. I wondered why Mum never had it well with this woman. It occurred to me that Mum never gave herself the chance to get to know her. I wondered if it was wrong, this polygamy thing; this idea of having more than one wife share your roof and your bed at the same time, yet the women accept it and defer to one another. And to think that most women who were involved in it these days were all educated made it all baffling. Aunty Agii was already a director with the Federal Airport Authority of Nigeria when Dad met and got her pregnant. Her father was a retired civil servant.

Now, I thought so much about Mum, always, and tried to wrap my mind around why she changed and at what point she changed. I used to believe it was the colour of Nigeria and what the country threw at her that changed her the way the colour of different vegetation changes the chameleon to either green or grey and helps it to blend in. I remember now that Mum started to change when the men started coming to visit Dad in the house at Independence Layout in Enugu.

They came in the evening. The first day they came, I was

sitting with Dad in the sitting room, as they talked in hushed tones. Dad had told Mum to prepare cow-leg peppersoup. As she and Smart cooked, the aroma of the peppersoup filled the apartment and made my mouth water. Dad's visitors came in various expensive vehicles. None of them came with drivers. The cars were driven into the compound and parked beside each other. When they sat down, they talked about sports, farming, and how everything was becoming costly in Nigeria, and they blamed it all on the government. They were served peppersoup and wine. When the plates were cleared, they sipped their wine leisurely and talked in hushed tones.

'James, now tell us. Will you accept the general's offer?'

'No.' Dad sipped from a glass of brandy. The man who asked the question was seated opposite him. Dad placed his glass of wine on the table and said, 'It could have terrible repercussions.'

'Mr James Egbufor, it is not too much to ask. The general has been good to us and our business. Most of the products you import are contraband, but no one raises an eyebrow at the wharf when your goods come in because you are protected by the general and his men.'

Dad looked around the sitting room, ignoring me as I sat at the dining table pretending that I was not listening. Perhaps he thought I was not paying attention or that even though I could hear them, their words would make no meaning to me. Since Sudan, I had always sat in the sitting room when Dad discussed with people.

One of them, the one they called Chief Kutuga, said in a low voice, 'James Egbufor, this military government is not working. Things are not working. I think that the *offer* is good. What we plan will make things work. As soon as the general and his men *oust* the government and takeover power, they intend to return us to democracy. The offer is awesome. Gbogbotigbo, you will be made a minister. Plus, your business will flourish.'

The way he pronounced the word 'oust' made me raise my head. I would check it up in the dictionary later and shiver.

'Wallahi, we will own the government,' another said. He was the tallest among them, a northerner.

Dad replied the tall man, 'I have given this a lot of thought, Alhaji Usman. Can we do this?'

'Why can't we do it? General Babangida is the Head of State. He has been since nineteen eighty-five. Nothing is working in this country. No road, no water, electricity. Students are protesting almost every month and their lecturers call for strike actions every quarter. Wallahi, we cannot develop like this as a nation, believe me.'

'Alhaji Usman is right. Let us think about our nation first and not what we stand to gain or be pushed back by fear. Some of us need to sacrifice ourselves for the country. Countries that are making steady progress today like India, Malaysia, Indonesia, and the UAE were all pivoted to greater heights by men like us in their country, who looked beyond the ordinary, beyond their wealth and family and personal safety. They took drastic actions to make sure that their nation moved forward. We cannot continue to meander like fishes between one military regime and another, each one worse than the other, James,' Doctor Daniel Adele preached. He was a tall, fair, and handsome man. He unbuckled his belt and stretched out his legs on the stool before him.

'Now, all of you seem ready,' Dad said. 'But what of Chief Fegun Wale? Which side is he on?'

'Gbogbotigbo, he is on our side on this.'

Dad scratched his beard with his left fingers and smiled at the word 'gbogbotigbo' which Chief Kutuga never stopped saying. Dad's forehead stiffened into lines. He was the youngest among the men. This Chief Fegun Wale was Dad's business rival. There was no evening that he returned without mentioning the man to Mum.

'James, we have been ready since eternity. We need to do this, and we need your help.'

The aroma of food lingered in the room.

'And why, if I may ask, do you people need me so much?'

'James, you are new in this country; no one knows you. In just some months that you came in, you already have a successful business. You returned to Nigeria in nineteen eighty-nine, and we helped your business to grow. This is nineteen ninety-one, less than two years and you are a billionaire. Chief Fegun Wale is a brand in this country. If he gets into this so much, the plans may leak.'

'I don't like him. He thinks I am too much competition. He tries to stifle my business.'

'We will warn him off, wallahi.'

'That is not all. James, you are unknown to anyone. If we hit this government now, we hit them hard, and no one will know where it is coming from. Gbogbotigbo, no one will know how the coup was financed, at all, at all,' Chief Kutuga said.

'The general has a lot of money to finance this himself, doesn't he?'

'He has money, James, but not a lot of money. Even if he has enough to finance this, we are sure that as soon as he starts making a lot of financial transactions running into hundreds of millions, the government will begin to watch him closely. Besides, does he have hundreds of millions of naira to finance such a high-scale coup that will overthrow Babangida's government? He doesn't.'

'He doesn't. Only businessmen can do that. Only businessmen like you, James, have that kind of money,' Doctor Daniel said.

'And Chief Wale.'

'Yes, and Chief Wale.'

'Businessmen are the ones who finance coups everywhere in the world. The soldiers execute and carry out the operation, yes. But ammunition needs to be bought, colonels and generals and army commanders need to be bribed beforehand, soldiers too. Gbogbotigbo... we are talking about a lot of money.'

'Plus, journalists,' Mister Isaac Uwaifo said. He was a journalist by profession, but a millionaire. He owned two independent newspaper firms and a television station in Lagos.

'Ah, Isaac, Look, if we need to do this, hmm, *everyone* must have a role to play. I cannot fund everything. You are the journalist. You should take care of that end.'

The men in the room nodded, they knew Dad was consenting since he was already talking of sharing responsibilities.

Chief Kutuga, who was the anchor-man and the direct contact to the general, said to them, his tone lower now than before, 'James is right. And James, we know that, as soon as you agree to do this, gbogbotigbo we will give you our budget.'

'Why can't I see that budget now?'

'Because, gbogbotigbo, we don't want to scare you, James.' He smiled.

Dad's eyes were alert. 'Oh!' He paused before saying, 'Look, how do I recoup my investment?' He was now sitting on the edge of the cushion.

'My friend, you are already thinking like a businessman!' Mister Isaac Uwaifo said. They all laughed.

Doctor Daniel stood and refilled their glasses. 'I am not surprised. You are an Igbo man!' he teased.

'If we must overthrow the government, we need to act fast. As soon as we succeed, you will be made the Minister of Trade and Investment, with carte blanche to initiate and execute series of contracts, enough to recoup your money. You will also make a lot of profit on top in less than a year.'

Dad was calm. He studied the faces of the men one after the other.

A voice said in a whisper, 'Your duty will be to fund the lobbying of the important people, military personnel, civilians, labour unions, and human right groups and to provide the funds for importing and transporting arms, gbogbotigbo. The duty of Mister Isaac will be to lobby and control the media. Then, leave the action to the general.'

'You have explained this before, Kutuga–'

'I want to erase your doubts. We are making serious progress. We only need your commitment. The general counts so much on your support.'

'How do we transport the arms?' Mister Isaac Uwaifo asked.

He looked at me, but I pretended I was not paying attention.

'Leave that to me. Gbogbotigbo, I control every man in the Nigerian Port Authority and Customs. No one will blink an eye when the containers carrying our seedlings arrive.'

The room was surrounded again with silence. The air conditioner hummed.

'This is becoming interesting,' Dad said.

'Wallahi, it can only get interesting, sir, if you agree to this plan, kawai!'

'Yes. You gain financially. You also gain politically. Think about it, James. Let me tell you, James, no matter how wealthy you are, without political power in Africa you are nothing. For example, you may be driving a Rolls Royce, but if a mere state governor is passing with a Peugeot 504, you have to clear by the side of the road for him. If you want to board a plane, they can displace you for a minister, a governor, a senator, even an ordinary local government council chairman. In Africa, power counts, not money,' Doctor Daniel explained.

'Do I want power? That is the question you should've asked me, Daniel.'

'Who doesn't want power?' He laughed.

'Look, power kills a man's conscience. And what is a man without conscience? He is like dead wood.'

'Even dead wood has its use, James. But I don't agree that power strips a man of his conscience, rather I think power makes man aware.' The journalist explained.

'Aware of what?'

'Aware of what he is, who he is in the society. It is second to enlightenment.'

'I think it is greater than enlightenment for power finances knowledge,' Doctor Daniel contributed.

'And power kills knowledge—'

'Only in places like Africa. And that is what we strive to change. We can nurture some kind of power that will pursue illumination.'

'Is it possible? Is this not merely rhetoric?'

'Do I sound unserious to you, James?'

The journalist said, 'We all are educated people. We have no friendship with darkness.'

'Look, my concern is to have our nation grow economically,' Dad said.

'Alhamdullillah! You share the same aspiration as many of us then, James.'

'We might pretend as hard as we can that we don't love power because the opportunity has not presented itself, but our hearts know better than our heads that when the opportunity comes knocking, we will leap and grab power with all tenacity and ...' He clenched his fingers into a fist and continued, 'Drink its profits and savour it.'

'That is true, James. What Daniel said is true. We have enjoyed power in Nigeria since independence. We know that it is true. You are younger and with wealth, but as soon as you have power, you will understand that not even the gods will blink at you. You can do anything; kill and be killed for, steal and be stolen for. Churches will honour you, mosques will pray for you, communities will crown you, and God will bless your handiwork, gbogbotigbo... just wait and see.'

Dad's hand went to his jaw. He sat back, thinking.

SIXTEEN

Dad looked around and said, 'Leona! Is it not too late to be reading now? Go and sleep, okay?'

When I was leaving, I heard him tell Mum, 'Now, Dear, you are still up? I thought you'd gone to bed?'

Smart walked into the sitting room to retrieve the wine glasses and plates and clean up the place. Mum stood up from the armchair she was sitting on in the lobby and approached him.

'What is the problem, James?'

'What is what?'

'The meetings that have been going on—'

'They are meetings.'

'This is the second time those men have been here. It amazes me that we have only been in this country for two years and you already have friends with such evil in their hearts, huh?'

'How do you know my friends have evil in their hearts, woman? Do you listen to our conversations? Why?'

'Tsk. Because they do. We know why they come here. We know what you people are planning. What you are planning is evil.' She approached him. 'And when did you start barring me from listening in on your conversations?'

'Oh, woman!'

'When?'

'Shut up!'

'I won't shut up in my house o.'

Dad scoffed. 'What do you know?'

'Huh?'

Dad was silent.

'May I remind you that I have a degree in International Relations. That—'

'Spare me!'

'And don't ever tell me to shut up again, James.'

He glared at her.

'James.' She went close to him. 'You are planning a coup, a treasonable act, huh. It is evil!'

'Look, tell me what makes a coup evil, Mary.'

'Because you will kill people—'

'People, Mary, who have killed this nation in many a million ways, people who kill every day, who kill innocent youths, who starve children even though there are enough wealth and resources to go around; people who assassinate laureates and priests and academicians; people who stifle the growth of businesses and kill the economy, and on and on.'

'Yes. Yes. But you are not God, James! By sponsoring a coup, you kill not just these people you mentioned, but countless innocent men and women and soldiers, huh. That is evil, James!'

'Well, you don't know what you are saying, Woman.'

'I know what I am saying.' Mum's voice softened. 'I know, James. Tsk. I lost two very dear people to war... plus Yaya's children. I know that what you and your friends plan can lead us to war, huh?'

Dad turned and began to walk back into the sitting room.

'You run away when your conscience begins to tell you the truth.' Mum followed him into the sitting room. Her voice became sober. 'Listen, James. We ran away from trouble in Sudan. Tsk. We have a good life here. Why are you not content? Why do you court trouble?' Mum's voice was pleading and calm and soft.

Dad said with sarcasm, 'Look, I am content.'

'My father, whom you loved so much, died in Sudan, in the presence of you and your daughter. Leona watched some *people* murder her grandfather. Why? Because he collected money from the government and betrayed his people. It messed our lives up. We would have been killed. I am still hiding though I am in a distant land. Why do you want to tread that path, James, eh?' She closed her eyes. Dad stared at her. He could not say anything. 'Why do you hearken to vain promises of wealth?'

'I have wealth. Look, Mary I am drawn to the plight of my countrymen and women.' He sat down forcefully on one of the cushions.

'Oh, how saintly you are, my husband! Tsk!' her voice rose, then died slowly, 'Please, I beg of you, don't do this.'

'I need to contribute to saving my nation. We need to progress, to transit to democracy.'

Mum knew he was lying. It had more to do with the quest for wealth and fame.

'But there are repercussions. General Babangida is evil. What if this coup fails, huh? Eh?'

'It won't fail.'

'What if this plot leaks before the coup?'

Dad hesitated. 'It won't leak, Woman! And, please leave me be!' Dad hurled the words at her. There was silence. 'Or do you plan to hand me over to the authorities? Do you?'

Later that night, I was in my bed trying to sleep when the door opened, and Mum came in.

'You are still up?'

'Yes, Mum.'

'Okay.'

She sat on the bed; and I sat up, facing her.

'Tsk. Leona,' she called. 'Your father is trying to become a politician. And I don't like the kind of friends he keeps.'

I did not know what to say. I was not used to Mum coming to discuss issues with me. She just always expected me to keep aloof. In the house, no one asked me to go in when important issues were discussed. They would argue, quarrel, and debate on important as well as mundane issues, and pretend I was not present. I would ask no questions and talked only if I was talked to. Ever since we escaped assassination from Sudan, my parents began to regard me with some sense of responsibility. To them, I was not just a child, I was more than that; a person who had experienced the world as much as they had, some iron that had passed through a blazing furnace and came out unbent and stronger.

I was their pampered little child. I was not sent away when important issues were being discussed but my opinion was never asked for nor needed. So, I was surprised when Mum came to talk to me. Perhaps she was beginning to realise that Dad was slipping away every day. He was no longer that jovial family man we knew back in Sudan who would play with his wife and daughter, go on trips with us, and tell us stories. He was now a serious businessman. He travelled anytime he wanted without telling anyone and came back when he wanted. He took decisions without discussing them with Mum. We only knew about his actions when they were being implemented. It was as if in his country, Nigeria, his wings sprouted, and he could fly higher than he ever imagined.

'But Mum, will he be fine? Will they kill him like they killed Grandpa?'

Mum recognised the worry written all over my face and the strain in my voice. 'Leona. No. hmm? They cannot do that.'

She caressed my shoulder. 'This is his country. This is his home. They cannot.' She was silent, then as if in doubt, she said, 'Tsk. I hope they don't.'

She took my head to her breasts.

'Dad has changed, Mum.'

She was silent for a while. Then she said, 'He has been busy, swamped with business and politics. You are all I have now. You know, eh?'

'Yes, Mum.'

'You are growing into a woman, Leona. Do you know that?'

I forced out a smile.

She looked into my eyes. 'You know, as you grow up, you look more like Yaya.' She smiled. I made a mental note to look at the medium-sized photo very well the next day when I go to her room. 'She was very beautiful. Tsk. I used to be envious of her. Growing up, I lied against her several times to get her in trouble, for looking beautiful.'

'Mum?'

She smiled beautifully now. 'Yeah. We were children. She was the most beautiful in the village. Tsk. Many men were already setting out cattle for their sons to come for Yaya's hand in marriage, back then. And her beauty was her undoing for she was married off early, as soon as she finished high school.'

'Mum, why did she not leave her town before the war came?'

'The war had just started. The soldiers invaded her town, early morning while they were asleep and massacred them… she was planning that morning to travel back to where she was teaching at a boarding school. Tsk. If only she had left the day before. Her husband was safe because he had travelled to buy goods for his shop. The shop was burnt. Their house and car were burnt. The adorable children... everything... gone.'

I did not know what to say.

'Oh. How our mother loved Yaya. She loved her so much. Sometimes I think it was good our mother died early... that she was not alive to learn of what happened to Yaya.'

There was prolonged silence.

'Leo. You have to be careful. Okay?'

'Mum, careful with what?'

'With life.' I stared into her eyes. She looked away and said with seriousness, 'With boys too. You hear?' I looked away. She held me by the arms and looked into my eyes as if searching for assurances that I would be cautious with boys. If only she knew what was to come. If only she knew. 'Turn off the light and sleep,' she said.

I did and the room became dark. I saw her silhouette on the wall behind her. Outside, crickets chirped; birds sang incoherently, and cars hooted. We heard some voices rising and falling from the sitting room, and the faint sound of the leaves on the ube tree by the window as they swished gently to the breeze.

'Whatever you need to know, about life, just ask me. Always.'

'Yes, Mum.'

'Ask me because I am your friend.'

'You are my mother, Mum.'

She climbed on my bed and rested her back on the wall. 'Your mother is your friend too, you know? Eh?' I stayed calm, wondering what she meant. 'Let us start with you calling me Mary. Will you?'

My eyes widened. 'No... Mum.'

She raised her eyebrow.

'But that is your name, Mum. I cannot call you by your name. Dad will be angry.'

'Tsk. Don't worry about your father. Ha! Call me Mary, always. Understood?'

I fell asleep later, in her arms. I was excited and sad at the same time.

That night I had a nightmare that I could not describe. When I woke up, she had gone to her room.

SEVENTEEN

Smart had put off telling me what she wanted us to talk about; what she said Mum told her sometime before she died. I did not want to seem too eager, so, I let her be. The night that Aunty Agii came and while I could hear Dad and his friends exchange banter in the sitting room and Aunty Agii laugh loudly too, my door opened and Smart walked in.

She was dressed in oversized jean trousers folded a few times. I thought they may have belonged to Mum because after the funeral she opted to take all of Mum's belongings that we wanted to burn or give away. I was now used to seeing her dress in Mum's clothes and shoes and some jewellery without having to swallow hard.

'Madam Agnes was calling you.'

'To do what?'

'To say "Hello" to the visitors.'

'Mstcheew.'

I sat up.

Most of Dad's friends and visitors never stopped admiring and staring at me; some even swallowed saliva while looking at me, and sometimes, Dad noticed. There was never a time I visited Abuja that I did not have one offer or another from them; mostly old men whose desire for girls young enough to be their granddaughters flew overboard. They went extra miles to get my phone number, called endlessly, and offered to pay money into my account and buy me heaven and earth.

'Don't worry. We will keep the affair a secret. Your father will never know,' they all promised.

Adulike said I was being childish. 'Come on, babe. You want to be a model, right? Your dad is refusing you go to any agency. These wealthy men can give you all the money you need, fiam, that you wouldn't remember this modelling dream of yours.'

Everywhere I went, heads turned. It is difficult trying to keep your head straight when you know how people react to seeing you, knowing that you are beautiful and the effect your beauty has on people is another daily challenge, more difficult than trying to keep up with the doctor's advice to run some kilometres every day.

Smart stood by the door.

'You don't want to sit down?'

'No.'

'Tell me what you want to tell me.'

She sighed. 'By the grace of God, sometime before Madam died, before she was killed, she told me that some people had been blackmailing her for long.'

'You too believe Mum was killed?' I was frowning now. She did not answer. 'So why would she tell you that?'

'Leona, Madam was always lonely. After many years, by the grace of God, we became friends; not that we were close, but sometimes when she returned from work and was settling in her room, I would be helping her remove her sandals or unzip her gown, or rub some ointment on her body, and she would be talking to me.'

'I see,' I thought she was blabbing.

'Then, she said she wanted you to grow into a strong woman. She once mentioned that if you were strong, you would never allow anything happen to her. Madam was seeing you as someone older. I didn't understand that.'

'She did?'

'Yes. Yes.' She nodded as she responded. It sounded like what Mum would say.

It was like what Grandpa once told me in Sudan, the day we were attacked by bandits, 'Never allow anyone take advantage of you.' I came out of the bed and sat on a chair, thinking.

'Why would she tell you this?' *What does this mean?* I wondered.

'Only God can say.'

I saw tears in her eyes now. She was quite close to Mum, I realised.

'Madam told me a lot of things. Before she died, she was talking a lot to me, mostly when she returned from work, not when she was preparing for work or during weekends. If Madam didn't go to work, she wouldn't talk to me... tell me those things, I mean.'

I wondered if Mum was depressed but did not know it. Why would she be talking to Smart and telling her things? Of all people to talk to, why Smart? Yet, I wondered who was left to talk to. I was away at the university, visiting only during vacations or when I was ill; Dad was away on business or political trips, and when he was not engaged in those, he was with Aunty Agii or my school mother whom he later married. I recoiled at remembering that. Mum had only a few friends ever since we came to Nigeria; she could not bring herself to keep many.

'So, do you believe someone killed Mum?'

Smart looked at me for some seconds as if she had not heard me.

'The day Madam died, nothing was wrong with her o, at all. She came back from work and... and... before she left for work, she was all enthusiastic about the progress the factory in Sudan was making. She was on the phone with someone while entering the car, and she was talking about it. When she got back, she could barely walk. She said she had stomach trouble.' No one had ever told me this. I gawked at Smart. 'I gave her Gelusil tablet. She didn't want to eat anything. Leona, Madam told me to tell you that she wasn't happy. That she was sorry.' She looked down.

'She did?'

'Yes.'

'Sorry for what?'

'I don't know.' She began to cry.

I stood up hurriedly.

'She made me leave when I tried to ask what she was sorry about.'

Smart had been leaning on the door, and she slipped to the floor, sobbing now. 'When I checked back, shortly afterwards because my mind wasn't at rest. I felt this heaviness. I was thinking something had happened to my madam. And I hurried upstairs and...' I sat back on the bed. 'She had foamed in the mouth.'

No one had ever told me this. I had gone to model for a pharmaceutical company when I got the call that Mum was dead. It was the day scheduled for the last photo shoot. Dad did not want me to register with a modelling agency, but Mum had talked to the owners, asking them to see me when she heard they were looking for models. They saw me and agreed to use me instantly. It was a one-off project. When I got the call and hurried home, she had been rushed to the hospital. I did not see her until when we flew to Sudan for the funeral and Dad insisted I looked into the coffin to see her for the last time. After she died, Dad forbade me from modelling.

'Why didn't you ever tell me this?'

'I don't know.'

We were silent for a long time.

Smart was done sniffling and coughing intermittently. She wiped her face with her palms.

'I am sorry, Leona. It is God's will.'

I nodded.

When she was about to leave, I asked, 'The man who comes to the house to see you, does he want to marry you?'

Caught unawares, she paused. 'It's not... it's none of your business.' Her voice was stern.

'I don't mean any bad, Smart.'

She opened the door and walked away.

I fell back on the bed and covered my face with my palms.

'Screw you,' I whispered to myself.

EIGHTEEN

It took a long time, but finally, the tears came. The circumstances surrounding Mum's death were unclear. Was she poisoned? Who did? The Wales? Her business partners? Could it be anyone in the family? One of Dad's wives? I was not sure about Senior Elizabeth, my former school mother, but I knew Aunty Agii would never do such a thing. Did Dad know more than he was telling me? Could it be why he wanted me to marry Akinola Wale? Recently, I had been researching the man. He was six years older than me and now that his father was incapacitated by a stroke, he was running his family's business, Dragons Investment Incorporated.

The tears had stopped flowing, but my heart was beating so fast. The last times my heart beat this fast were after Onyinye told me that her sister wanted to arrange for us to have sex with some boys and on the day that we finally did. After Onyinye told me what Rosa was planning, my mind became muddled with ideas and thoughts, so strong that they engaged my heart in a drum-beating fight. My heart pounded on my chest, causing fear mixed with anxiety and expectations to fill my head, and I could not obliterate it from my mind.

Mum had asked me to always tell her everything, but how could I tell her what Onyinye told me? There were things that were never said, and not to one's mother, not even if the mother was the kind that wanted you to call her by her first name. I wondered if Mum was scared that she was losing Dad to politics and business and luxury and did not want to lose me also, hence the incident of coming into my room to cuddle me until I fell asleep and suggesting that I call her 'Mary'. How would I feel calling her by her name in the presence of friends, instead of 'Mum' or 'Mama' or 'Mummy', or whatever other children called their mothers? I was worried, but she would force the name into my mouth, like she used to force food into my mouth when I was much younger—and used to abhor food—and hold my mouth shut until I swallowed.

When I got into my bathroom, the night after Onyinye made her suggestion, I pulled down my clothes and closed my eyes and imagined how it would feel having a man on top of me. It would be painful, I thought, but pleasurable, I imagined; otherwise, people would not be doing it. That night, I was in my room ironing my school uniform and listening to 'I believe in you' by Don Williams from Mum's huge stereo as it travelled through the walls of the house into every room and every ear. Mum loved the stereo so much; it was one of the things she had smuggled into the car trunk when we were leaving our house in Khartoum.

It had followed her to Omdurman and was brought back from Sudan; and she had promised to give it to me when I got married. When I was done, I went into the bathroom and filled the tub with water. I added some bathing fruit mix from a huge plastic container, one of the materials Dad imported into the country. When it lathered so well and frothed, I dipped my naked body into the tub, still shivering at the thought of what Onyinye suggested.

Then, I thought of Kosi. In school, we all had a boy we were attracted to. I was attracted to a boy named Kosisochukwu. I had a crush on him. I loved him. There was nothing I did without him. I always told Smart to prepare fried plantain for me to take to him in school. He was my husband, and everyone knew it; our class teacher, Anya Four Taati, inclusive. When I did badly in Mathematics, Kosi put me through during school breaks, but that was not often because I was always with my friends. It was while we discussed Mathematics that he told me about himself; his father was a civil servant with the Nigerian Railway Corporation, and his mother was dead. He was always late in paying his tuition, and he did not have enough textbooks. There was nothing I would have loved most than for Kosi to visit me, but Dad would have a heart attack if a boy came to the house to see me. My parents guarded me like a fowl would her chicks. They always wanted to know what I was doing and where I was at every point in time. The only visitors allowed me were Onyinye's family; but my parents never knew that Onyinye and her sisters were corrupt.

All my friends had their 'husbands' too, and just as we discussed the boys, they discussed us too. After school hours, we held hands and walked to nearby shops before our cars started arriving. There, we bought and exchanged snacks and lollipops, and joked and played with them before going home. And every morning, we exchanged love letters and poems. Some of the girls whose parents had telephones in their homes called when their parents were not watching, except Onyinye whose parents never cared about what she was doing as long as she was happy. I never spoke with Kosi after school hours because they had no telephone in their house. Other boys in school bullied him. Kosi once told me that the boys were speculating that he was having sex with me. In our school, everyone discussed sex more than we discussed our books, but our teachers and parents thought we knew nothing about that.

Aunty Agii's knock on the door of my room jostled me out of my thoughts.

'Can I come in?' She opened the door. 'You've been crying?'

I sighed. 'I didn't ask you in.'

'Sorry, Nne, I can leave.' She smiled her apologies.

'No.' I sat up. 'Stay.'

She stood by the door, unsure. 'Your dad said to ask you to come down.'

'Why?'

She smiled, 'Someone is here to see you.' I looked at

her questioningly. 'Akinola Wale.' I sighed. 'You should see him, Nne m. He is cute, so-so cute, Nne. I think your dad is trying to match-make both of you, or his dad is the one trying to. I don't know whose idea it is, but I do know they think if you two get married, the family feud would end.'

'Why are women always the sacrificial lambs?' I did not know when I said that.

Aunty Agii hurried to the bed, 'No. No. Why would you say that?' She patted my shoulder. 'Your father wants the best for you, I am sure.'

'Hmm?'

'Look, no one will force you to make a choice you do not want. Okay? At least, I won't allow that.'

I looked up at her and she nodded. If only she knew.

'I can't see him.'

She was silent for some seconds. 'Okay.' She stood. 'This modelling thing… I think it's good. I think you'll fit in well.'

My eyes flew open. I beamed, 'You do?'

'Nne, eh, you have the figure, shape, and all. I have talked to Chief about it.'

My eyes sparkled to life.

'He said okay.'

'Oh!'

'So, do you know where to start?'

'There is this agency in Lagos that has contacted me. They seem desperate that I come to audition in their firm. I think the auditioning is just a formality though.'

'Good. In Lagos? You can stay at the house.'

My heart leapt. 'Thank you, Aunty.'

'Mbanu. I bu nwanne m. Anytime.'

The excitement was like when Kosi and I first kissed after our common entrance examinations and I had not seen him for a while. I went to visit Adulike who lived on the same street with him; I had to plead with Mum several times before she allowed me to go, under the watchful eyes of Smart.

It was a sunny morning. I rarely saw my friends since we were not going to school anymore, but we talked on the telephone; therefore, when we got an opportunity to see one another, it was always fun. We gossiped until late in the afternoon, ate ice cream and popcorns, licked lollipops, ate chocolates, and watched the latest fashion shows on television. All of us wanted to become models, including Ezinne who was fat, like all those American women we saw in comic shows on television.

That morning, I went with Onyinye.

'Make sure you are in the same taxi with them, huh? Understood?' Mum had told Smart, holding her own left ear.

'Yes, Madam.'

'Understood?'

'Yes, Madam.'

'Make sure they don't talk to any boys. They can't begin to talk to boys at this age.'

'Yes, Madam.'

'That is why you must keep an eye on them.'

'Okay, Madam. By the grace of God I will do as Madam has instructed,' Smart responded, her arms on her back as she stood in front of Mum.

'Grace of God? Eh, Smart? Tsk. I don't want to hear stories afterwards and you tell me it was because 'grace of God' wasn't with you. Please o!'

'Yes, Madam.'

We had fun at Adulike's place. They lived in a bungalow with a towering fence that had a red gate, and a huge dog named Papi. The dog liked me, but I hated dogs, and I always told her to make sure the dog was locked in before I came.

In her house, we gossiped and played around. Smart waited for hours and got tired, and since I had all day, she took permission to run an errand.

'Don't go anywhere, Leona. I will be back before one hour, you hear?'

'Don't worry. We are not going anywhere.'

We suspected that it must be her boyfriend she was off to visit. It was the opportunity I had waited for. When we heard the sound of the gate as it closed, Adulike followed her and watched as she crossed to another street; then, she came back and called on us, and we left for Kosi's house.

It was in the afternoon and Enugu was always hot. The area where Kosi and Adulike lived was quiet except the noise of the commercial motorcycles. The street was dusty because the road was not tarred, and the buildings were dirty too. We got to the building where he lived and as we climbed the stairs to his flat, I was nervous as Onyinye rang the doorbell. Then, the door was thrown open and his friend, who was also our classmate, called out his name and said, 'Talk of the devil and she appears!'

'Who is a devil?' I asked.

'So, you stupid boys were discussing us, eh? So, boys now gossip? Umu nwoke ana akukwu asiri?' Onyinye asked.

We laughed, but my heart sang and beat fast in the knowledge that they were talking about me. I wondered if he thought about me at nights like I did; if he saw me in his dreams, chased me about, and kissed my mouth until he woke, like I did in my own dream every other night.

'Who is that, Ebuka?' Kosi called from within the house.

'Ghosts. Who brought you girls here?' Ebuka gawked at us.

For some seconds the sitting room was filled with silence. Kosi was wearing a yellow-coloured polo and a boxer short.

'Can't you offer us seats?' Onyinye inquired.

'Sit down.'

Kosi tried very hard not to look at me. My hair was newly braided, and my face looked slimmer. My lips were large and the colour of chocolate. My body was fit perfectly into jeans trousers. I was also wearing a striped top that exposed my shoulders. Adulike had on a skirt and a worn-out shirt, while Onyinye wore a pair of jeans trousers and a blue shirt that clung to her body.

Instinctively, we scanned the sitting room. Parts of the sofas were torn, here and there. The floor was covered with a new blue rug that matched the colour of the wall, but the wall was stained with mosquito blood. On the wall, there were old calendars and almanacs from various government agencies and ministries and a few framed family photographs, and about six or seven framed photos of Jesus and those of the Virgin Mary. There was a large cabinet on which rested a small television and a turntable. There were no curtains, and there were no dining table and chairs.

'Come, Leona. I don't like this place,' Onyinye whispered to me.

'I don't too, but we better not be stupid.'

'Let's leave,' she said in a hushed tone. Adulike gave her a nudge.

'I made vegetable pottage,' Kosi said. 'Can I get it for you girls?'

'Don't bother,' we managed to say after hesitating.

I was surprised that he cooked because I did not know how to light a stove. Learning this about him mesmerised me. I fantasised about him, and in my mind, I could see him, grown up, in boxer shorts, and stirring something in a pot in a large kitchen, while I clung to his back, kissing his neck and giggling.

'Then, what do I offer you?' he asked.

'Offer them oranges, the ones your sister kept in the refrigerator,' Ebuka, advised.

'Oranges then?' Kosi asked.

'N… no, we're okay,' Adulike answered for us.

'We are okay,' I said.

He went inside and came back with a huge photo album. We began to look at pictures of when he was born, and when he was a child. We saw his mum and I looked at him, and he nodded. We saw his parents' wedding pictures. As we were looking at the photographs, my friends stood up to go, giggling as they left. I said I would stay a while. We had rehearsed this before coming.

'Remember your chaperon, before you get carried away!' Adulike called.

'Smart? Forget her.'

'Eh?'

'I won't stay long. I will be right behind you.'

When they were gone, we talked a bit. Ebuka also left when it seemed we had ignored him.

We were now alone, and the room was charged as if a heater was turned on. I felt sweaty inside me.

'So, how have you been doing?' I asked, with the Sudanese accent that occasionally escaped my lips when I was nervous.

'Fine. I still read. Do you still read?' he asked.

'Yes,' I lied. 'I missed you,' I said, taking him by surprise.

He looked up at me; he was shy. My beauty captivated him, and as my eyes met his own, it charmed him.

'You look beautiful… like an angel, Leona,' he said. His voice was cracked.

'Yeah. And you look …' I said and tossed the album on the centre-table. I shifted and was close to him. He remained rooted where he was sitting as if in a trance. He did not make any move to shift his arms. It was as if he was affixed with nails to that position. We said nothing for what seemed to be up to three minutes and just stared at each other in the eyes. Shy. Nervous.

'Did you miss me this one month and some weeks?' I was nervous and afraid of what I was trying to do, but I wanted to try it again after Onyinye's sister made the arrangement. He wanted to open his mouth and utter some words, but my charm seemed to have stolen all the words in his brain.

The clock in the room ticked away the seconds, and the solemn quietness made the scene obscene, hush, and fetish too. Spirits lurked around. They enchanted us. We were just an inch apart. I brought my lips close to his. They met, he made as if to throw back his head, but my charm was irresistible. That instant, he inhaled deeply and closed his eyes. I brought my hands like Rosa, Onyinye's sister, had illustrated. I touched his laps. He quivered. I threw myself on him, pushing him to the floor. It was hurried and uncoordinated.

He was pulling up his shorts and saying, 'What have you just made us do?' when I hurried out of his house.

I dreamt of him always after that day, but I did not see him again until my last year at the university. By then, he was already a seminarian.

NINETEEN

Adulike called to tell me that my father's wife was threatening her. I wondered why Elizabeth was threatening
to pour acid on my friend. Why? We all attended the same
secondary school. Elizabeth was our senior and my school
mother, which meant that she was like my self-appointed
chaperone. Once freshers came into the school every new
term, senior students picked those they wanted as their
school daughters. They got to keep their provisions and
pocket monies safe for them, and if one was unlucky to have
a greedy school mother, all their stuff would be gone. But
school mothers were protective against bullies. So, Senior
Elizabeth was my school mother and we had a good relationship until she came to stay with us at Enugu on vacation and
my father fell in love with her.

I always felt edgy anytime someone mentioned Elizabeth;
my heart sank into my stomach and begin to pound heavily
like a pestle against a kitchen mortar, with a sound akin to the
thunderous noise of a cannon shot at a great chief's funeral.
We rarely saw each other and anytime we did, I stared her
down, my lips pursed in hatred, until the intimidating beauty

of my face and eyes scared her to submission or she looked away. Then, she would tell my dad how I was a witch and lie that while in school, rumour had it that I flew at night. My hatred for her climbed one million flights higher when she lied to my dad that while we were in school, I slept with other girls and Dad called Mum to report me to her.

'Leave my daughter alone, James, huh. You and your harlot of a girl should leave my daughter alone. Tsk.' Mum never referred to either Elizabeth or Agnes as wife.

'So, if your daughter misbehaved in school and picked up an odd behaviour, I shouldn't caution her?'

'Thank God you didn't say "our daughter", James. You said "your daughter". Tsk. You have seen other women who would give you your most-longed-for male children; so, leave my daughter for me. I don't want them to pierce my only eye with their witchcraft.'

'Mary!'

'Leave me. Please! Tsk.'

Dad never mentioned the issue again, except to Onyinye's mother who then asked Rosa. Rosa told her not to mind Elizabeth, that she had always been jealous of me. So Onyinye's mum reported her findings to Dad and that was that. But what Rosa never told her mother was that it was Onyinye who was indoctrinated into the act in school by her own school mother, and that she knew about it but did not think it was wrong. Rosa had always been like that, free-minded.

I hated Senior Elizabeth for snatching my dad from

my mother, though she was not the one who first did the snatching. It was Agnes who first took Dad away—that is how Mum said it.

It was around the time when Dad was always talking about me, about Sudan, and the fun we had together travelling everywhere. He would gush about my beauty, possibly telling her that no children of his from other women would equal my beauty; this infuriated Elizabeth, I was sure. But I hated her mostly because she did not try to make friends with Mum like Aunty Agii did. Agnes respected Mum as the first wife and wrote to her, rang her, or sent messages across if there was anything that had to do with the family that she wanted to be discussed, though Mum ignored her, never responding to her calls or messages, and put down the phone whenever she heard Agnes' voice. Elizabeth was not the kind of woman to patronise. She was all out to get whatever she wanted. She was beautiful in her own way too—fair, average height, and classy. I loved that she was classy.

When I got into Mr Bigg's where Adulike was waiting for me, she had worked herself into a temper and was boiling with rage.

'Warn that your mother oh! Warn her!' she yelled as I walked into the eatery. Other people in the café must have been speculating on why my friend was screaming like that in a public place and asking me to warn my mother.

'Hey, calm down, girl. Ah! Ah!' I sat down, my gown sweeping the floor. I placed my handbag on the glass table. 'But why are you crossing her line na?'

'Ha! Me I no cross any line oh. See, babes, I like your dad. It's no secret. Every John and James knows that, including you, his daughter. Unlike her, I've always made my mind open. I am not a sneaky leech. I say what's on my mind.'

'I know. Calm down, girl.'

'See. Your dad and I have started texting each other.' Her voice was lowered now. 'I got his phone number from my dad's phone, and we talked.'

'And Elizabeth snoops and finds out her husband is doing, with some other girl, what he did with her that made her his wife?'

'Yes o, babes. And she is upset. She called me. Imagine? "Eh, Adulike Obiora. So, you are the one coming on my husband, eh? If I find you one inch closer to my *Minister*, I will kill you. In fact, I will pour acid on you. Your smeared face will appear on every tabloid in this country." Imagine that. What does she think she can do?'

'And what did you say to her?'

'I told her to go fuck a cow.'

'Haba, don't you think that was harsh?'

'Harsh? Come on, she said she was going to kill me… pour raw acid on me.'

'She didn't mention raw, I am sure,' I was smiling.

'Acid is acid, raw or not.'

'Well, I think you used harsh words yourself.'

'Which side are you on, Miss Egbufor? I am your friend, babe.'

'I am on your side, trust me. Who she be wey go make

me no dey your side? Well, Elizabeth is a serious runs girl. The only people she couldn't threaten were Aunty Agii, and my mum, when she was alive. They were in before her, but she thinks every other person wants to make her lose her source of cake. You know, she fears that just the way she hooked my dad, other girls might do the same.'

'Ehen. Before nko? She wants everything all for herself? No o.'

'Ha! Come oh, have you forgotten it's my father we are talking about here, Adulike?'

'Ehen?' She looked at me in the face, but I could see the hints of a smile.

'You shouldn't even be making passes on my dad. You are supposed to be my friend.'

The hints of a smile disappeared, and her face became blank. Her expression could have meant anything—frustration or shame. She looked down on the table, then raised her face and smiled conspiratorially.

'I know. I don't mean any disrespect, Leo.'

'Then, please stay off my dad. Elizabeth's is enough insult already,' I said deliberately making my voice even, I hoped it was bereft of any emotion.

She said nothing. We were silent for a while.

'Can we go order some food? I am famished.'

She stayed put.

'Hey!'

'I am not hungry.'

I went to the counter and ordered some food.

'Okay, I will leave your dad.'

'Better.'

I began to eat.

After a while, she said, 'But Elizabeth would think it was because of her warnings. Mstcheew!'

Then, I knew she was not going to leave him.

TWENTY

Adulike and Dad had something together, and she sent some evidence of their romping to Elizabeth. I do not know what happened, but I think they went on a date and Adulike sent a photo of her in bed in a hotel with Dad asleep in the background. Elizabeth threw a fit, calling Dad all sort of names and tore his papers, the one on the table when she barged into the house.

I was in the kitchen preparing dinner when it happened, on a day that did not start off as a bad one. Earlier, Akinola Wale had called, and we talked. He sounded like a nice man and mostly discussed formal issues with me, and I was reeling in the euphoria of his call. The velvety nature of his voice mixed with the thrill that I was considering dating him to avenge my mother's death was giving me some kicks when a car sped into the compound and someone threw open the door. I hurried out in time to see Elizabeth hurl her phone at Dad who was reclining on the sofa, watching *NTA News at 9*. She yelled until her rage got the better of her, and she tore the documents Dad had on the table.

She was dressed in tight-fitting leggings and a black singlet, and just as her fair-complexioned body radiated off the lights in the room, her loud yells bounced off the walls like a tennis ball.

'How dare you!' I screamed at her.

Dad said nothing. He looked tired and shaken. He was not used to people challenging him that way.

'How dare you barge in here like a criminal... like a prostitute that didn't receive her pay?' I strode into the centre of the room as she turned swiftly to behold me.

'Hey!' Dad warned.

'How dare you!' She folded her hands on her breasts and gawked at me. 'Eh? Ashawo! Ashawo kobo kobo!' I called.

'Hey!' Dad shouted at me.

'Cheap prostitute!' I continued.

'Mind your language, Leona,' Dad cautioned. 'She is my wife.'

'Look at this one!' Elizabeth jumped as she said the words, pointing at me. 'So, you are here to defend your friend, abi? She is the one who is a cheap prostitute.'

'You agree you are a prostitute but not a cheap one?'

'Gerrout!' she yelled, approaching me.

'Get out of this house. My mother made it clear to you to never come here or to the house at Enugu. What are you doing here?' I demanded, approaching her.

'Your dead mother cannot do anything more than my dirty pants!'

'Hey! Enough. Look, if I hear you mention my *late* wife

again, if I hear her name in your mouth, I will *skin* you alive!'
Dad warned.

'Don't mind her, anuofia!' I said, venom in my voice.

We were a few feet apart, measuring each other. Her eyes
bulged, the veins on her head and face all clear and vicious.
Dad stared at both of us, his eyes moving from Elizabeth to
me, confusion all over his face.

'If you don't get out this minute, I will kill you,' I said
calmly. She looked at me, took a deep breath, and stepped
back.

'Idiot!'

'I know. Out!'

She stood her ground.

Then, Dad's thick, Igbo accent boomed, 'Out of my
house. Now!'

She turned and their eyes locked. 'And if I refuse?'

'Look, young woman. If you don't get out of here this
minute, I will cut you out of everything, hmm. No allow-
ances for you and your boys.'

'Eh? Okay na! Do that! Go ahead and do that! Do your
worst!' she fired back.

I turned and headed for the kitchen, while she back-
tracked out of the house, yelling all the way.

After she left, I called Adulike and rebuked her on the
phone. She was calm all through. I knew she went out with
my dad to spurn Elizabeth, but I had asked her not to. She
ought to show me some respect, I told her. Now I wondered
if I had any friends after all. Why would my friends want

to sleep with my dad for his money and still hangout with me, look me in the eyes, and laugh out loud with me as we discuss girls' stuff? I could not understand that. It did not help matters that I called Onyinye before I slept, and she laughed her head off, making me feel stupid and childish.

'What's wrong if Adulike wants to fuck your dad, babes?'

'Wants to or already did.'

'What is wrong with that? Abeg, babes, this is the twenty-first century, damn it.'

'Good night!'

I threw myself on my bed. Onyinye was the most changed of us all. The one who was most daring, most experimental; the one who allowed her school mother touch her in her bunk while she slept at night, and later began to enjoy the act and never stopped. The one who would defend abortion in front of Kosi, knowing that Kosi was a seminarian and his faith abhorred taking life in anyway. She would say that a woman had the choice to do to the foetus in her stomach as she chose; she would go lap-dancing in Lagos, not for money but because she wanted to feel the touch of men and know if they would be as sweet and exciting as girls.

We were changed so much by our experiences as children. Most especially, we were changed by Rosa who was as beautiful as Onyinye. After Rosa was born, it had taken a long time before Onyinye came, hence Onyinye's name: 'Gift from God'. Their parents were good-looking, especially their father. He was dark-complexioned and broad-shouldered, and he spoke quietly and convincingly. He used to call me his daughter, and each time I was in their house, he would tell me stories of Burundi, where he lived as a young man.

Rosa was as tall as her father and as fair in complexion as her mother. She walked like a model, and like her other sisters, she carried herself with so much elegance that made us jealous of her. Whenever I was in their house, she stared at me, checked out my hair, felt it, and sighed. Other times, she patted my head and commented on how tall I was. She said that my legs were straight and too long and asked what I intended to do with legs like that. Then, she was eighteen and in her first year in the university.

Rosa was attached to Onyinye. She shared all her secrets with her. In turn, Onyinye shared them with me, and Rosa was aware of this. Rosa liked men just as she liked clothes, and she never stopped discussing them with us.

'Don't do this… don't do that… don't say this or that to a man asking you out for the first time… and if he is already your boyfriend, look him straight in the eyes while talking to him and pretend you like him so much so that he would do anything for you.' She told us. 'Boys? Hmm. Boys do not deserve to be loved; they deserve to be played with. Toy with them and let them go. They are wicked and ingrates. If you give them a part of your heart, they claim the whole and before you know it, they claim your body and sleep with you freely, without as much as giving you a kobo to buy soap to wash your pants.'

I did not like listening to her, but I could not stop because what she said was both revolting and intriguing. Each time I encountered her, her words played themselves repeatedly in my mind after I got home. At home I would force my mind to imagine Kosi on top of me, doing all those things Rosa said, touching me breasts—which Rosa said was the best feeling in the world—and making me giggle. Then came the day we were deflowered. That day, I played Ludo game with Smart while country music played on Mum's stereo. The television was turned on, broadcasting some news about the military and how the government wanted the monthly nation-wide sanitation to be taken seriously. I was expecting Onyinye's call so, I sat in the parlour, waiting while my heart beat a drum on the wall of my chest until the telephone rang a few minutes later.

'Leona, you can come. Now! Now! Oso! Oso!'

I heard the nervousness and the urgency in her voice; so, I ran out and walked the length of the street to Onyinye's compound. I carried an umbrella because Smart insisted.

Onyinye's compound was large just like ours, but the entire ground was covered in concrete and it had no trees or carpet grasses. Many cars were parked in front of the massive storey-building. Her father loved fast cars and bought them like he was buying groundnuts from hawkers along Ogbete Market. The French windows were open, and the front door was ajar; so, I walked straight into the sitting room. In the sitting room, I saw Rosa and two other boys. The two boys were my height, but probably older than Rosa though they did not look more than twenty-three years old. They were her colleagues at the university. Rosa introduced me and the boys gawked. They asked Rosa what she said was my age, and she told them. They said it was unbelievable. They asked if my parents fed me fertilisers once in a while, and Rosa laughed out loud, her high-pitched voice hitting the ceilings. I smiled and looked down at the terrazzo-covered floor. We were discussing when Onyinye came down from her room. She began talking about the latest fashion, eager to show off in the presence of the boys.

'These boys are nice,' Rosa whispered into our ears.

I saw the dark one lick his lips, and I became afraid. The fair one looked gentle and rarely talked.

Winking at the boys, Rosa suggested we go inside her room and we did, reluctantly.

'Come on, girls. Don't be scared, you hear? Don't back out now, eh. You'll do this and thank me, years later. You will see.'

The boys followed behind. Rosa's room was spacious, and she shared it with no one. From her room, one could see a large football pitch where some street boys played football every evening and on Sunday mornings. Onyinye shared a room with her other sister who was studying at the University of Nigeria, Nsukka, and who visited home occasionally. The other two elderly girls had separate rooms too, but they were rarely around. They were working in some big cities.

We sat on the bed and got talking. I stroked one of Rosa's teddy bears, while the fair boy found a novel by the lamp stand and began flipping through it.

After some minutes, Rosa said, 'Remember all we talked about, Onyinye.' She flipped her hands as if, like us, she was nervous. 'Leona, just relax, eh. My sweetheart, don't disappoint me oh. Oh?' As I looked around the room and noticed that the boys were conversing, my body quivered slightly, and I sweated underneath my clothes, even my palms were wet. Onyinye and I stared at each other in a second, and I saw in that moment, a deep lust in her eyes. It was from that day that I got to know one when I see it in people's eyes. I did not know what to do, and in as much as I wanted to leave the room and run home, I also wanted to experience whatever would happen. There was the inexplicable attraction to the feeling of having a boy on top of you, caressing your flesh, and taking your breasts into his mouth—Rosa had told us about this over a hundred times. A part of me yearned for that feeling, that experience, yet I was so scared. Some days before, Rosa had preached to us at length about sex, using lots of offensive words that I did not like. The words and her descriptions stayed with me since.

Then, our educator walked away, closing the door behind her. Onyinye was led away by the fair boy. I did not know where they were going. I became more afraid but tried to hide my fear. Already, Rosa had told us that boys liked it when you were afraid, that it made them feel like heroes. I did not want him to know that I was afraid of him. I played with my fingers and used my toes to scratch the floor. He came closer to me.

'Jesus, you are so beautiful.'

Silence.

'Your name is Leo... na?'

I nodded.

'That's such a beautiful name. I think I have seen you, somewhere before.'

'Where?' I raised my face to look at him. He took my hand.

'Somewhere.' He caressed my hand.

Grinning, he said, 'How much will you pay me for what I am about to do?'

'Ah?'

'For what you are about to enjoy?' he asked. He was now breathing steadily.

I was taken aback, and I could not wrap my mind around the words that just flew out of his mouth. So, I looked down on my toes, but not before I saw arrogance in his eyes and in his smile and remembered Rosa's words; 'Give a boy your heart, and he wants your body.' I added mine in my mind. *Give him your body, and he wants your money.*

'I'm leaving.' I stood, and he dragged me down and turned me swiftly to face him. He was muscular and his hands were painful. Then, he relaxed them on my arm and caressed me. It became soft. 'What... what are you going to do to me?' I asked in defiance. I looked at him steadily in the eyes, and he looked away.

'You are as beautiful as an angel,' he muttered. I said nothing. 'You can be my girlfriend. I know you have no boyfriend. I will always take good care of you… perhaps, marry you. All you need do is to take care of me as well.' His voice was unsteady.

'How?'

'Just take care of us. Your parents are rich, I know. Bring money, and I will take you out to many places here in Enugu. I heard you are about to go to a boarding school. You will give me money, and I will always visit you and buy you things, a lot of things like teddies, fashion books, clothes.' He was gesticulating so much, and his voice was edgy. 'When you get to school, you will see how difficult life is over there. You need someone who loves you, who is ready to be visiting every time, to bring you whatever you need, anytime.'

'Okay,' I said because I did not want to hear more. I was sure that I was dealing with a daft. I wanted to leave, but I was scared. I could hear my heartbeat. He took my lips to his mouth. It was like eating over-ripened avocado pears. I removed my mouth after what seemed like forever, shivering like I had a cold, yet wanting him to kiss me again. By this time, I was already on the bed, and he was on top of me and had unbuttoned my shirt. 'Is it going… going to be… painful?' I said softly. 'Please don't.'

'Relax.'

'Please…'

'Relax, girl.'

'I don't want again.' I was trembling. There was lots of saliva in his mouth, yet I wanted his hands on my body. As if in response, his hand touched my nipples, and I got lost.

'Please stop. It will be painful.'

'Shhh!'

'I am scared.'

'It won't be painful. If you refuse, I will force you. Then, it will be painful. I have locked the door, you know. But if you relax, I will touch you gently until you won't know when we start. You will enjoy it so much. Are you not enjoying... it... now?'

I could barely hear him, as he placed his mouth on mine again. This time I did not remove my mouth, but my entire body was shaking. His lips enveloped mine and his tongue travelled a thousand miles inside the cities of my fresh mouth, while he slowly undid my zip and traced his hand inside me. I moaned and felt tears in my eyes.

It rained that day in August 1991. Days after, I was still sore and in pains. I hid in my room and came out only when my parents were not around. Smart suspected because she always asked me why I walked the way I did, but I told her I fell and injured myself.

'You know, Leona, you should use hot water on yourself.' She said, smiling.

TWENTY-ONE

JULY 2005
ENUGU, SOUTHEASTERN NIGERIA

Each time I visit Enugu, I always feel some sort of melancholy. I never liked the town, perhaps because it was the first place we went to from Sudan. I loved Khartoum so much and the memories of the joy I shared with Grandpa and the love that radiated between Mum and Dad made me feel that Enugu was the reason everything got broken in my family, in my life. In Sudan, Grandpa and I visited various cities and towns, and he was not afraid to take me to the north. We would travel for many days, and I would miss school, and Mum would complain.

It was in Enugu that my nightmares started. Rosa got the boys to do what they did to us, and Dad impregnated Agnes and fell into the hands of my school mother, Elizabeth. It was in Enugu that Grandma came to make Mum cry; she never liked her—no matter how much Mum tried—because she was a foreigner, and it was where Dad was kidnapped by General Abacha's men and imprisoned.

The taxi was a new Lexus, painted yellow, and the driver was an elderly man. He was tall and his grey hair reminded me of Grandpa. Nothing had changed since I left, four months earlier. My plan was to return to Enugu and prepare for Lagos where I was going to check out the Emily Rose Modelling Agency that had asked to see me. I was going to live with Aunty Agii. I was also desperate to get to Enugu and check out Mum's stuff, perhaps I would find something. I had been thinking about her so much lately, since I spoke with Smart.

At the house, I struggled to drag my bags through the gate. Madam Imo was in the porch doing some vegetables. I had called to tell her I was returning, and she had warmed up, told me how lonely the house was, and asked what I would want her to prepare for me.

She looked bigger than she was when I last saw her.

'What have you been eating, Madam?' I asked her as we hugged.

'Ah! Munwa? Me? I don't eat anything.' She looked herself up and down. The folds of her stomach were visible through her white singlet, and her massive sagging breasts were threatening to burst out of the brassieres.

'It is you I should be asking. O ngi... look at you, Leona. You grow every time. I n' eto. Now your mother would be envious of your height if she was still here. Look at you, eh, bikonu.' She was holding my two arms, looking at me this way and that.

'Abeg, Mama. Leave me, biko.' I was all smiles.

She took the bags, and I followed her in. It was Mum who started calling her 'Madam' when she was brought by her friend for the job. She was too big, Mum complained. Why would a woman be this big? She would tell me this when the woman was not listening. She was older than Mum and because Mum did not know how to address her by her name, Evelyn, she called her 'Madam Imo' after her home state, Imo, and we all began to call her that. After Mum died, she wanted to stay, and Dad agreed so she would take care of the house. Dad was not in good terms with his people, except his mother; so, they rarely visited the house.

I called Kosi to inform him that I had arrived, and he was excited. He was at the Bigard Memorial Seminary and had said he would make out time to come to the house. Now, he said he could not wait to come the next day.

'I miss you,' I said. I pictured him—his afro, his ringed neck, his deep brown eyes, oh, how I loved his eyes. I missed the way his hands wandered on my body, knowing every part, every nerve and muscle. I missed the magic his fingers did while deep inside me, making me moan, causing me to smile to myself days afterwards.

After I ate, I took the key that was always hidden behind the louvres in my room, hurried to Mum's room, and opened it. It was just the way it was when she was still here. The curtains, thick and wide; the drawers, chocolate in colour; and the massive bed, taking up most of the space in the room. I saw some rat drops on the bedspread and found myself sneezing and removing some cobwebs that had got caught in my ponytail. Then, I dusted the bed, sat on it, lay on my back, and sneezed again as more dust got into my nostrils. Everything in the room stared at me, all around. There were a few photos on the wall—one of Dad and Mum at their wedding, and another one of when I was little. I saw Mum everywhere, and my memory flashed back to July 1993 when I returned home for the long vacation. Mum was looking so tired and had lost some weight. One evening, she came into my room, sat on my bed, and said nothing; she just lay down and stared at the ceiling the way I was doing now.

I remember placing my hand on her shoulder.

'Mum, is everything all right with you? What is bothering you?' She was brooding. 'Mum? Is it Dad?'

'Tsk-tsk, Leona.' She sat up. 'I don't know what is wrong with your father, huh. I don't know, but he is becoming a different person every day. He is distant. We don't talk anymore. I don't see him often. He has forbidden me from working since we returned from Khartoum, and I am tired of staying at home, but if I complain he doesn't want to hear.'

'Mum, why don't you find a job or start a business without his consent?'

'Without his consent, you say? My daughter, it's not as easy as you think, huh,' she sighed. 'We are subjects to our men. Tsk. When your man says don't do *this*, you don't do *that*. When he says sit here and don't stand up until I return from the bar, you don't stand. Tsk.' She sighed again, this time louder and longer, 'If you disobey your husband, he can send you packing. And then, what would you do? Besides, your father's people hate me enough as it is. If they hear that I disobeyed him, they would have something to capitalise on.'

'What will you do then, Mum?'

'Nothing. Your father knows I cannot go back to Sudan. He knows that things are so bad in Sudan. He knows that even if I decide to go to Sudan, I have no one there to protect me. Your father knows all these.'

'Of course, he knows.' I was helpless. I felt so bad that Mum was passing through some heartbreak and I could not do anything to help her. My stomach rumbled as if in protest. 'And that is why he treats me like a rag, Leona. He travels for a lot of political and business meetings and stays one week, two weeks, sometimes a month, and I don't see him or hear from him.'

We were calm. I saw sadness in her eyes. I saw tears too.

'I don't know what to say, Mum.'

'Don't worry, child. We are survivors. Dinka people are. We will survive.' She forced out a quick smile.

'Yes, Mum,' I smiled back.

'Mary, Leona.'

'Yes …' I looked away, and she smiled.

'That's heavy in your mouth, hmm?' she rubbed her temple. Out of the blue, she said, 'Your father was involved in the annulment of the last election.'

'Oh. How did you know that, Mummy?'

The June 12 election was a big thing. It happened just

a month earlier, and we were in school. On the day of the election, we were all in our hostels. There were no lessons because most of the teachers went to vote. People had trooped out en masse to vote because Nigerians believed in MKO Abiola; he was the messiah we had waited for. He was a billionaire and a man of the people, and everyone felt that true to his words, if he became a democratic president, things would change; and he would tackle corruption and take the economy to greater heights just like he did his business empire. To hear that Dad had a hand in the annulment was a big blow to me. I wondered if Dad had that kind of clout, if he wielded that kind of influence.

'Dad? How can he have had a hand in that?'

'Your father is a wealthy man now, Leona, you see. Tsk, I don't know what happened, but he has some friends that come here to meet with him, not often as they used to, and I overheard him on the phone after the election, talking with some dignitaries. He had a hand in it. I am just scared.'

'I thought Dad was not in support of the Head of State?'

'He is not. The last time I knew, your father was planning a coup,' she sighed. I heard the sound of a toilet flushing in another room. 'He and his cohorts feel that if democracy thrives in Nigeria, they would lose their investments. The plan was to overthrow Babangida's government, but that plan has changed now. I fear, they are working on something bigger, tsk, something I sense will have devastating effects, ha. I think your father has conflicting business deals with one Yoruba chief like that, one Chief Wale. And this chief and

Abiola are friends. Your father feels that if Abiola became president, this chief would ruin his business.'

'I am scared. I don't want what happened to Grandpa to happen to Dad.' I snuggled close to Mum. She embraced me.

'I am scared too, my angel. I sometimes wonder if your father did not see what happened to your grandfather. If he didn't learn any lessons from that, but we have to be strong.' She looked away. 'There are mosquitoes in this room, I will get an insecticide later. We are lucky to be alive today. Your father doesn't acknowledge that.'

Throughout the time I was at home for the long vacation of 1993, I rarely saw Dad. He barely noticed me, but he said that if I needed anything, I should ask Mum and that he left enough money with her. He had changed, like Mum pointed out, but he still allowed me to embrace him and peck his cheeks. He still kissed my forehead and said that I was eating too much beans in school and growing taller and dwarfing Mum. He laughed while saying this; then, he escaped into his room or library until he left the next day. By this time, Dad had some bodyguards, some young men with hefty chests and broad shoulders, who wore sunglasses and talked to no one, not even to respond to greetings. I suspected that he warned them to stay clear of me and not to even look at me or respond if I talked to them. Dad's behaviour marvelled me until November when the interim government of Ernest Shonekan who became the acting president after the annulment of the June 12 elections was truncated, and Sani Abacha announced himself commander-in-chief.

When the news reached us in school, I knew Dad had a hand in it, and I was worried sick.

TWENTY-TWO

I sat up and began to search through Mum's many handbags and travelling bags. I found the keys to her drawers in one of the bags and lots of money in both the handbags and travel bags, which I stacked on the floor, currency by currency to count later. I wondered if Dad had ever searched through Mum's things. Perhaps he had but did not think he should remove the money; perhaps he never did go into the room. What did he care?

I removed the files stacked in the various chests in Mum's drawers and studied them carefully. When I was done going through the drawers, I opened a heavy metal box containing her wrappers—expensive wax fabric, I made a mental note to select the ones I would take to Lagos and sew nice gowns out of. As I lifted the fabric one after the other, a white envelope fell out. I opened it and found that it had some dollar notes in it. I kept that on the floor. Then, my hand felt something that I pulled out and dropped.

'Jesus.' I cried, holding my breath and hyperventilating. After I summoned enough courage, I went closer. The thing was like a stone, round and smooth, and had three feathers of some bird tied to it with white and red threads. *What's this?* I wondered.

I was scared of searching further. My knees wobbled; so, I sat on the floor, thinking. *Who was Mum? What did she become within the short years that she ran Dad's business?* Sweat formed lines on my forehead, entering my eyes and soaking up my cloth. I began to remove the materials from the box, paying attention now, while carefully flipping the well-folded materials and clothes to discharge anything that may have been hidden in them. At the bottom of the box were some massive camphor balls.

I stood akimbo, thinking. Then, I brought out Mum's handbags and purses and began to flip them upside down, discharging their contents; and different brands of makeup, old Nigerian coins, old naira notes, folded papers, receipts, prescriptions, flight ticket stubs, letters, bank notes, cheques, tellers, and cheque booklets popped out. I sorted them out and read the letters; most were handwritten, and others were typed. There were memos pointing to business activities in Sudan.

I drew out a chair and climbed on it to be able to see the top of the wardrobe. There were bags, and I hurled two of them to the floor, sneezing. The ceiling fan let out a shrill sound and picked up as I turned it on and went to go through the bags. The black bag had files and books and papers; so I went through them. I flipped through the books first and moved to the papers; they turned out to be vital banks' information, so I kept them aside. I did have lots of bank visits to make. I was Mum's next-of-kin and no one had ever bothered checking Mum's banks. There were cheque books too and bank statements printed, over six years earlier. Next, I went through the files and saw, hidden in one—perhaps what I was looking for—an old VCR tape. My heart skipped. Inside another file was a paper envelope containing photos of Mum in bed with a man. The man's stomach looked massive, his moustache looked full, and his face was either blurred or scraped off. I wondered who he was. Was he Chief Fegun Wale? If he wanted to blackmail Mum, would he send her photos of them in bed together? It made no sense. My heart pounded.

The other file was bound with a white twine and had no inscriptions on it. I undid the rope with shaky hands and found three documents detailing a container that arrived Lagos, the day it arrived the Apapa Seaport, and the Customs report with description of items in the container as 'pharma-ceuticals and crates of ammunition'.

What was Mum doing with those?

I recalled Dad's words. These were the reasons Mum was sleeping with the man who imprisoned her husband, the reason for the other nude photos that trapped her. I wondered if the documents got her doing it to avoid being exposed, and whether when she could not take it anymore, she killed herself. I knelt, my head between my laps, and sobbed.

I knew Dad had a hand in the coup because when I was

about leaving for school late in September 1993, there was this clandestine meeting that took place in our house.

It was around one o' clock, and I was reading in my room when I saw the gate being opened. All of Dad's bodyguards were out, talking excitedly but in hushed tones. I turned off my light and peeped from my window. A car drove into the compound, and four men came out of it. I recalled Chief Kutuga as he shook Dad's hand. Then, another man shook his hand and hugged him. He was heavyset, but I could not see him clearly. I ran out, gently opened the door to my room, stood by the staircase, and waited—for the time they would come into the sitting room so I could eavesdrop from the door. They entered the sitting room, and to my surprise, walked into the library and bolted the door.

It was only Dad, Chief Kutuga, and the man who went in. I suspected that the other two must be bodyguards and that they were standing guard outside with Dad's men. I tiptoed downstairs and approached the door. Then, I placed my ears to it, cautious… scared.

They were talking, but the huge door prevented me from hearing everything.

'I have come personally… No. No. Chief, don't say that. No.'

I did not know whose voice it was.

'Look, you have done me great honour; to have the next head of state and commander-in-chief in my home… You have done me great honour.'

'Pleasure is all mine… Yes… That is…'

Their voices were breaking. I peeped through the keyhole, but they had turned off the light in the study and could only see each other with the help of a flashlight. It was as if they were studying something spread on the table, a lot of papers.

'Three hundred million in naira.' I heard Dad say. 'Then, two hundred naira...'

'Immediately, General here announces to the... that he has taken over... the Commander... gbogbotigbo, then... yes. You will...'

I was scared and my legs were trembling. I could feel sweat trickle down my legs to the tiled floor. *Could the other man be the general they always mentioned in their previous meetings? Was there now a change of plans?* I wondered.

'You don't know... indebted to... I am, sir... for this honour.'

'Look, it is... honour and pleasure, sir. You... good to my business.'

I heard the ruffling of papers and shredding of documents.

'General is a man that never forgets those that... during the rainy season... he remembers good deeds like... all the time.'

'Chief James Egbufor, you are about to do me a great honour. Never forget this... Insha' Allah... repay...'

I tiptoed back to the stairs and waited for another fifteen minutes. I heard the door open. The third man came out first, and I saw the side of his face. He had tribal marks.

I went downstairs to the visitors' room where our old VCR machine was and inserted the tape after it took me some long minutes to get the wires fixed into where they belonged. I heard Madam Imo humming. I knew that song. Where had I heard it before? I paused.

> Eje m igho okwuru.
> Ighomi igho okwuru igho
> Ejem igho okwuru
> Ighomi igho okwuru igho
> Okwuru eju nkata
> Ighomi igho okwuru igho
> Onye g' ebu?
> Ighomi ighomi igho okwuru igho.

I began to sing to myself, quietly, allowing the song to calm me. I recall now that it was Dad, back then in Khartoum, when he used to sing me to sleep. He always sang this song that Madam Imo was humming now. He said it was one of the songs they sang in the playground in the village and that it made him nostalgic. He always wanted me to belong to his place, to learn their songs and folklore; he told me it was a folkloric song about a woman at a time of famine who gave her only food to a dying traveller and went to her small farm to harvest okra. It was supposed to be just a plant that should yield a few okra, but she harvested until her basket got filled and she needed help to carry the basket.

Straight away, the camera zoomed in on a room. There was an air conditioner humming, and a woman, slender, tall, on top of a fat pot-bellied man. The woman's hair looked long and beautiful—like mine. The man was moaning loudly in grunts. His face was technically blurred, but the camera zoomed in on the woman's—her eyes wide open, her mouth tight in a pout. Her body was not moving; rather, the man was moving beneath her. I turned off the television and removed the tape. My heart was doing one hundred and eighty kilometres per hour.

SECTION III

TWENTY-THREE

JULY 2005
LAGOS, WESTERN NIGERIA

Lagos had always held this fascination for me. It is like a giant sea animal—its mouth wide open, swallowing everything on its way, fishes of all sizes, crabs, seaweeds, and gulping water steadily. And I think it is this feature of Lagos that keeps people continuously on their toes, moving and walking fast, exploring and breaking grounds, and rising from poverty to riches, from wealth to more wealth, before sometimes descending to the abyss of penury. It is in many ways different from life in Enugu where everything is quiet, smooth, and easy, where there is less hustle; and it is much more different from Khartoum. Though the time I spent in Sudan was during my childhood, I still always feel the difference in the colour of its vibe and energy in ways that are appealing.

Aunty Agii came to pick me from Murtala Mohammed Airport, dressed in a tight skirt and a sleeveless top, looking all younger than her age. We hugged, and she appraised me, commenting on how everyone was gawking at me in admiration.

'Nne, I maka.' She held my two hands. 'You are too beautiful.'

I giggled. I was already in love with this easy-going step-mother of mine. She helped me wheel my bags to the lot where her Honda CRV was parked, idling. The driver came out and took the luggage to the boot. He stared at me all the time.

'You never see pesin before, abi, Mustapha? Abeg enter moto make we go!' Aunty Agii snapped at her driver.

He grinned, ashamed, and hurried to the car; and we slowly snaked out of the traffic of the parking lot and found our way through the narrow road that led to the expressway.

'You've been to Lagos before, Nne?'

'Yes, Aunty. Ah ah!' I smiled at her.

'Of course. Of course.'

'Umuaka a, the boys have been expecting you, but they are not at home kita. They are in school.' She flashed her disarming smile.

'You wouldn't believe if I told you that after they left Abuja, I missed them. You are lucky to have them all to yourself always.'

Her face became brighter.

'We are lucky to have them, Leona. They are your broth-ers. We are one family, anyi ncha.'

'I know.'

She turned to face me. 'I am unhappy that I wasn't able to get along with Mary. Ogbawarum obi.'

'Mum was a stubborn woman.'

'Every woman can be stubborn if pushed.'

I thought about what she said.

'We passed through a lot.' We were in traffic now and hawkers were thrusting their wares at us. We ignored them. 'Mum was never like that, but I guess it is quite difficult seeing your husband change before you, with his quest for power and fame and wealth. She couldn't understand why he didn't learn any lessons from what happened in Sudan.'

'What happened in Sudan? Biko, gwam,' she looked concerned. 'Everyone in this family keeps mentioning this thing that happened in Sudan.'

I was silent for some seconds. 'Mum's father... she loved him so much. We all did. He was killed in Sudan by the rebels he was a part of... before our eyes.' She turned to look at me. 'We escaped assassination too. Mum couldn't go back for a while until Dad was in prison, and she took over the business. Then, she was in control of funds and President Al-Bashir became her friend and gave her protection.'

'I do not know much about that side of the family. Your father never discusses them.'

'He doesn't. We don't.'

'Even why he was imprisoned.'

'But you met him before he went to prison?'

She smiled and her face beamed. I wondered how much she loved my dad.

'We met the year he left prison. He was in our office for

business. I think he was trying to re-establish himself. He did mention your mum and told me how much help she was in keeping the business running while he was away.'

'He did?'

'Oh, yes. Why?'

'He never showed gratitude that Mum ran the business.'

'But he did. He never stopped talking about your mum. Eziokwu.'

I wondered if she was telling lies to protect her husband.

'I think he is ever grateful to her,' she said, and I was surprised.

I always thought he did not care much about Mum and all that she did. I wondered if his idea that we avenge Mum's death truly came from his heart. I was beginning to believe it did. We were silent for some time. She asked if I was hungry and I said, 'Yes.'

When we got to the house, a massive mansion in the Lekki side of Lagos, and the gate was being rolled open, she said, 'I do love your dad.'

'Wow!' I responded.

She looked at me and smiled.

'But then, aren't you worried that he has another wife and children?'

'I am not. Mbanu. I guess love doesn't know these things.'

'And I used to think—pardon me for saying this—that women who get involved in polygamy are uneducated.'

She laughed. We were coming out of the car now.

'Not anymore, Leona. Many women get into polygamy

because they love the man. Eziokwu ka m n' agwa gi. If you find a man interesting, say in many ways, and he is married and offers to marry you still, as our custom allows him, you wouldn't refuse because he is married to someone else.' She beckoned that I follow her, leaving the driver and the gateman who had hurried to join us, to get the bags out of the car. 'I think that the west, just the way they now try to criminalise Islam, did same for polygamy because, just as Islam isn't their religion, polygamy isn't their thing, and our people follow the west blindly.'

We were in the sitting room now. It was massive but had only a three-piece settee, making the place spacious and free. A plasma television hung on the wall and massive air-conditioners stood by the corners of the room. The staircase coiled down almost to the centre of the sitting room, making it palatial. The tiles were smooth and shiny, causing the light ricochet off their surface. I could hear the sound of utensils moving in the kitchen and perceive some aroma. I could not place it—egusi or ogbono soup? I swung around, and my eyes beheld a painting on the wall, huge enough to be mistaken for a window. It was the painting of a nude man. It was magnificent.

'My favourite,' Aunty Agii said.

'You love art?'

She nodded.

'Gee nti, if polygamy was their thing, they wouldn't have made it seem as if it was such a big and unforgivable sin, and our people would have copied it wholeheartedly the way we now embrace divorce, abortion, homosexuality, and so on. So, you see, I don't care what people say to me, as long as I am happy.'

'I don't think we copied homosexuality... has it not always been here?'

'Well, it's subject to debate.'

I sat down and said, 'In many ways, I think you are right. I feel that it's better for a man to be married to two or three women and live with his children, training them in his ways than divorce their mothers and scatter them far apart. It doesn't make sense.'

'Abroad, the rate of divorce is mind-blowing. It kills the sanctity of marriage. I wanted to live in the same building with Mary, but she didn't even want me around.'

'Please don't blame her.'

Someone, a lady in her late twenties or early thirties, came out and greeted Aunty Agii.

'Chi baby. Kedu?'

'Odi mma.' She sat on one of the stools. 'Is this Leona?'

'Yes.'

'Welcome. Nnoo.'

'Thank you.'

'Take the bags to her room, Chinwe. Please.' She took one of the bags and struggled with it through the stairs. When she left Aunty Agii said, 'My sister.'

'Oh. She looks like you. That waist.' I rolled my eyes.

'Oh, we do have massive hips. She laughed. 'So, just like some men are, I would say, prone to divorce, some are polygamous in nature. And if a man is rich and strong enough to have two, three nkita ara in the house at once and can feed and control them, why not? Besides, men hardly feed women these days. Take, for instance, Chief's three wives. Mary was wealthy and industrious. I am a senior civil servant, and with your dad's help, I now have a few small businesses of my own. Elizabeth, I heard, owns and runs a boutique successfully. What would make us want to kill each other?'

'Nkita ara? You think women are mad dogs?'

She clapped her hands. 'No. Nooo! Far from it. I don't mean it that way, but if you keep women together under one roof and they belong to one man, no matter how lovely and friendly they are to one another, they are bound to quarrel and fight. No? O asi?'

'Over sex and attention?'

'My grandfather was said to have married eleven women. They all lived in one big compound, like a kraal. Each had her own small hut and cared for her children with support from the man. It was said that they took turns cooking for him and the day you were to cook was the day you would sleep in his hut.'

'Is that your culture in Abakaliki?'

'That is the culture mostly in Igboland.'

'And he made love, every night, to them? Because I can't imagine this or that woman thinking this was her night and her turn would come after another ten days or so and the man must have to satisfy her.'

'That, I do not know. I do not think that it was all for the sex.' She took the remote and turned on the television and flipped to Channel O.

'I think that the way we see sex now is different from the way our ancestors saw it. To them, it was for making children; to us, it is more of pleasure and satisfaction.'

'Oh.'

'I guess so. Bia, do you want anything chilled, say Fanta or Malt?'

'Dalu. I am fine.'

'Alcohol? Do you drink alcohol?'

'Oh, yeah,' I nodded. 'I do.'

'Let me get one.' She made to stand.

'Perhaps when I have eaten.'

She continued where she left off. 'Leo,' Tuface Idibia's video was playing on television and she was nodding to the tune. 'There are studies on this. Our forefathers had rules guarding sex. A man was not supposed to suckle his wife's breasts, they believed it would make the woman infertile. There were others. I also think that he was not to put his fingers into her and to pull out while he was about to ejaculate, and so on.' She smiled. I was seriously grinning too and staring at her. 'All these and more led me to believe that they approached sex differently.'

'It was all about the man's pleasure then. As long as the man climaxed and impregnated the woman, no qualms.'

'Ehe nu. Possibly so.'

'The world has always been chauvinistic.'

'Perhaps they didn't see it so.'

Chinwe finished taking my bags upstairs and when she came down, she said, 'Someone dropped a message for you.' She eyed me playfully. 'His name is Akinola. Said he will come in the evening.'

'He came here?'

'Yes,' she said.

I caught her wink at her sister.

'Oh, how did he know I was arriving today?'

Aunty Agii laughed. 'Your father. That would be my guess.'

'I see.'

Chinwe walked away.

'So, what if a new man arrives in the village, say from a more civilised part of the world, skilled in the act of pleasuring women, do you not think that there would be some sort of trouble?'

'Of course, but there were rules against adultery and fornication. Everyone stuck to her man even if he didn't measure up; and rarely would a woman have extramarital affairs, or would a young girl fornicate.'

I nodded. 'I see… Thank God.'

She laughed and stood abruptly, eyeing me sceptically. 'Thank God you weren't born then? Hahahaha! Me too.'

She began to head inside. 'Let's go check out what's cooking. And when we're done eating, you tell me the real story behind Chief's imprisonment.'

I rolled my eyes and followed her.

TWENTY-FOUR

'So, Dad never told you why Abacha put him in jail?'

'Mba nu. No, he never did. That was your father's darkest period. Each time I raise the issue, he broods and gets sad. The only thing he said was that he was put in jail forcefully, without trial.'

I nodded. We were eating in the kitchen. 'So Chinwe made this delicious añara soup?'

'Yes. Chinwe can cook for the world.' I laughed at the easy way Aunty Agii used her words. 'Tell me why your dad was put in jail. He never talks about it.'

She dropped the moulded fufu in her hand to stare at me, all attentive. I considered for a split second what to tell her. I was not going to tell her that Dad, her husband, was involved in a coup, but I skipped that part and began to eat slowly while telling her the story. She could see that it was difficult for me and she was patient, not talking or prodding.

'Dad was a good friend of the Head of State. Their friendship dated back to before he took charge, before the coup. In 1995, Dad got a contract to build silos in almost all the states in Nigeria, including those states that had no need for a silo. The silos were to house products like maize and groundnuts and rice. Dad had hardly commenced the contract when one day, a phone rang in the house, Mum answered, and the voice on the other side of the phone asked if she had read the day's papers. Mum informed the caller that she hardly read papers.'

My mind went back to that day, years ago.

'Who are you please?' Mum asked the caller.

'I am your husband's friend.' It was Mister Isaac Uwaifo.

'Oh, sir. Sorry, I couldn't tell your voice.' But Mum told me that by then she was already sure that something had happened to Dad. Otherwise, why would he call around seven in the morning asking if she read the papers?

'Well, Madam. It is too early anyway but make sure you get today's papers.'

'Is everything all right?'

'It is Chief.'

'Who is Chief?'

'James—'

Mum never got used to calling Dad by his new title. She inquired if everything was all right with her husband.

'The Head of State... he ordered the arrest of your husband. He was arrested early yesterday evening around seven o'clock. We have been trying to track where they kept him but—'

'Oh my God! Oh my God!'

'Listen, we are making all efforts to track his whereabouts.'

'Oh my God! Is my husband… is he still alive?'

'Madam, now, please don't think about that. We believe he is still alive. Abacha cannot kill James.'

'Why did he arrest him then?'

'They said he embezzled contract money, Madam.'

'Did he embezzle the contract money? Did James embezzle the contract money?'

'You won't understand, Madam. You see, your husband… he sponsored… he was involved in many projects for the general, which helped the general in a lot of ways. We are talking of millions of naira.'

'But, sir did he embezzle the contract money, hmm?'

'Your husband just started the contract a month ago. We are not sure he embezzled any money. We think it is a ploy to take him out of the way. Besides, the contract was supposed to be a means for James to recoup—'

'Recoup what?'

'Madam, listen to me.'

'Oh my God!'

'We will find where he is, but we are sure that the Head of State will not kill James.'

'Tsk!'

'Buy today's papers. And stay indoors. We will contact you.'

The next day, a Peugeot 404 came to the school, and our form teacher called me out. I did not know the men, but they had a letter from Mum. The letter said I was to follow them. We drove straight to Dad's village and on the way, I could not stop thinking that it was as if what happened in Sudan was playing back, that the life we ran from had come back to haunt us; and this time, I worried there would be no escape.

We spent about three nights in the village, and all through that while, Grandma hardly said any word to Mum. She said Mum brought bad luck to her son. Then, one morning, a white Volkswagen beetle brought a man to the village; he was Mister Isaac Uwaifo. When Mum saw him, she rushed out of the house, and they embraced. It was awkward because Mum never knew him well before then, but he was the one helping us out. When you are hopeless, the little sun rays at the end of the tunnel could mean so much.

'Any news about my husband? Have you heard from James? Is Abacha going to kill him?'

'Not yet, ma'am.'

Grandma came out and joined them, then. Grandpa was in the sitting room. He rarely came out of the house because of his arthritis.

'What do we do about my son, eh?'

'What do we do, sir?' Mum re-echoed Grandma's question.

There were tears in Mum's eyes. She looked emaciated and taller than her height. I was standing beside Mum, confused at all that was happening. Grandpa could be heard talking to himself. One or two neighbours had come but stood a short distance away.

He talked in hushed tone, 'Listen, we must act fast. James

wants his family to be safe. James had some backup plan ready since 1993. We have made arrangements—'

'What kind of arrangements?' Grandma asked.

Mister Isaac hesitated. He was not a man that could trust just anyone.

'Well, Madam,' he said, addressing Grandma. 'We have been instructed to relocate his wife and daughter from this place.'

He turned to us and said, 'Pack your things in five minutes, no more, no less. Ensure you get only a few things.' We ran off immediately. 'Don't worry about money!' he called, while he paced around the compound. Neighbours escorted Grandma into the sitting room. She was sobbing.

In the car, he said, 'They killed Alhaji Usman's son this morning at the University of Ibadan where he schools.'

'Who is Alhaji Usman?' He did not respond. 'My God!' Mum immediately drew me close to herself.

It took a little over two hours before we got to Abakaliki. There, we entered another vehicle, an army coloured Toyota saloon car, driven by a man in camouflage; there was another man seated in the front. They did not respond to any of Mum's questions and probes. At first, when Isaac Uwaifo handed us over to the soldiers, we were cynical, but he said we had no choice and there was no time left for scepticisms. When we were transferred into the Toyota, Mum asked the soldiers, 'Who are you?'

No response.

'Good day, sirs!' I greeted and there was no response.

'Where are we going?'

The car drove off at high-speed, and Mum sighed her usual way. We were stopped at about three checkpoints before we got to Ogoja; and each time, the soldier sitting beside the driver spoke to the soldiers on the road, and we were waved on with a salute.

What he said was, 'Wife and daughter of a colonel.'

It was an eerie experience, worse than what we felt on the evening we were driven to Omdurman.

At Ogoja, there was another vehicle, a Land Rover jeep, waiting by a lonely road. A soldier was leaning on it, smoking a cigarette, and another was inside.

'Sorry we ignored you, Madam. We had our orders,' one of the soldiers who brought us said, as we were about to enter the new vehicle.

We got into the Land Rover that took us to the Calabar seaport, where a flying boat was waiting, ready. There, the soldiers handed us over to one of Dad's bodyguards. It was when we saw the bodyguard that our hearts stopped racing. Before then, all the while that we travelled, Mum had held my hand, almost crushing my fingers. We finally got to Limbe by boat and were transported to a family house in Yaoundé, where we lived for close to seven months.

'So, it was when you got back that your mum began to run the business?' Aunty Agii was pouring me wine now.

'Before we returned, they had traced where Dad was being held. Mum bribed some soldiers and she was allowed to visit him. She told him she went to the office and everything was a mess and that she wanted to take charge. He refused. They quarrelled. Mum never visited him again until his release, but by then, the business had grown. If not, there wouldn't have been anything left for him to return to.'

'Agu nwanyi!' Aunty Agii placed the bottle hard on the glass table. 'That's what your mum was, lion woman!'

In the evening, while Okwudili and I were playing in front of the house, a sleek Porsche drove into the compound. When the driver came out and I saw him, my heart skipped. He was handsome, so handsome that I could not close my mouth for some seconds. Thank God he did not notice because he was busy bringing out some paper bags from the car.

He was tall but I was taller by a few inches. He was chocolate complexioned and lean. He had no noticeable broad shoulders, but he looked all handsome and angelic. He walked to me, smiling.

'Good evening, Leona!'

I knew then that it was Akinola Wale.

Why on earth hadn't I Googled him before? He took me unawares. He was the son of the man who messed up my mother's life. The son of my enemy, and by extension my enemy too. *How was I supposed to be pleasant to this man, and love him, marry him? No.*

Smiling mischievously, he said, 'I am Akinola. The one who has been calling—'

'You sound as if you've been calling always.'

'I call once a week.'

'Most times it could be once in two weeks.'

'I am a busy man.'

'I can see,' I snorted.

'You'd prefer I call more often?' He was still smiling. There was silence. Then, he handed the bags to Okwudili. 'You are so beautiful.'

'Who told you I am here?'

'Your aunty... step-mum.'

'Agnes? Ah' *And she lied to me. What else does she know?*

'You didn't know?'

'Never mind.'

'Do we go in?' He inclined his head to look at me, pleading. His eyes were brownish as if he had a headache. His face looked dull but that did not belie his handsomeness.

'I didn't invite you. Your host should welcome you.' But my heart was sounding like an old generator, and my stomach was churning. He was handsome, far more than Kosi. There was no comparison—his hair was well shaven, his face smooth and comely—he looked appealing. And his ears, neck, his mouth—everything was perfect. My God, I could eat him. I felt like I was falling in love with this man. However, I had to force myself to hate him, to hate him enough to kill him.

Just then, Aunty Agii came out in tight bum shorts and a tiny sleeve top. I wondered why she was wearing that kind of top when she knew she was massively endowed, but she had come to save me in the awkward situation I found myself in.

'Hi, Akin!'

'Hello, Aunty.'

'Come in, now! What are you two discussing outside? You people have not even met properly, and una don dey talk, see am? Nekene.' She rolled her eyes.

'She refused to invite me in; she said I am not her guest.'

'Haba, Leo! Okay, come on in, you are my guest.'

They shook hands, and she dragged him with the right hand and me with the left and led us inside. My legs were finding it difficult to move. I was in a dilemma.

TWENTY-FIVE

Monday mornings in Lagos are always chaotic. The traffic is often thick and congested, with cars stretched over two, three kilometres, stuck, and their horns blaring incessantly, while Danfos tried to sneak their way out of the traffic, hitting road curbs and denting people's cars and causing a commotion. It is a usual sight to see two people, one finely dressed and the other not-so-finely dressed, engaged in a shouting match and sometimes a fist fight, and a lot of people trying to separate them at the same time, most times causing multiple fights to start, with everyone hitting everybody and pickpockets taking advantage of the situation.

It was my first day at the Emily Rose Modelling Agency, and I was being driven down by Aunty Agii. Already, she had called them and made all the arrangements on my behalf; and luckily, we had escaped the traffic and got there in time for my appointment. The agency was located on the ground floor of a high-rise building. I walked into the small reception area and there were girls seated on sofas. There were two other girls behind a desk; so, I walked up to them and introduced myself. They did not look surprised to see me, and they directed me to the manager's office.

Waribagha was a dapper middle-aged man who came across as boisterous. He came over to meet me and shook hands, studying me with something more than a professional appraisal. I was sure I saw him lick his lips.

'Just like in the photos! You look exquisite.' He beamed. I later learned that 'exquisite' was a word he used often. 'Please, sit. Sit.'

He walked back to his seat, drew out a drawer from his table, and found a file. He placed it in front of me. 'Your file.'

'Okay.'

'Emily Rose Modelling Agency is the largest in Lagos, meaning, it is the largest in the country. It's owned, as you may already know, by two women, Emily Whitman and Rose Hedrick, both from the United States.' I nodded. He stared at me. 'You are so *damn* beautiful. *Exquisite!*'

'Thank you, sir.'

'Don't call me sir, Leona. Call me Waribagha.'

'Okay.' I wondered what his other name was.

'You are admitted already. Our madam, the CEO, I understand, was a friend of your mum, your late mum. She told us she'd been doing everything possible to have you with us.'

'Okay.' I nodded. All smiles.

I looked around the office. The wall was painted sky blue. An artwork of a woman carrying an empty calabash by her side stared at me. There were framed photos of models in various poses on the wall—dark, slim, plump, fair girls, all looking serious and beautiful.

'Do you have any training?'

My eyes returned to him. 'Yes, I do' I stammered. 'Catwalk. Poses. Makeup. Speech modulation. I try.'

'Where did you train?'

'I have a friend, Rosa. She is a model here in Lagos. She used to train me while I was in secondary school when she was home for weekends or holidays.'

He laughed and scoffed.

'Do I know this Rosa?'

'I don't know. Rosa Ilo.'

'Of course, I know her.' He scoffed again and waved his hand.

I jumped in immediately, eager to please him. 'Then, there is this agency in Enugu where I paid for some training. I also practice.'

'It's all right. It's all right. Well, today, this company that owns Luxury Soap will be here to audition our models. Let's see how much practice you've had for yourself. If you get it, you are lucky. It will throw you to the limelight. Nigerians will marvel seeing your face. They would wonder where you have been all these years. You are twenty-five?'

'I am. Just turned twenty-five.' I wondered if I was too old.

'We would have loved it if you were younger but... don't worry.' He smiled. I beamed at him. 'Go to the reception and ask for the personnel department. They will brief you on how we work here. They have your contract. Normally, you should take it home and go through it, perhaps with a lawyer, I must add. But most girls don't and when things don't go their way, they come barking, forgetting they signed the damn contract. But since the Luxury Soap auditioning is today, I suggest you go over the contract and if you find it okay, you sign, we sign, and you join and be auditioned for it. Who knows?'

I grinned and beamed.

He stared at me.

I have to be careful with this man.

'I must go to personnel then.' I stood, stretched my gown. He looked at my legs.

'Okay.' He stood. 'From the reception, there is a hallway to your left, second door by the right.'

I smiled. 'Thank you.' I was sure he was still staring as I left.

I did not read the contract. It was over twelve pages. I just made sure my name was spelt correctly, 'LEONA CHIZOROM EGBUFOR', and I signed.

Representatives of the company that owned Luxury Soap came as Waribagha said, to audition all the models at the Emily Rose Modelling Agency and select their brand ambassador. I was taken to an inner reception area, a large hall-like room with reclining leather sofas and throw pillows. The television affixed to the wall was showing DSTV's E Channel. I said 'Hello,' to the girls who were already seated, before I sat down. They all looked at me like I was a ghost, which made me uncomfortable, but I was taller than most of them and more beautiful as well—of that I was sure.

The girls all looked frantic and anxious because any of us who got selected to model for the company stood a big chance of winning the Miss Nigeria Beauty Pageant, 'If they chose to enter for it.' I had overheard someone say at the personnel department.

I crossed my legs. A few of the girls talked in hushed tones. Then, the door into the lounge was thrown open, and heavy scents of cologne rushed in first and mingled with ours. We stood up, and Waribagha walked in, followed by some men. He began to talk, and the girls straightened up. I noticed then that he was bald and had a bad posture.

'Good morning, ladies,' Waribagha said.

We responded, our voices in a high pitch and in unison like a flock of birds, while the men with him scanned the room, admiring the girls.

'Today is a special day. These are men from Luxury Beauty Products Company Limited, the owners of Luxury Soap. We all know why they are here. I advise we comply with them. All of you here stand a chance of being selected for the job. Just show them the talent you have and make this agency proud. Gentlemen, please meet *my* ladies,' he said, throwing up his hands and bowing his head slightly.

They asked us to sit and we did; and their lawyer gave a brief talk about the contract, its terms, and benefits. We nodded mostly while he spoke. Then, we went for a tea break and came back after an hour. The selection process was tedious. They first walked around, asking questions, and checking for marks and disfigurement, as if the agency would take on anyone who had a spot on her body. My heart never stopped racing, the whole time. My phone beeped and it was a message from Akinola. I hurriedly scanned through it. He was wishing me success on my first day at the agency.

The men also checked our catwalks and our postures, before they retired to the sitting room where each of us was invited privately for questions and interactions. After that, there was a photo session in the agency's massive and richly equipped studio. They gave us different clothes, and we posed and took pictures. We also undressed down to our underwear in their presence, while the agency's cameraman took snapshots.

Undressing in front of contractors hired for auditioning was nothing to the other girls, obviously; but I protested and they all stared at me as if I was a moron, until another woman who worked with Waribagha and had a name tag, Paulina Sonuga, asked me to calm down.

'Other girls do this, always. And in this agency, we have a *good* reputation. We are professionals.'

Finally, I stripped. After the audition, the men—I was sure—would go home, dreaming and fantasising. It was something I was sure most men could never do without. I wondered briefly if men could survive without women. For what was a man without a woman? His happiness was shortened and his mind disoriented if he was denied the pleasure of a woman, even if that pleasure was only but imagined.

All the girls took their turns getting auditioned, and in the evening, after a long wait, they announced their nominations.

'It's been an interesting day, I must say. Mister Waribagha, you have a lot of talented, young professionals here.'

'We are the best!' he exclaimed proudly, beaming at the girls. He was sipping from a can of energy drink. His shirt was rumpled, and his face looked sullen.

'You all are great, first-class models, and we found it difficult making selections.'

We were seated, all twelve of us, watching him. He was the tallest among the men from the beauty company. He wore a blue suit, a tie, and shoes to match. He was hand-some. He looked like the kind of man I would love to hang out with. But then, there was Akinola—my mind went to him. He had asked that I call him. After a brief talk, as the hands of a clock made sounds, which indicated the time of day, he finally gave out the names of the three girls selected. By this time, it was evening, and the streets had become busier with motorists adding to the noise with their loud hoots.

'They are Adriel Adetokunbo, Leona Egbufor, and Joy Uwais.'

He paused for emphasis, and with a smirk he watched our faces, enjoying our surprises and disappointments.

'These three ladies are to meet with us in our office on the twenty-seventh of this month. Before then, we shall bring our official invitation letters to you and other necessary documents; then, sign an MOU with your agency. One person out of the three shall emerge as the brand ambassador for Luxury Beauty Products Company Limited for a year and six months, while the other two shall work with us from time to time.'

He paused to look at our faces and we could not hide the joy that radiated from our eyes, while the other girls stared in disbelief.

'Thanks for your cooperation today. Thanks, Mister Waribagha. It has been wonderful working with you. You have wonderful and brilliant girls. Your staff too is amazing. Thanks, again.'

I could not say anything. It was magical. While the girls talked in hushed tones, the men also did. It seemed they were arguing over something.

TWENTY-SIX

As we filed out, the first person who crossed my mind was Akinola Wale. Somehow, Aunty Agii had mentioned that I was going to be signed on by a modelling agency, and he had wished me luck and said that I call him afterwards to tell him about my day. Now that my day turned out good, I wondered if I should call to tell him I got signed to the agency on my first day; found a contract already drafted and waiting for me, which I signed without looking at twice, without even reading what was in it; then, coincidentally, there was an auditioning and I got short-listed for a major deal. I thought perhaps it would be reasonable if I called him to tell him that my day did go well, and I was on my way to achieving my childhood dream—to become a supermodel.

But why was Akinola the first person to cross my mind after this success; not Kosi, not Onyinye, not Adulike, and not even Aunty Agii who was supportive, who convinced Dad to allow me a chance to pursue my own dreams? I was supposed to hate this man, hate him enough to want to harm him for what his father–his family—did to my mum. But all day, his face kept coming to me; and during the auditioning, I kept thinking about how cute he looked and how he talked a bit loudly, enthusiastically, showing he was a lovely and carefree person. I wondered if he knew that I was forcing myself not to like him, yet pretending that I did love him, in order to get him to marry me so I could kill him. I wondered if he knew what had happened between my mum and his father and if he encouraged it—if the plan to marry me was a family plot to ruin me as they did Mum. Clearly, I was not thinking straight, but I found myself dialling his number.

A female answered and told me he was busy.

'Oh. Sorry for bothering him.'

'No, wait. You are Leona, right? He asked that if you called, I should take the phone to him. I was just going to tell you that he is busy and that you would have to hang on for a moment; so, I give him the phone.'

'I see. Not to worry, I will call later.'

'Please, no—'

I hung up and threw my phone into my handbag. I was standing under the threshold of the building, in front of the office, waiting for a cab, as it was drizzling lightly. Why did I call him in the first place? Now he would act all important.

Fuck him and his wealth and his protocols!

My phone rang, and I could not hold back so I fished it out of my bag. It was him. I wanted to take the call, but on a second thought, I threw it back into my handbag and got into the rain. Adriel walked up to me as I headed for the road. She said, 'Hello,' just as a cab approached.

'Seems like this rain is not stopping anytime soon,' she said.

'I think so. Heading which way? We might have some difficulty finding a taxi.'

'Lekki area.'

'Oh. Me too. Let's share one then?'

'Fine with me.'

As we stood to wait, I tried to get her to divulge as much information as possible about the agency. I wanted her to tell me about the girls and the owners and how strict they were and all. A taxi stopped and we boarded, and as we drove home, I learnt she had been with the agency for more than a year and was not a darling to the other girls.

Adriel was a tall slim twenty-three-year-old who looked quiet and content. She wore a pair of denim trousers and a white shirt.

'You'd love this place,' she assured me.

'I bet I would. This is what I have always wanted,' I agreed. The driver was entering and coming out of potholes.

'So, you live in Lekki?'

'Yeah, I came to live with my father,' I lied. 'My father lives there. I used to stay in Enugu before relocating to Lagos because of this modelling thing.'

'So, how is Enugu?'

'Have you been to Enugu before?' I asked.

It began to rain so heavily, and the cabman slowed down. The wiper was moving fast, slashing at the mass of water that was dropping on the windscreen and blurring the driver's vision. I could not pull my eyes away from the wiper. It made me forget that she was talking to me.

'Leona!' she called out again and nudged me. I came back to consciousness.

'What is wrong with you? Are you okay?'

I turned and looked at her face and she saw fear in my face.

'What is wrong with you?' she asked again. 'Are you feeling cold?'

She unconsciously held my shoulders with her long arms, while I shivered. It was as if we were sisters or that we had known each other for long, but the wiper reminded me of the day in Omdurman when Grandpa was stabbed. Instead of the rain pouring on the windscreen, I had pictured blood, and the wiper slashing at it.

TWENTY-SEVEN

It rained into the night. Some trees behind the windows of my room swirled so much that I could hear the swooshing sound from my room. It seemed as if the wind came along with spirits in various shapes. I saw one—large, with protruded eyes and a flabby stomach. It danced in front of the window and made my head swell. I felt my head growing until it reached the size of my bed, and I jumped off the bed. More spirits came and they danced inside the room. They had long fingers, and each of their hands had eight fingers. Their faces were at their backs, but their eyes were in front. I screamed and they entered into me all at once. The coldness of the breeze that came as the sky sent down drizzles made me shrink myself into a ball and gaze at the ceiling, moaning, crying, dying, and seeking help, but I could not scream. It was as if my mouth was sealed shut.

The lights in my room were on, and I could not keep away the images of the wiper slashing at the rains and how the water turned into blood and moved to the sides of the car's windscreen. It made me see Mum; she was bleeding, someone was slashing at her with a big machete, and blood was spurting from all of her body. Then, I saw the day we ran to Cameroon, but it was a different time. There was blood in the car too and I wondered where it was coming from. My mind wandered to Omdurman, blood spurting from Grandpa's body as he lay on the sandy earth, and the blood from a young bandit Grandpa once shot in my presence.

When I woke up, I could not think clearly. Tears stood in my eyes, and they stung so badly that I blinked several times to push them out. I wondered what was happening—it was not a dream at all. I wondered if I was hallucinating. Yet, it felt all familiar as if I had experienced the same thing before, perhaps at Enugu. I thought about the difference between hallucination and déjà vu. Then, my phone rang. It was so loud that I nearly bit my tongue in fright. I was dazed, but I began to search for it. It was on the bed, by the pillow.

I recognised the voice. It was the voice that had been questioning my resolve to avenge my mother, the voice that still chimed in my ears and sent heat waves through me.

'Sorry about this afternoon.'

His apologies made me angry. I wanted to hate him, needed reasons enough to hate him so much that the hatred would fertilise my resolve, and I would grow with unmatched strength, enough to attack and kill him at sighting him, enough to send him seizures or cancer just by thinking about him. But now, he was giving me reasons to not hate him, to bury my disaffection. But what about my mother? No doubt, they were the ones who killed her. Dad was right; I would have to pay my adversary back in his own coin.

After I regained myself, I asked, 'Why do you apologise?'

'For not taking your calls when you rang earlier. I was busy and had instructed my secretary to take all calls, but I left strict instructions that yours be passed through.'

'I have heard.' I stood and stretched myself. I was so exhausted. 'So?'

He laughed. His laughter was velvety, like if you touched it you could feel some powdery texture that would leave you gasping. It did leave me gasping, but I willed myself to hate this voice, this laughter. I wanted his voice to turn to something fiendish enough to make me want to defend myself and kill him—that way I could argue that it was in self-defence.

'Now you know that I did not intentionally avoid your calls. I was thinking about you all day. I couldn't even concentrate on the meeting.'

'You better stop thinking about me.'

'Why would you want me to do that?'

I pictured him smiling, his jaw tightening but smiling all the same, like Dad's—but Dad rarely smiled, since we returned from Sudan, and more after he was imprisoned. He would look grotesque if he did. He seemed always to be brooding. Even when he was in the news, he always looked ahead, not staring at the press, his jaw set tight. I guess politics could turn you into a statue like that.

'Just stop thinking about me.'

'Well, I will try. Can I see you tomorrow?'

'Why?'

'Because I want us to hang out. There is this new spot I'd love to show you.' He sounded excited. 'And I would love you to get to know me for who I am. All right?'

'Don't you have better things to do?'

'Better things? Better than seeing your beautiful face? No.'

'I'll think about it.' I peeped out the window. It was pitch dark.

There was no electricity anywhere in the neighbourhood. 'See ya.'

'When?'

'Whenever we see. But definitely not tomorrow.'

Each time I heard Akinola's voice, something ran through my blood and made me feel like hyperventilating, and I had to pinch myself to be sure I was still alive. I thought about telling Aunty Agii this plan of ours, but as liberal and open-minded as she was, I knew she would never consent. And how could you tell someone—even if the person was your mother—that you were planning to kill a human being for whatever reason? It was not an idea that was appealing. Sometimes, I asked myself whether I wanted to kill this man. I called Kosi instead, and we talked briefly. He said he had just got back from Mass. I asked if he thought about me, and he whispered that during consecration while his eyes were closed and he was supposed to be praying, he was thinking about what we did in Enugu. I laughed and called him naughty. He said he would call back and hung up.

When I went downstairs for dinner and met Okwudili and Johnson perched on the edge of their seats eating, I nearly laughed. Their mother was angry at how they had messed up the table. I got my food from the kitchen and joined them. The two boys rushed to my sides instantly.

'What?'

'Meat.'

'Ah! What? Oya, halele! Go back to your food. Both of you. Now!' their mother shrieked. They stayed put. I smiled and divided my fish into three parts and handed them a part each. 'Hei! Chineke! These boys won't kill me.'

'They are just boys, Aunty.'

I began to eat. It was amala and ewedu, cooked with fish. 'You will teach me how to make this,' I said innocently, but Aunty Agii crooked her head this way and looked at me sheepishly, smiling at me.

'You definitely need to learn how to make amala and ewedu.'

The way she stared at me, I knew she was up for some mischief.

'Why?'

'Because your husband would love it if you can make that.'

'Why? Who is my husband?'

'Ha! Akinola of course. Ha! Don't tell me you haven't accepted, biko?'

'Mba. I haven't. No.'

'Oh?'

'We haven't even seen again.'

'You should see him. Does he call?'

'I just finished talking to him. He wants us to go out on a date.'

'But, Nne, why do your lips shiver? What's wrong? You are scared of this guy?'

I looked up sharply, stung at having been discovered. Not that I was scared of him. Rather, I was scared of myself, of what I was going to do if I allowed myself to fall in love with this man, or if I allowed him to fall in love with me. It was a great heart-wrenching dilemma, having to debate every day what to do with him; whether to accept his proposals, whether I would be strong enough to avenge my mother if I accepted, whether killing him was the proper way of taking my pound of flesh. Sometimes, I wondered if it was best that I get into his family and kill his father. I wondered why Dad never planned to kill the man; after all, he had used the phrase, 'an eye for an eye'. Or could it be that he wanted his son so Chief Fegun Wale would suffer just like we did when Mum died?

'What's bothering you? O gini?'

'Nothing. I don't seem to cherish the idea of marriage, now.'

'And who says you must marry him now?' She had finished eating and was now washing her hands by the basin affixed to the wall.

'He wants marriage.'

'Gi kwanu? Do you want marriage?'

'I still want to do a lot.'

'Like?'

'I want to pursue my modelling career.'

'You can pursue your dreams even as a married woman.'

'Not every man would be comfortable seeing his wife's face on billboards and magazines et al. What if he is the kind of man who doesn't give women the chance to be who they love to be? He is wealthy, a billionaire. He might make me a housewife, a trophy.'

'In this age? Mbanu. He knows better. You are smart and from a wealthy home too. He can't treat you anyhow.' She towelled her hands. 'And girl, that's why I ask that you get to know him; then, know what to say.'

'You sound like he's asked for my hand in marriage. He hasn't.'

I was silent. Now, this was why I never wanted to tell Aunty Agii about our conviction that they had a hand in Mum's death and the plan to make them suffer.

'Not every woman is lucky like you, Aunty. You are married to a man who is too busy to ask if you are doing this or that, to question your career.'

'Negodu nwatakiri a.' She rolled her eyes. 'Well, what you call luck might not be that to me. Leona, you see, life is different for different people. I do not cherish that I do not live with your father.' She looked at her boys. 'Come, let's go to my room.'

I carried my plates of food and followed her.

'We want to come along, Mummy,' one of the boys said.

'No. Stay there. Finish your food and go inside for your bath. Your sister and I have some things to do inside, and I don't want you coming to disturb us. Inugo?'

They nodded.

Her room was the biggest in the house. It should be the master bedroom, but she took it since Dad did not visit often. There were portraits hanging on the wall—she and Dad dressed in traditional attire, those of her boys, and one painting of a half-nude, large-assed woman whose skin was so dark they could be compared to the flesh of coal. She indeed loved nude paintings.

'The best life in marriage is when the partners live together. This life,' she spread out her hands, 'This one is temptation. Every day, you meet handsome men, married and unmarried, some of them ask you out; and you live in this big house where you have a room for yourself, all alone and can do anything you want. It could be tempting.'

I wondered when this conversation drifted to this.

'Do you feel tempted? To cheat on Dad?'

'Sometimes.' She smiled.

'And have…? Never mind.'

She smiled at me. 'I haven't. Not because I am a saint, but because your father is a public figure and has ambitions. If I do anything silly and it gets out there, he might be ruined. You see, in marriage, you make sacrifices, and mostly for your family, not for anyone—not your father, mother, or friends.'

I wondered if she was reading my mind. I sat up on the

214

bed. I had stopped eating. I placed the plates on the floor.
She sat down and we faced each other. Her hair was covered
in a dark net; she was wearing her usual singlet.

'Let me tell you, Nne, there is no gain in staying single
or divorced.'

'What if you are in a bad marriage? Won't you leave?'

'If you can't make it work, you leave. But first, you try to
make it work and you try as many times as possible, as many
years as possible. Your father is married to me and the *other*
woman. Whatever she does or says, I don't take it seriously.
I am concerned with making my marriage work. I married
when I was thirty-seven. That is considered *very-very* late in
the east, right?'

'Right.'

'In Igboland, to marry well over thirty is considered
late. People ask questions and gossip. They say 'Negodu, she
could not get married because she had aborted all the babies
in her womb', so young women do everything possible to
get married in their twenties. But I am educated. I studied
overseas. I was rich and had a good job and didn't care about
marriage until your father came along. I married him not
because folks were asking questions but because I loved him.
He was this serious and tenacious and smooth—'

'Smooth?' I winked at her.

'Your father bu fire… he knows how to treat a woman
right.' She laughed.

I did not. I was jealous, jealous for Mum. Dad was
not smooth with Mum almost all the time they were

married—except when we were in Khartoum. I wondered if the part of him that loved Mum died the day he watched the rebels kill Grandpa, and if this smooth part of him was rekindled when he was with another woman.

'Bia, am I embarrassing you?' She asked me.

'No. Not at all.'

She smiled.

'Well. So, if this boy, this Akinola shows you that he loves you and is serious to settle down with you and you find out that he is the kind of man you want, don't rush into his hands o, make him understand your priorities and be sure he is ready to allow you to pursue them. Inugo?'

I nodded.

TWENTY-EIGHT

The days that followed were filled with a lot of activities—meeting family relations in Lagos, nightclubbing, dinner parties, modelling sessions, and rejecting dates and invitations from men. At that time, each time a man proposed to me, I remembered what Chief Fegun Wale did to Mum and my hatred for men tripled. Every character they exhibited triggered some sort of unconscious defence, tending to prove to me that they wanted nothing but their own happiness and could go to great lengths and chicanery to achieve that, especially betraying and killing women both physically and emotionally.

The last audition for Luxury Soap came, and I emerged the winner. The judges were unanimous in their decision. Aunty Agii threw a big party and invited her friends, almost all of them— even Dad flew in that evening. He had grown to love parties. You could not live in Nigeria without loving parties, especially if you were a reputed politician and a renowned millionaire respected by your country for spending three years in jail, fighting the military government and for working to entrench democracy—that was what Nigerians thought of my dad. Only few of us knew better.

Aunty Agii said she had to host the party so that the 'Who-is-Who' in Lagos would get to know about me. She convinced Dad to come so that rich and influential folks would attend the party and meet me too.

After the party, when her friends were done cleaning the sitting room and everyone had left, she walked up to Dad and sat on his laps. Dad and Mister Isaac Uwaifo, his old-time friend, were sitting on a long couch, talking in hushed tones.

'Hey, woman. I couldn't keep my eyes off you all the time. This backside of yours seems to grow every time I am away,' Dad teased.

'Inukwa? Perhaps I have some macho boys pumping it out for me.'

Mister Uwaifo laughed. 'Give it to him, woman. James thinks he has wit.'

Dad laughed. I sat on a dining chair and listened.

'Well, I know my wife.'

'Are you sure?' she asked.

'I am sure.'

I heard their mouths click in a kiss.

'So, who was the lady in red?' she asked.

'"The Lady in Red" is a song by—,' Dad tried to say.

'Spare me that, James. Asi! Asi! Lie lie! She is one of your Lagos girls, right? I was watching you all the while as you made contact with her, as if you were telling her where to meet you.'

'Perhaps I am planning on a third wife.'

'Fourth,' Mister Isaac Uwaifo corrected.

They laughed. I wondered if Aunty Agii was serious.

'Woman, I think your eyes were playing tricks on you. If I want to play games, I would do that in Abuja.'

'Where your other wife will burst your head? I know her quite well. And I know you wouldn't try anything stupid in Abuja, so you come to Lagos where you have the loyal, easy-going wife to push around.'

I smiled. Aunty Agii did not know about Adulike then.

'No. Ha! I am a saint oh. Look, I don't chase girls. Besides I am too busy for that.'

'James is a busy man.'

'What would you say before, Oga Uwaifo? You are both partners in crime,' Aunty Agii accused, jokingly.

They laughed at her. She stood from Dad's lap and sat on another cushion.

'If I catch any girl around you in Lagos, I will skin her and use her carcass to sew agbada for you.'

'Agu nwanyi!' Dad teased. 'You won't dare.'

'He said you won't. Meaning he would do it in a careful way so you wouldn't know,' Mister Uwaifo said, laughing. He stood, 'You people will not kill me with banter. I am leaving for my house.'

'This is no banter o. I am serious, James.'

'Don't worry, small girl. Look, I am clean. I am a Minister of the Federal Republic, you know.'

'Ministers do the worst.'

Mister Uwaifo was already at the door. Dad hurried to meet up with him. I heard him telling the man that he would leave by first flight the next day.

Aunty Agii met me in the dining room and smiled.

'Your father is like a boy. I so love him.'

I smiled back at her, jealous for Mum again. I wondered if she could see them, playing, joking— if she felt jealous wherever she was.

When Dad came back, he joined us in the dining room.

'You want anything, Nna?' Aunty Agii asked.

'Cake, if there is still some left.'

'Of course.'

Aunty Agii went to fetch some cake.

'So, my girl, congratulations.' He ruffled my hair.

'Are you serious? You are happy for me?'

'Of course. My wife… Agnes said I should give you a chance. She said you are happy and that you'll be good at modelling.' I nodded. 'You seem to have grown fond of her.'

'We are good friends, Dad.'

He beamed. 'Look, she is nice. I hope one day you come to hate me less for marrying her.'

'O, Dad. I don't hate you.'

'Another reason why I am glad you are here is because Akinola Wale is here and I hope he gets to win you over and we accomplish our small plot,' he said conspiratorially.

I raised my eyebrows in acknowledgement and wondered if he was not interested that I was in Lagos for modelling, but so I could get close to Akinola.

'I saw Mum's things, Dad.'

'You did?'

'Yes.'

'What did you see? Where?'

'At Enugu. In her room.'

'I never checked her room. Look, I couldn't bring myself to do it.'

He sighed. It was one of the few times he looked like he missed Mum.

'I do think they had a hand somewhat in what happened, Dad.'

He nodded at me approvingly. 'Good.' Aunty Agii walked in. She dropped a large saucer before us. We picked up pieces of cake and began to eat. She took some icing and put it in her mouth. 'Good. Now you are coming around, my girl.'

Dad stretched his hand across the table and placed it on mine.

I was quiet.

'What's that?' Aunty Agii asked.

'Nothing, Agnes. Leona and I are just talking.' He stood. 'I'm going to my room.'

When he left, she asked, 'What's that? He seemed happy with something you said or did.'

'I told him you and I are now pally-pally, and he is happy.'

Aunty Agii beamed at me and hurried to join her husband upstairs.

TWENTY-NINE

I had a dream that night. I visited Enugu and Mum was in the house. Enugu, in the dream, seemed different—the streets, the roads, the environment looked different. I felt I could touch the town if I stretched my hands from the cab window. The idea of touching the city roamed in my mind, and I thought that if it was possible for a man to touch whatever he wanted—to touch feelings, happiness, existence, even death– it would have been a wonderful thing. There were rainbows so close that I could touch them and smell their colours. The rainbows followed the cab until we got to the house.

We drove into Independence Layout and meandered through those streets that Onyinye and I passed many times while taking walks in the evenings and while going to play volleyball at the 82 Division Army Base during school vacations. The gate was so long my eyes could not see it all. It was thrown open by a man I had never met, probably a new gateman. I hurried out of the cab to meet Mum. She was at the porch with some Sudanese who looked dirty and dishevelled. Mum was looking old, like she was in her seventies. She had a wig on, I suspected to cover her grey hairs. She smiled at me and there were no teeth in her mouth. That scared the shit out of me, but we hugged still. She was crying now. Then, the beggars came and hugged us both, telling me, 'Thank you. Thank you.', but it was not in English. They were speaking some language that I found difficult to understand. I woke up.

Everywhere was quiet, apart from some noise outside. I parted the curtains and saw Aunty Agii hug Dad and kiss him briefly. Then, someone opened the car door, and he stepped inside and the person hurried into the passenger seat and the car zoomed off towards the gate. A backup vehicle followed. I watched Aunty Agii stare at the direction of the gate until I could not see the vehicles. She turned towards the house, and I closed my curtains.

I wondered why the Sudanese in my dream were thanking me. I recalled the times I returned to Enugu from the university and Mum was hosting some Sudanese and Niger refugees who roamed the streets of Enugu. There were so many of them in Nigeria and Mum liked to invite them to the house, each time she met with them. She would be driving along Okpara Avenue and when they came to beg, she would speak Thuongjang, a little Twic, or Rek; and they would be thrilled. If they did not understand, she would greet them in Zaghawa. She could not speak Fur, and they would have to use Pidgin English to communicate with her.

Sometimes, she would ask them into her car and bring them to the house, and Smart would empty pots of food for them and empty bags of garri and rice for them to take along. Mum also gave them money. Sometimes she dropped them off or asked our driver to do so. It was one of those acts of hers, which Dad hated so much when he was still living in Enugu.

'Look, you are turning my home into a refugee camp,' he complained.

'They need help, all the assistance they can get. Tsk.'

'And you are the Red Cross or the Centre for Human Rights?'

'Come on, James? I am not any of those, but I am their sister.'

'Sister my foot!' he would clap his hands in fury. 'You are a sister to those thieves from Niger and Chad?' Mum would remain calm. 'Listen, I am not asking you not to be a little sympathetic. Look, they are your people, yes; but stop bringing them to my house like this place is a refugee camp. Some of them are criminals, you know.'

'Ah! How can you even conceive that in your mind, James?'

The next day, two black tinted Toyota jeeps with thick armoured windows drove into the compound. I was in the sitting room by the window, watching to see who was going to alight. Then, a young man came to me in the sitting room and informed me that their boss sent them to fetch me.

225

'Who is your boss?'

He was staring ahead, not looking at me; perhaps embarrassed by my outstretched legs on the sofa. I was dressed in mini-skirt and a brown-coloured singlet.

'Akinola Wale.'

'Oh. He didn't call me,' I said to myself, but he heard.

'He said you can call him.'

'Why does he want to see me?' I blurted out before it occurred to me that there was no way he would know. 'Never mind.'

He did not respond. I took out my phone and searched for Akinola and dialled his number. I was fuming but maintained my cool. He apologised for the short notice and said he wanted to surprise me.

'Your surprise better be good.'

'Trust me,' he sounded arrogant.

'How did you even know I would be home?'

He whistled, and I sighed, ended the call, and went upstairs to change. Then, my phone rang again, I hurried out of the bathroom and answered the call.

'Dress casually, darling. You kill me each time I look at you. You intimidate me. I want to intimidate you today.'

I scowled. 'Aah! You should have pre-informed me.'

'I told you I want to intimidate you. I think I am already succeeding.'

'Where are you taking me to?'

'It is a surprise, sweet.' The way he said the words made me feel older.

They drove me to Marina, and my jaws dropped at seeing a big yacht that was basking in the waters. They helped me into a speed boat, and we rode the short distance to the yacht. I instantly knew it belonged to Akinola. News had it that he lived in affluence and was a little extravagant when it came to acquiring luxury stuff.

Aunty Agii never stopped talking about how she read in this and that magazine and tabloid about how Akinola acquired this art, that painting, this speed boat, or car. The yacht was named 'Mary' and painted dark red. I wondered at the coincidence of the names, and I made a mental note to ask him what the name meant to him. The inside of Mary was painted lilac, and the colour sparkled. There were lights and air-conditioners everywhere. I could count about six staff inside, all of them dressed formally. A young woman of about twenty years old led me to a large lounge where Akinola was seated. The lounge had over six sofas, brown in colour. There were paintings on the wall, five of them. He stood as soon as he saw me, smiling awkwardly.

'Thank you for coming. Are you afraid?'

The floor was covered in a thick woolly rug that swallowed the sound of the feet and eased walking. Everything sparkled. It felt like heaven.

'A bit,' I replied. A sound came from some speaker somewhere; jazz music, I think. 'I am most delighted. I've never been on a yacht before.'

'You intimidate me with your looks.' He inhaled the scent of my hair perfume. I caught him take a breath.

227

'You haven't had a photo shoot in a yacht?'

'No. I'll keep that in mind now that you have pointed it out.'

'Never mind—'

'Oh, don't worry. I am a new model.'

'But you are already gaining fame. You are on all major tabloids in the country and beyond. I follow the news.'

We were still standing.

'I hope I keep getting lucky.'

'Of course. You won't believe your eyes when offers start flooding in. That is the way of fortune—money begets money, success births more and more success.'

'You talk from experience.'

He smiled and blinked when our eyes met again.

'This is beautiful.'

'No. It is more than beautiful. This is my goddess. I told you I was going to intimidate you today.'

He wore a sparkling white polo shirt and loose designer trousers, with ropes to hold it to his waist. He was barefooted.

'Please sit.'

We sat on the same sofa. The girl came back with two men. They brought plates containing assorted meals and set them on the long glass table. An elderly man returned with four bottles of Champagne in buckets of ice.

I could see shrimps in what appeared to be soup. I picked one and threw it into my mouth.

'Sorry,' I laughed.

He laughed and nearly fell off the sofa.

'I didn't even wash my hands.' It tasted so good. 'So, what are you doing?'

'I want to celebrate your grand entry into the world of affluence.'

'You do that in a crazy way.'

'Yes. Yes, 'cos I am *crazy* about you.' He turned and looked closely at me, and I moved to the sofa opposite him. He smiled at me. 'I won't eat you, sweetheart. I have enough food on the table to fill my stomach.'

I smiled. 'You a heavy-eater?'

'Not at all. Most of the food are for you.'

'To impress me?'

'Yes.'

I laughed aloud, 'Well, I am impressed, and the shrimps taste good, hmm.' I took a spoon to the soup and tasted it. 'Hmm.'

'Before we eat, let me show you around.'

'Oh! Okay.'

I rose like a child on her first trip to the zoo and floundered; my knees were shaky, and my eyes swooned a little. I was overwhelmed. There were two spacious rooms inside the large boat, and each had a family-sized bed and more paintings. One of the rooms had a dresser with a mirror and chests for clothes. Each had bathrooms en suite, painted white; they were impeccable. The lights in the rooms, and in the veranda and lounge, sparkled. He took me to the deck.

I was amazed to find out that the yacht was moving with great speed, faster than a vehicle at a hundred and twenty kilometres per hour.

'I didn't know this was moving.'

'You are not supposed to know from the inside unless you look out of the window.' We sat back at the table, and he dished the meal. After we ate catfish peppersoup and drank half of a bottle of Champagne, he said, 'Have I succeeded so far in intimidating you?'

'I've never been so overdone in my whole life.'

'The pleasure is all mine, sweetheart.'

'I think you are trying to seduce me.'

'Oh! Then, I have failed in that regard, for by now you should have been making love to me.'

'Make love? Ah!'

'Haven't you made love before?'

'You want to know if I am a virgin?' I grinned and pretended to look away.

'Well—'

'I am not, but it is close to a year I was with a man last.' *Now, why did I say that?*

'Makes me jealous.'

'You'd prefer a virgin?'

He said nothing, and I guessed he was hoping I was one. I did not care. My mission was not to love him. I hoped I was succeeding in doing so.

He looked at me with love. 'Your sincerity kills me. I fall more in love with you every second.'

'Love?'

'Yes.' He began to eat some ice cream.

'I don't believe in that.'

He smiled, probably thinking I was not serious. 'Tell me, who is the man with the good fortune to enjoy those lips?'

'Who are the ladies that have been sucking you off?' I replied sarcastically.

He beamed. 'I might be a virgin.'

'Go tell that to the birds.'

'Why do you not believe?'

'You are a globetrotter. And you must fuck not less than one woman per city you visit.'

'Fuck? You use the F word with ease.'

'Because I am not a child.'

'You are twenty-five; you were born in nineteen eighty, on May eighteenth.'

'You have done your research. What else did you find?' I was now reclining back on the sofa, sipping from a glass of wine. I was cautious of the alcoholic content.

'Many things, but they don't matter.'

'They should.'

He fingered the bracelet on his wrist. 'I should get to know much about the girl I intend to spend the rest of my life with.' He added quickly.

I wondered if he knew about Kosi. And now that I remembered him, I was already missing him. I wished he was the one seated opposite me now, staring at me on this sweet, romantic voyage. I stared Akinola down.

'It would be an honour to have you stare at me like this, every morning when I wake up,' he teased.

'When did the idea of marrying me get into your head?'

'My father and your family have had so much in common for many years. Your father is a friend. My father told me that he would love to cement the relationship. He told me about you.'

'You are acting your dad's script then?'

'No, no.' He was leaning towards the table now, his long eyelashes fluttering. 'No, I have to be sincere. It was first his idea but when I saw you my heart skipped.'

'When was the first time you saw me?'

'I came to Enugu on a business trip—'

'And you spied on me?'

'Oh, yes.' He beamed.

I cursed under my breath.

'I hope to be your friend, get to know you better on a more personal level, and convince you to be my wife.'

'Are you asking me to marry you, Akinola Wale?'

'Not yet, ma'am.' He gulped his drink and poured another for himself.

I wondered if he was excited or anxious.

We sat in silence for some time, while I contemplated a lot of things. My heart chimed a bell, each time I stole a glance at him.

'My grandfather used to make me feel so exceptional back then in Sudan.'

'I know that part of you. Have I made you feel exceptional, Leona?'

'I don't know how to describe how I feel.'

He leaned towards me, 'I would love to hear that I make you feel great.'

'It's not that. It is something else, something different,' I said. 'What did your father tell you about... my family... my mother?'

'Like what?' he was on guard.

'They were business partners.'

'He only has good words for your mum. He says that she was a tenacious woman who knew what she wanted. She was a lion, he would tell me; not a lioness, but a lion.' He stood and came to my side, placing his hand on my shoulder. 'The day I came to your house and we met for the first time, I said to myself, 'This girl will make you the happiest man alive.' I knew from that day that I could sell all I have to acquire you and make you mine.'

'Acquire me?' I dropped my cutlery.

'Not in that sense, but like one acquires a precious thing, like diamonds. You go to great extents to get it, greater extent to keep it safe, and admire it every night before you sleep and every morning after you wake. You know what I mean.'

Then, he sat down.

'It sounds to me like a chauvinist idea—seeing women as objects. You compare me to a precious stone that you can buy in the Asian market.'

'You are entitled to that opinion, but to me, you are a rare gem that I can travel thousands of miles to possess, to acquire, if you allow me use the word again.'

'You should have said "possess" the first time.'

'Is it not after you acquire something that you come to possess it? In this case, the process of convincing you to return my love, convince your family and friends to accept me, and possibly we coming to do the traditional rites, is the acquisition process.' He winked.

'You should delete the word, "acquisition". I have a problem with it in the context you are using it.'

He appeared to ponder about it. 'My bad. I'm sorry, Sweetheart.'

'It's a wrong word. You can't acquire a human with a soul. Can you control the soul?'

'If I have your love and attention and devotion, can I say that I have some control over your being?'

'Being not soul.'

'The being is comprised of spirit and soul and body. The three make us up.'

'The human being, as it is, is a complex matter that can't be understood. It's an element too difficult to study, especially its pattern. It's not something you can understand entirely as you study it then say, I have known it so well, and it's now mine, mine to *acquire*. I mean, even if we become friends and we are together for years, you can't say for sure that you've known me well to now possess me.'

'I—'

'Unless you are limiting possession to just the societal definition of it, in relation to having my name attached to yours and people see us as one part and we define what happens to each other's' life.'

'More than that.' I began to eat again. 'You mean a lot to me.'

'How much?'

Our eyes met, and he looked away.

'I can't explain it. I don't want to compare you to anything, but you are so free and pure and beautiful. Like a...witch.'

'Are witches beautiful?'

He laughed. 'I know in Nigeria we relate witches with evil and ugliness and dirt in all physical attributes. You bewitch me, all of me.'

I drank from a glass of water. He did the same.

'The other day,' he came and knelt beside me. 'When I asked you out and you accepted, I felt on top of the world, and...' he smiled proudly, 'I had the name of the yacht changed—'

It dawned on me then. 'You did what?'

'Yes. My office is on the paper works now.'

'I saw the name... Mary? After my mum?'

'Yes.'

I fought tears from my eyes.

'I hope I keep her memory alive, for you.'

'You are so kind, Akinola.' *But I am going to kill you.*

THIRTY

My phone rang just as we were stepping out of the boat. Kosi was in Lagos. I brightened up while receiving the call, asking when he got into town and what he was in Lagos for, all the while shifting away from Akinola, but I was sure he noticed.

The Range Rover cruised into the compound and Akinola waved his goodbye. I rushed upstairs to my room and changed into another dress. Kosi was booked into a hotel with other seminarians, but he had promised to smuggle me in.

'Don't ask at the reception. Walk straight upstairs to the second floor, Room Two One Two.'

Kosi was pacing the lobby in front of his room when I came up. He was dressed in black trousers and a white shirt, unbuttoned. He looked just the same—average height, broad-shouldered, but now darker. His afro was lowered and a line crossed from the left side running to the back; it was his signature hairstyle from when we were in primary school. When we got into the room, he hurriedly closed the door behind us, and we fell into each other, kissing, caressing, and undoing our clothes.

'Kosisochukwu m…' I moaned.

Early the next morning, I prepared to leave so that none of his colleagues would see me sneak out of his room. He did not look happy.

'Come on, Darling, I need to go. But wait o, I'd like to ask you again, are you sure this is what you want to do?'

He hit the mattress with his fist. 'You have asked me this, many times, Leo.'

'I know.' I hugged him, placing my head on his chest. 'It is just that I miss you, and you don't seem happy, Darling.'

'I am happy as a Reverend. I am unhappy that I can't have you. I miss you.'

We were beyond the point of talking about the rightness of our actions—if it was sinful that he was going to be a priest and yet we were having sex.

'I wish we are allowed to marry.' He stretched his hands in surrender. 'What will happen to all this beauty?'

I said nothing. And while dressing up, he asked, 'The man you talked about? Are you sure of what you are doing?'

I wished I could open up to him. 'I am sure.' He sighed. 'He is already talking marriage, Kosi.'

For a moment, I thought if I said that he would be spurred to change his mind about becoming a priest, and I would not hesitate to say 'yes' to him if he wanted me to be his wife.

'I will pray over it, Leo. The will of God will be done.'

'I don't want you to pray over anything.'

'What do you want me to do, Leona?'

'I want you to marry me.'

His jaw dropped. He knelt on the bed. 'You amaze me,' he said tiredly.

'How?'

He came to me and took me into his arms. 'I want to. I love to but I can't.'

'You can. You can leave.' There were tears in my eyes.

'I can't leave priesthood unless they discharge me, unless I'm not called. But this is what I want to do… what I always wanted to do.'

'And how long do we continue to do this?'

'I don't know.' He hugged me tightly. I willed myself not to cry. I loved him so much. I loved that he loved and adored me, but sometimes I questioned why he loved the priesthood more than me. I wished it was not so. I wished he could tell me he was leaving the seminary to be with me. And now, I wished that was the case so that I would have something to hold on to and not succumb to the temptation of marrying Akinola and killing him afterwards.

That morning, when I left the hotel and got to the house, I received a transaction notification on my phone. Luxury Soap had paid in the first instalment of the contract money. I was officially a millionaire.

In the evening, Dad called Aunty Agii just as she returned from work. She dropped the call on him and yelled down the roof.

When I rushed out, she said, 'Your father thinks I am stupid.'

Then, she told me what he said. Elizabeth was in the

hospital and she had no one to take care of her. Dad asked if Aunty Agii could come to Abuja to stay with her for a day or two. I laughed so loud that she dropped her handbag and stared at me.

'Ara o n'apu gi?' she asked. Her forefinger poked at her head, inclined to an angle as she asked if I was insane.

'Is she not your junior wife, eh?'

'Biko, get out!' she stomped out.

Akinola called more than five times and sent tens of text messages every day. He said when he thought about me, he stopped whatever thing he was doing; and for someone like him, it was terrible because he was assiduous. I wondered if it was true, because a man would say anything to a woman just to win her heart. He was falling deeply in love with me, day by day—that I knew for sure; but to think he could not do anything just thinking about me was amusing. The most terrifying part of it all was that he was succeeding in making himself likeable. I still could not understand why he had the yacht named after my mum.

And when I rang Dad about it, he seemed to take a moment before responding, his voice sounding off-key. 'Look, he was just showing off.'

'Not to the extent of naming that beauty after Mum.' I raised my left hand as if he was looking at me. 'Dad, that is *huge!*'

'Perhaps the yacht was bought with our money. Can't you see?' He sounded childish.

'Oh, Dad! Don't be ridiculous.' I hung up.

The day before, Aunty Agii told me that Akinola's goods were seized by the Nigerian government. She wondered why Dad would want me to marry Chief Fegun Wale's son, yet not protect his business interest. I shrugged it off, and she followed me to the kitchen asking if there was something I was not telling her.

'Akinola didn't even tell me that.'

'Obviously, he doesn't want to get you thinking about it all.'

'I am old enough to form my own opinions.'

'Well, I think he knows that, but he doesn't want you asking your dad about it. He made me promise not to ask Chief, but he is worried and curious. I guess he has information that your dad's ministry has a hand in the seizure.'

'Well, Dad doesn't forgive easily.'

'Nne, is there something you people are not telling me? This feud shouldn't still be on.'

'I am telling you something huge.'

'What?' Her eyes twinkled as she listened.

'That Dragons Investment wants to sign me on. They have spoken with my madam at the agency, and we think it is a big one.'

'Dragons is Akinola's business empire, right?'

'Yes.'

'Good. Ifugo? It means we have a man who will value your career and cherish your dreams.'

'You are rushing into conclusions, Aunty.'

'Don't be ridiculous. You were scared about this earlier.'

'Still no guarantee that he won't change when we get married.'

'Oh, I don't think so. Calm down, Nne. This man probably asked his company to contact your agency. The deal with Luxury Soap would just be chicken change.'

'Let's see how it goes.'

THIRTY-ONE

Arrangements were made and Emily Whitman flew into the country for the meeting with Dragons Investment Incorporated. Around midday, Emily, Waribagha and I walked into the huge complex that housed the most successful business empire in Africa. Located on the island, the fifteen-story building had three large glass doors leading into it. I noticed security cameras everywhere as a security man led us into the reception area. It was an extra-large lounge, with cushions aligning the walls. There were three huge television sets at different parts of the lounge, barely audible but showing various news channels. There were countless people in the lounge, over twenty of them, waiting for meetings, interviews, and God-knows-what. They all turned and stared at me, while a few bent and whispered, gossiped, and conferred with each other. I wiggled my waist with added effects, and some men swallowed saliva.

The ladies must be calling me all sorts of names.

Waribagha was enthusiastic. If the deal pulled through, I would be the face of Dragons Investment, representing all their products from pharmaceuticals to plastics, foods, sugar, salt, noodles, and what-have-you, plus the telecommunication network operating in many African countries. The deal would run into millions.

Waribagha was about to introduce himself to the receptionist when she said, 'I know you, Aunty. Good afternoon.' She was looking directly at me.

'Good afternoon. How are you?'

'I am fine, thank you. My Director has been waiting for you. A minute, please.' She took up the intercom and dialled. 'Please sit here. It has been reserved for you.'

There was a three-in-one leather sofa beside her with a white fluffy pillow. An air conditioner was directly behind me. I liked that. People gawked. I could see them conversing still. Waribagha stood by Emily like a devoted bodyguard, while Emily took my hand and placed it on her lap. She was delighted about the deal and was surprised that Dragons Investment had requested for me specifically.

'Don't be nervous, Dear,' her American accent was smooth and lush.

I wore an Ankara sewed into a big gown that extended to the ground and swept the floor as I walked. My neck was adorned with beads that were as long as a Santa's beard. On my arms were bracelets made of costly gold that jingled as I walked and tormented the eyes of onlookers. I was confident. A tall man, who walked as if he was hunched, came out from one of the four elevators in the lounge.

'My pleasure meeting you all,' he said, extending his hand. I took it. Emily stood and they shook hands; Waribagha, too.

'My pleasure,' I said, flashing a wide smile.

'You look prettier seen alive.'

'I have always been alive.' I smiled.

Emily laughed and winked at me.

'I mean when seen physically and not on screen or on the pages of newspapers and magazines,' he said, laughing slightly.

'You flatter me, sir. Thank you.'

'Please follow me.'

We rode an elevator to the fourth floor of the complex. The elevator opened to a long corridor with offices and young people dressed in suits walking hurriedly along. Each one stared at us as we walked past. His office was large and had a set of brown couches, which I thought was the place where he held important meetings. The room was cool and comfortable, and the television was tuned to Bloomberg News. There was a laptop on his desk. His secretary, a fat lady in her mid-thirties, who looked smart, her hair gathered in a bun, opened a bottle of chilled white Bordeaux.

After the lady left and we sipped our drinks, he said, 'Pardon my stupidity, I forgot to make an official introduction. My name is Johnson Wenger. I am the Director of Publicity, Dragons Investment. Soon we shall be meeting with the President and the Executive Officers.' He did not sound Nigerian though he looked it.

'Once again, my pleasure meeting you, Mister Wenger,' Emily said.

I smiled at him. Waribagha extended his hand again. I

wondered if he would at least keep calm for a minute and stop pushing forward his hand and his big head. I wondered too if I was the only one who noticed that Mister Wenger could not stop staring at my breasts. I wondered if men would ever admire women for their personalities and successes without linking their physical attributes. It was a shame that men admired the physical endowments of women more than they honoured their achievements.

'Dragons Investment Incorporated began in the mid-eighties. It was started by Otunba Fegun Wale.'

'Otunba is the Yoruba word for chief, right?' Emily inquired.

'Yes, Madam. His son is in charge now. Otunba Fegun Wale toiled laboriously and took the business to great heights, one that is reckoned with and respected all over the world. Today, it stands tall as one of the largest and strongest business empires in Africa. It owns several business ventures: Dragons oil, Dragons Foods Limited, Dragons Drugs Limited, Dragons Sugar, Dragons Cements, Dragons Construction Company, and so on. We have grown big, and sometimes it is difficult to keep track of the businesses. Otunba Fegun Wale is a household name in Nigeria. He is one of the richest men in Africa.'

'The richest, we heard,' Waribagha said.

Mister Johnson Wenger smiled.

'I heard the branches extend to lots of countries around Africa.' I wanted to get him talking. I savoured the drink.

'We have branches in all the thirty-six states of Nigeria,

fifteen African countries, and two Asian countries. We have one in New York and another in London. We have gone multinational. The current president is rated one of the richest men in Africa, like his father. We know that in the Forbes released next, he will be announced the richest young African.'

He took a cigarette from his suit pocket. I asked if he could put it off, please.

'Why?'

'I am sorry, but it disturbs me, and it is not good for your health,' I responded.

I wondered if Emily approved of my action. I knew she wanted the job more than anything else, but she did not know about me and Akinola.

'If Dragons Investment produced cigarettes, would you not model for us?'

'It's business—'

Emily butted in, 'Of course, she would. Our duty is to promote and own the clients' products like it's ours and make it shine. She would.'

'I can model for anything or for anybody.'

'But you can't model nude, huh?' He looked at me; then, at my manager, and finally at Emily.

Emily's face turned serious. 'Our agency is a professional one, and as professionals, whatever brand we take, we tweak to meet their standards,' Emily educated him.

The man looked lost.

I smiled. 'If Nigerians did not have negative sentiments

for models exposing sensitive part of their bodies, I would not mind modelling nude. But if I do, though ninety-nine percent of you men will like it and stare at the pictures for eternity, some will worship me even, but they would also be the first to come to the public and throw stones.'

He began to laugh, nodding his head, 'Very true.'

The door opened and his secretary threw in her head while holding the door.

'They are ready in the boardroom, sir.'

'The boardroom is on the sixth floor,' he said. 'Please let's go.'

'After you,' Emily said, smiling.

The elevator opened into a corridor that looked exactly like the one we saw before.

A huge man dressed in a black suit with an earphone plugged to one ear, which made him look like a state security detail attached to the country's president, opened the door and muttered greetings. I saw two other men sitting on chairs in the veranda. They studied me, not with lust but with consciousness. The men in the room, numbering over a dozen, did not stand as we entered, an indication they were Mister Wenger's seniors or equals. He greeted them and drew out a seat for me. He was a pleasant man. Waribagha waited for Emily to be seated before he sat beside her. Emily smiled at everyone, while Waribagha held our files and thumbed through the papers, his hands sweaty.

A young girl, who I guessed was an intern, came in carrying a tray of tea and coffee which we helped ourselves to. Another entered with a tray of snacks, and just as we were about picking them, the security man opened the door. Akinola was looking smart in a blue suit. He was followed by a pretty, young, and tall lady carrying files and phones. My heart skipped. *Was she his secretary? Why did he have such a beauty as a secretary?*

The doorman latched the door while talking on the earphone, and before the door closed, I noticed that the other two bulky men who were studying us earlier were standing with the doorman. As Akinola walked in, all the men in the room, both young and old stood to their feet and remained standing until he sat down. I was flabbergasted. Emily and Waribagha stood with the others.

The young lady dropped the files on the table before him and sat by his side. One would think she was his wife, both of them looked angelic. Akinola was beautiful, in a way that if a woman referred to a man as beautiful it meant he was extraordinarily handsome. His long, squared face had an ease and relaxation about it. I could not stop staring at him. The last time in his yacht seemed like ages ago.

A man, in his late sixties, with a pockmarked face and grey hairs spoke up.

'Good day, gentlemen and ladies.' There were about seven ladies in the room. 'I welcome all of us to this brief-ing. Indeed, this will be a brief meeting because our presi-dent will be travelling to South Africa tonight. We shall try to make this quick so that he can leave to prepare for his journey.'

He nodded at Akinola who flashed him a smile. Our eyes met, and he grinned. I kept my gaze at him, and he was forced to look away.

'I do not think we need an extensive introduction. We shall just introduce some few persons, starting from myself. I am Donald Agbohomire, CEO of Dragons Investment here in Nigeria—'

'And Donald didn't add that he is a chief,' Akinola said. Everyone in the room laughed aloud.

'I am Chief Donald Agbohomire.' Everyone laughed again.

'My lady,' he spoke to me. 'The young man who brought you here is Johnson Wenger. He is the Director of Publicity. He and his team shall be working directly with you and your people. The young lady seated here is the secretary to the president of this firm. While the gentleman by my side is the President of Dragons Investment, Mister Akinola Wale.' He paused.

'Chief said I am a gentleman, okay o,' Akinola remarked jocularly again.

Everyone laughed. I knew then that even if he said that he had just killed someone, they would still laugh. He nodded at me, and I smiled. My heart fell into my stomach, long ago.

'Soon, if he agrees, we will make him a chief.'

'Ah, no, Donald. Abeg oh!'

They exchanged a few banters.

Johnson Wenger began, reading from a document before

him, 'Ladies and gentlemen, please let me introduce our guests from Emily Rose Modelling Agency. The gorgeous lady in our midst is Miss Emily Whitman, one of the founding partners and the chief operating officer. She is one woman who is bringing lots of innovation into the fashion, beauty, and entertainment industry in this country.'

They all nodded while looking at Emily. Emily beamed at them, her teeth shining like the sun.

'Please, ma'am, go ahead and introduce your team, though we all know the lady with you.'

Emily thanked them for extending their hands of friendship and for singling me out to work with. She chirped, 'Leona is a new gem we discovered a few years ago, but she refused to come into the industry until some months back. Since then, she has been making heads turn. She is born to do this, to use her beauty and style to market for people. And brands that have chosen her haven't regretted it one bit.'

She turned to me, 'Miss Leona Egbufor.'

I stood. There was applause as the men looked at me in admiration.

I said hello and sat, while the president looked me up and down. I wondered if Akinola was intimidated more by my height than by my beauty. I was intimidated by his beauty too but most especially, by his wealth. Emily smiled again and sat but not before introducing Waribagha as the company's manager who would work with them if the deal clicked.

'Sir, do you have anything to say?' the CEO asked.

The president looked up from an open file and smiled. I wondered if he lived with a dentist.

'Thanks for gathering here once again. This is the fifth time we are having a meeting this past eight days that I have been in the country, and I appreciate all your hard work and kindness. I do not wish that we stay long. You may carry on, sir.'

After that, he remained silent throughout the meeting, nodding occasionally. They discussed the things they wanted me to do for them. My face was to appear on over twelve products, including their sugar, salt, drugs, brands of noodles, and cosmetics. I was also to feature in various advertisements for the company. The contract cost and further details were to be discussed with the publicity department headed by Mister Wenger.

The main reason for the meeting was for the president to see the lady who was to pilot his empire's brand. I wondered if they did not know—as I was sure—that it was their president's idea after all. Akinola's secretary was busy typing away on a laptop and occasionally whispered into the ears of her boss. I could not stop looking at her.

Was he sleeping with her? I wondered. *How close was she sitting to him? Did I see her lips touch his earlobe when she whispered into his ear? The nerves on my forehead bulged, causing me a headache.*

THIRTY-TWO

I wrapped myself in a light blanket, lazily in my bed. I was yawning like a dog when my phone rang. I stretched and yawned again as I answered.

A voice said, 'Good morning, ma!' It was a female. 'Good morning.'

'Please, ma'am. This is Dorothy. Sorry, the introduction yesterday didn't mention my name. I am Mister Akinola Wale's secretary.'

I sat up. *Why was she calling me?* 'Oh! How are you doing… Dorothy?'

'Great, ma. Uhm, sorry if I woke you up. Did I?'

'Never mind. I heard your boss was to travel to SA. How was the trip? Did you travel with him?' I stretched like a weary cat and pressed the phone tightly to my ear, waiting to hear what her response would be and hoping she would say no.

'Yes. I did.' Reflectively, my fist clenched. 'The trip was fine, ma. I want to ask for your permission to connect you with my boss. Please!'

Was Akinola trying to make them believe he was meeting me for the first time at his company? What was he doing? Was this some sort of future image positioning thing so that when the press got wind of our friendship, his office staff would gossip that we first met at a briefing when his company wanted to sign me on?

I was thrilled. I had found it difficult to keep him out of my mind.

'Why not? Go ahead.'

'Please hold on, ma.'

'Okay.'

'Ma, I want to let you know that my boss couldn't stop talking about you.'

I was startled, 'Is that so, Dorothy?'

'Yes.'

'He is a man of importance. Men of importance don't stop talking about women.'

'Oh, no, ma. This is different. My boss has never talked about any lady with me, since I started working for him five years ago. Now please hold on, ma.'

It was also possible that Akinola had told Dorothy what to tell me to make my head swoon.

I said nothing. The voice came, 'Good morning, Her Excellency!'

'I am not the wife to the president of any country,' I responded in giggles.

'You could even be president, someday. How was your night, ma'am?'

'It was fine, though I won't tell you about it. You will laugh at me.'

'Please do.'

'No! I do not know you that much to be sharing stuff as personal as dreams with you.'

'What?'

'Oh yeah.'

'I am Akinola Wale.'

I laughed. He did too.

'You will get to know me. I called to let you know that I arrived safely.'

'That is nice of you. You must be a busy person?'

'I am not. Technology has made everything simple, and I have a dedicated and loyal team, people still loyal to my father though.'

'How is South Africa?'

'Fine. And Nigeria?'

'I don't know if Nigeria is fine.'

He laughed. 'I miss you.'

'Eh? Is that so?'

'Yeah. Can't stop thinking about you. You got my SMS yesterday?'

'Yeah. You said I looked like a duck in my gown. I know you didn't mean that.' I imagined him grinning.

'I meant it.'

'Oh, come on. That's no way to treat a lady; especially someone you'd love to see become your wife.'

'Ah!'

'So?'

There was silence. He stammered, 'You… are… you are the most beautiful girl I've ever seen… since I was born. You are beautiful and elegant, nothing to be compared to a duck.'

'I got you!' I laughed. 'Now you are praising me, eh, Akinola?'

'But of course, I don't want to get you thinking I'm a dumbass.'

'I don't think you are a dumbass. By the way, how is Mary?'

There was a pause. 'The yacht?'

'Of course. The other Mary I know is long dead.' I sighed. He did too.

'Mary is fine. You seem to love this *my* Mary?'

'Yes, I do.'

'Okay. We can arrange another meeting.'

'How many South African girls have you spoken to since you arrived there?' I hated myself for asking.

'Two hundred, and I ended up kissing half of them.'

'By now your lips would be chaffed.'

He laughed. 'I miss you.'

'Thank you.'

He was delighted. 'That's a good start. You are more beautiful than what I have seen here, you know.'

'Oh?'

'The press will soon be talking about you when my publicity guys are done with the plans they have. They shared them with me and were surprised at my enthusiasm.'

'That's cool. I love the press.'

'I don't.'

'You need them for your business.'

'I don't like them. My father loved them. I am a recluse.'

Something was hitting itself on my window, perhaps some bird or a lizard. I drew the curtain to check, and a bird flew away and perched on a masquerade tree nearby. I thought the bird was perhaps seeing its reflection on my window, and thinking it to be another bird, was trying to play or fight with it. I stood by the window, watching as other birds flew to the tree.

'Sorry that you are a recluse.'

We laughed.

'That is a lie. Well, not a recluse in that sense, but I avoid the media. A man like me should, otherwise, they will mess me up.'

'In my own line of business, we need them; so, we love them and hate them, I have come to learn.'

There was a long silence.

'I couldn't stop thinking about you since yesterday. If I were the pilot, I would have crashed the plane.'

I began to laugh again. He laughed too.

'I should allow you to prepare for work, you know.'

'No. If you grant me the honour of doing nothing else but listening to your voice alone today, I would be fulfilled. You are an angel, my angel.'

'I am?'

'Yes.'

'Do you say that to all the girls you meet?'

'Oh, don't be funny. Do I have time for women?'

'Am I a man?'

'You are different.' He sounded childish.

It was beginning to drizzle. I heard the boys making noise, while preparing for school, and their mother shouting to get them to be quick.

'I am to travel to Saudi Arabia from here, but I wish to see you. My head has been spinning since yesterday. Will you allow a visit?'

It took me by surprise. I began to sweat and used my left hand to push out the blanket. Then, I looked around for something to dress in as I was naked.

'I don't know what to say,' I said to Akinola. I wondered if he could hear the nervousness in my voice.

'What are you doing?'

'Just stepping out of my bed,' I lied. 'What are you dressed in?'

'Kai! Young man?' I raised my brows. I imagined him grinning. My phone was held by my shoulder to my left ear as I stepped into a long skirt.

'Okay. Will you allow me to visit you? If you agree, my jet will bring me to Nigeria tomorrow, and I can leave for Saudi after that.'

There was a pause. I pondered what to say.

'We can always see when you come back. I don't want you losing deals because of me.'

'I want us to become friendlier, Leona. I want us to build

a future together. We can't do that if we don't see each other more, talk more. Please, stop being distant.'

'If I was being distant, I wouldn't be talking to you on the phone, Mister Man.'

'You sound distracted.'

'I am looking for something to wear.'

'I guess that answers my earlier question then.'

'Shut up.'

'So, do I get to visit you? Please?'

'Okay then. Visit me, sir.'

He hung up without saying bye.

Rich men and their arrogance. I scoffed.

The phone remained on my ear for a moment as if to savour his voice. I felt like one who just took a cold bath on a hot afternoon. I cursed.

I thought about Kosi, and I wondered what he was doing. I felt sad that since Akinola entered my life, I called him less. The most surprising thing was that the more days passed, the more the plans Dad and I had vanished out of my mind. I felt ashamed of myself. Instead of planning on avenging Mum's death, I was busy thinking of the body of the man whose father killed her; the man who possibly knew what happened between his father and my mother, who possibly connived with others to kill my mum.

Chinwe came into the room. She said she wanted to do laundry and wondered if I had dirty clothes.

'That's so kind of you, Chinwe.'

'It's nothing, abeg.'

'We will wash together.'

'You are not going to work?'

'I will but not until eleven o' clock. I have an appointment with my boss to look over some contracts.'

'The one with Dragons Investment?'

'Yes.' I smiled. She beamed.

She never stopped telling me how she envied my work. When she sat on the bed, I knew she wanted to gossip.

'That your bobo try wella for you o. God knows how many millions you are going to rake in from this job.' She smiled at me, looking at me admiringly.

'Yeah.'

'Is he talking marriage, Leo?'

'Must it always be about marriage?'

'My sister said he wan marry you.'

If she knew, why was she asking?

She remained silent.

'He hasn't said anything yet.' I began to fold the clothes into the laundry basket.

'I married my husband because he was rich,' she said, suddenly and forcefully. 'It's three years since I left his house. I won't go back there again. Ever.'

'Don't say so, Chinwe. Pray he changes.'

'Men who beat women don't change. Show me one who ever did.'

My mind went to Sandy's parents. When we were in primary school, they fought even in the car, on the highway. I heard they still did.

'Nothing is impossible with God.'

Our eyes met, and she held my gaze.

'Forget it. You see, Leo. I am young. I am just thirty. I will find another man, and I will file for divorce, then.'

I shrugged. She was a lovely young woman, just like her sister, Aunty Agii, but she believed luck was against her.

'Three years. I have tried to fall in love with him again, but I cannot because of the things he did to me.'

I understood what she meant.

'Is he aware that you aren't ever going back to him?'

'I no know. I don't care. I once seduced his cousin with his money and slept with him.'

'What?' I stopped on my tracks. 'What?'

'Ehen! He was following every girl in town. The second time we did it, he nearly caught us. You see, Leona, there is nothing so special or extraordinarily beautiful about marriage, if not for children and to continue the tradition of family. Other gains of marriage can always be acquired even if one remains single. The stress of marriage is not worth it, cha-cha. I will advise, if I have the power to, that you stay single, if not forever, but for long. Try to enjoy your youth and your fame first. With your beauty, you can always get married at age forty or late thirties. Marriage is like a prison, and if you are convicted and confined into the prison of marriage, it cages you until eternity. I don talk my own.'

Was this not the same person eagerly asking me if Akinola had proposed and who was showing that she was envious of my luck? I wondered how Chinwe's mood and words changed per second, which was why she never stopped having issues with her sister.

'No, Chinwe! If I get married today and the man is not treating me well, I can divorce tomorrow. I wouldn't want to wait until I have another man who is ready to marry me before I file for divorce.'

In her leisurely way of talking, she said, 'No forget this na Africa, not Europe where celebrities divorce after two weeks of marriage. An African woman doesn't ask for a divorce. It is an abomination. Your people will abhor you unless there is another man ready to replace the other one. Else, your parents, his parents, your friends, and society will distance themselves from you, Leona. If a woman is tied into marriage, she is there o, final-final, whether good or bad. The chain is always difficult to break. If she breaks it, she becomes a nuisance to the society at large. And no matter her beauty, only a few men would like to marry her. Men will only resort to stealing her womanhood, her passion, and her money no matter how small they are. They will suck her dry like an orange and leave her. Fiam!'

'What are you saying then, Chinwe? You are the same person who wants to get a divorce as soon as you find another man.'

'But e never easy for me.'

'You are young. You married early, which is an advantage. You are just thirty.'

'Just thirty? Men haven't seen those standing, is it those seated they will see? Girls full everywhere. Many of them looking for husbands and no men available, not to talk of men who are ready to marry a woman who left her husband's house. This is Nigeria, Leona. Ha!' She became serious. 'If you asked me to advise you, I would say don't get married now. Enjoy your success. Start up a business and become wealthy. Marry in your mid or late thirties, and you will hold and control the world.' There was silence as she stared at me. 'Men be like chameleon o, Leona. They have so many hidden characters. After they put forward the good and colourful part of their charade, caress and pet you until you have resigned to them and crave for more and more love, na that time them go strike, bringing out that part of them that is rooted in evil.' She grimaced. 'By then, voom, you would have gone too deep. Why do you think they were evicted from heaven?'

'Ah, Pastor Chinwe! How do you know Lucifer was male?'

'The Bible, Leona. Lucifer is male.'

'One can never be so sure.'

'It was because of his cunny cunny way, his mischief that he and other men were evicted from heaven.'

'Were they evicted from heaven? I thought it was from the Garden of Eden?' I laughed.

'You don't go to church, Leona? Tufia!'

'Oh! You are funny.'

Chinwe had amazing and nerve-wracking mood swings. She could stay in the house for a whole day without talking to anyone, not even her sister or the boys; or she could wake up and sing all day, whistling and pulling down the roof; and sometimes she could be philosophical. I recalled she was the one who once told me that one can always do anything to escape a difficult situation, even if it amounted to killing.

She had said back then, 'You see this life, eh? It is so beautiful and so sweet that one's life should not be made miserable in anyway by any man, living or dead. Mbanu! Make I talk my own o, for me, it is better for a woman to kill a man than allow him stand on her path to enjoying life. Do you hear me? After all, we have been granted freewill by nature. And killing should also be freewill. No?'

THIRTY-THREE

I was in the garden, and the gentle evening breeze had seduced me to sleep. It was just before twilight and the birds had chirped and lured me into a dream about Mum. She was standing in the centre of the house in Enugu, yelling at Smart about something I did not know. I walked in, dressed in a pair of jeans and a polo shirt, and as soon as I entered, she turned away from me, making sure her face was invisible to me. I asked what the problem was, but she ignored me. I approached her but each time I did, it seemed she was distant and no matter how I tried, I could not reach her. Then, Grandpa appeared, dressed in his camouflage. He was by her side, reaching out to her, wiping her tears. I woke up, sweaty—beads of sweat settled on my brow and soaked the front of my shirt.

The breeze danced with my gown, lifting it this way and that, drying the sweat. I sat up and picked up the magazine I was reading before I slept off. It had fallen and pushed down my glass of garlic water, which had soaked the magazine. I sighed and flung it several times before spreading it on the floor to dry. Birds danced about, flapping their wings, and Aunty Agii's large tortoise crawled past. I thought about my dream, wondering why Mum did not want me to see her face. Had I offended her? Did she want me to kill Akinola or his father? Would she want that? It was also possible that she was not happy with me for being so gullible. Was I gullible? Was Dad trying to manipulate me?

I wiped the tears running down my face with the back of my palm. Then, a hand touched me, and I turned.

'Tears are costly.' The hand squeezed my shoulder. 'We think they can save us from our situations; though they sometimes do, it is rare. The more you cry, the more you muddle your mind, making it incapable of thinking out solutions to your problems.'

Then he said, 'Come on, Sweetheart. In the matters of death, tears are nothing, we end up making the dead sad by the volume of tears we allow stream down our face. The dead laugh at us, at our stupidity,' Akinola said.

I stared at his squared handsome face. Speechless. He squatted and rested his hands on my lap.

'How did you know I was thinking of the dead?'

'Why would you be crying if not that you are missing your mother?'

Then a question came to my mind. 'Did you know my mum?'

'Oh yeah, I did.'

I straightened up instantly, looking at him. 'What do you know about her? Where did you meet her?'

'I saw her a few times at Dad's office, and once in the house. But mostly, Dad talks about her. They were friends.'

'Your father told you that?'

'Well… have you had anything to eat?'

'Are you evading my question?'

'Why? No.'

I looked away, thinking. He had not sat down though there were chairs around.

'Do you know about the Grail Message?'

'Yes, but I am Catholic.'

'I know. You should read up about the Grail Message. When I lost my sister, I cried like a woman.'

'So women are known for crying—'

He laughed at little. 'If tears could bring back the dead, my sister would have returned to life. You see, the Grail Message adherents do not believe that one should cry when they lose loved ones because the more you cry and wail, the more you disturb the spirit of the dead, interrupting their journey.'

'I see. We women… it is difficult Akin, not to cry when we lose a loved one.'

'Men cry too. You loved your mother and I bet she loved you too but crying won't bring her back, darling.'

I looked up at him. 'What was your sister's name?'

'Temitayo.'

I nodded. 'You miss Temitayo?'

'Sometimes. She was very stubborn. She was older than me. I miss her stubbornness.'

I held his hand briefly. 'You did not tell me you were coming?'

'I wanted to surprise you.'

'You and surprises. Do you ever stop?'

'My heart is filled with surprises, but I might not have time enough...'

I thought for a while, and I said to him, 'One would think that with your influence and wealth, you would have a strong heart... never joking or playing or laughing.'

He raised his eyebrows and nonchalantly, he said, 'Influence and wealth are a burden to the one who possesses them, for as you toil to maintain and increase them, you make yourself vulnerable to evil and crime.'

'Are you evil?' I asked, fixing my eyes steadily at him, grinning.

'It is dependent on your definition of evil. Every man is evil. Women are more devilish than men, just follow their path and you'd find it's a broad way to hell.'

'Ah? Akin?'

'True. Their spirits are fiendish.'

'Well, I do not believe in hell, not even in the existence of souls and spirits,' I said, standing.

'And you are Catholic?'

We began to walk back to the house. He placed his hand on my shoulder and I shrugged it off.

'I am not a good Catholic. I can't remember the last time I was in a church.'

'Then you are doomed,' he responded. 'For the soul is

the essence of existence. The spirit controls our activities on earth and the hereafter. It is like the subconscious mind; if you learn how to control and influence it, there is nothing you cannot achieve. Even wealth and fame.' He looked at me and nodded convincingly.

We passed the kitchen veranda and walked into the living room. He went to the bar and poured some scotch into two glasses.

'Take a little liquor. It will clear your head of fears and worries.'

'No way, I am not strong enough for liquor,' I informed him. 'I am just twenty-five.'

He laughed. 'You? Too young for liquor? Well, twenty-five is not too young. You can't even imagine what others are doing at that age.'

'I don't want to know.'

He cocked his head. 'I don't trust that you don't take hot drinks. Is a criminal now too scared to touch a gun? You are mature for it. Take, go on.'

'Oh, you are impossible. You think I'm bad. I am not. I am innocent of a lot of things. Ignore what they are beginning to say in the media.'

He smiled.

'I knew they would come. As soon as we signed you on.'

'Yeah. I don't care.'

'You shouldn't.'

'Back to what you were saying, I do not believe in

anything.' I sipped the drink. It hurt my throat, down through the oesophagus and to my tummy.

'Not even in love?' The question took me unawares. I looked down to the floor.

'I don't know.'

My mind went to Kosi. I loved him. What love was greater than that?

'But...' I raised my head and our eyes met, he came closer and sat on the cushion beside me.

'But what?'

'Never mind.' I gulped the drink and put the glass on a side stool.

'I believe in love, Leo. And I am in love... with you.'

He held my gaze. He was dressed in a turtlenecked, brown-coloured polo and well-ironed trousers—the crease quite prominent.

'I have a professional relationship with you.'

'Ah! Please don't say that, Leona. That you have something to do with my firm doesn't mean I shouldn't be in love with you. You have nothing to do with me directly *professionally* that should make us not be in love with each other.'

'Who put you up to this?'

'No one.'

'Your dad?'

'Well, partly.'

I pondered what to say.

'Do you dream about me?'

'What has that got to do with the discussion?' I forced out a smile. 'Is that a step to falling in love?'

'Partly.'

'Well, I do.'

'Liar.'

'I do see you in my dreams, most nights. It is like walking with the winds. You are such a nice person. Your spirit is a good one, and I fantasise about you too.' He paused and stared at me for long.

'Oh, spirits again. What do you want with me?'

He sat on the edge of the cushion, looking me straight in the eyes.

'I want your happiness. I want your laughter in my house.'

'I don't get it.'

'I want your joy to be mine, Leona. I want to look in your eyes, every morning when I wake up and every night before I sleep. And when I wake in the middle of the night, I want the smell of your body to be the one I perceive.'

'The smell of my body can be a bad odour.' I smelt my skin in mockery.

'Come on, woman.' He stood up. 'You smell good.' He leaned close to me, and I pushed him away.

'Go joor.'

'See, when we were children in high school in England, there was this girl who went for weeks without bathing. She applied all sorts of deodorants and sprays to cover the odour.'

'But why?'

'She was just lazy.'

270

'Maybe she was prone to cold and flu.'

'No, I think she was lazy and dirty. She smelled like cow dung, and I called her that once. When I was in the village, we visited this family who lived in a hut and plastered their floor with dung. It had this kind of smell—not bad but not pleasant either.'

'How were they able to live and sleep in there?'

'Well, my friend said it was because it was just newly done, that after a few days the odour would be gone, entirely.'

'I doubt.'

'So I insulted this girl, Helena, and told her she smelled like cow dung, and the name stuck.'

'Interesting.' I smiled. 'You were stubborn, I can see.'

He drank his liquor in one gulp.

He leaned forward. 'I am tired of playing games, dear. I want us to be close.'

'How close?' I asked.

He drew closer. 'I want to spend the rest of my life with you.'

My heart skipped and began to beat so fast. I wished things were not complicated the way they were—that his father had not had a hand in Mum's death, that he had not blackmailed Mum into warming his bed, that he was not his father's son, and that they never had issues with Dad, with our family. He was so handsome, so brilliant, and wealthy and neat, and I wanted him so much, all to myself. But I did not trust myself. I did not trust that I would not harm him if I married him, if I was in the same house with him, cooking for him every day. I did not trust myself not to harm him for what they did to my mum.

'Did you hear me?'

'I heard you.'

'What do you say? Why do you look like this?'

'How do I look?'

'You look sad.'

I shrugged and sighed.

'I would love to marry you. My dad mentioned to yours that he would want to see us married. At first, I didn't understand, but having seen you, talked with you, and been with you, Leona, I want you more than anything. Please, don't think I am rushing you.'

'Okay.' The room appeared to be moving. *Was it his words or the alcohol?*

'Am I rushing you?'

'Yes,' I laughed uneasily.

'Sorry if I am rushing you.' His hand was rubbing my back. 'You can think about it. If you do not like to spend the rest of your life with me, no problems. Just that I am kind of confused. I am in love with you. I love you so much that I am willing to trade all that I have for you. You are—'

'Shhh! Do not say anything again. Ozugo, it's enough.'

He held his breath, then leaned back. 'Tell me you'll think about it.'

'I won't.'

'Come on.'

'Okay, I will.' I was grinning.

'See, I am going to ask properly later on. I hope by then you must be done pondering over spending your life with me.'

I smiled broadly. 'You should have waited and asked properly then.'

He grinned and gulped his drink. 'You know, if you say 'no', it will be in the papers, and people will stone you to death.' He looked serious.

'In that case, I am going to say 'no' and make headlines.'

We both laughed.

I became serious. 'You know, Akin. The way you laugh reminds me of my mum's friend, Margaret.'

'Oh.'

'Seriously. She was British and used to visit my mum in Khartoum to discuss her research back then. I think of her a lot, lately.'

THIRTY-FOUR

While Emily and I shopped for clothes at a boutique in Ikoyi, she chirped on about how I had brought luck and fortune to the agency, how my mum was her friend and had told her about her daughter who wanted to be a model, and how she did not pay much attention to my mum because she had met many others who would tell her about how good their daughters were and ask that she signed them on until Mum showed her my photos.

I got a call from my dad and excused myself to take the call.

'The president would like me to run for president of African Development Bank.'

'Are you serious?' I screamed.

'It's just a nomination, darling.'

'But it's a good thing. I will pray for you.'

'Thanks. Look, we need lots of prayers at this point. His Excellency, the president, still has to lobby other member countries and the governors of the bank, if it's to work.'

I laughed in excitement. 'That will be awesome. I would be happy to see you there, Dad.'

'I know, thanks. I will get it. Count on that.'

The way he said it, I knew Dad was going to do everything possible to get the position. He was now so ambitious that he could even sell his daughter. While in Sudan, he was the one who used to ask Mum to slow down when she rattled on about how she was going to be an ambassador in her country and how she was going to head one development agency or the other. And this was why when we were in Enugu and he began to get into politics, Mum could not understand what was happening and at what point the bee of ambition stung him.

'Your mum would have been delighted today.'

I paused. 'I guess so. Dad, I got to go. I am with my boss.'

'Oh. My regards to her. Look, I will ask Agnes to invite her for dinner the next time I am in Lagos.'

'When will you be in Lagos?'

'Next week or before then. Let's see how this weekend will be.'

'All right, see you then.'

'Yeah. Hey!'

'Dad?'

'The Wale boy? What's happening now?'

There was a pause. 'He has... he has... hinted he wants to marry me.'

I pictured Dad smiling. 'Good. Good.' I could barely hear him.

'Dad, but I am still not sure I... want to do this.'

'Look, it is your choice to make. You are old enough

to stand for yourself, to protect yourself and to redress any wrong done to you or to your loved one. Our people say, ife metutaru anya meturu imi, when the eyes cry, the nose cries with it too. That is the way of the world. Your mother isn't happy, Leona.'

'I've heard. Bye, Dad.' I cut the call and leaned against a shoe rack.

Emily came to me and asked, 'Are you all right?'

'Yeah, just excited. My dad called to say he is going to be president of African Development Bank.'

'African Development Bank? What do they do?'

'I don't know, but I guess it's huge.'

'Oh! That's good news.'

We walked down to the changing room where I could check out the clothes we got.

'He said when he is in town and if you are still in Lagos, he would like to have dinner with you.'

She paused to look at me. A group of young girls walked past, giggling.

'That will be awesome, my dear.'

She walked off, talking, as she walked, about Waribagha and how funny the man was. I followed her, carrying the clothes. She was walking, as she always did, like someone running out of time.

The Pontiac gained speed as Akinola drove into Banana Island where his family lived. The beautiful scenery filled with green lawns and canopied trees caught my eyes, and I tried not to stare too much so he would not notice. There were many plots barricaded and buildings coming up in them. I heard that a plot could be worth hundreds of thousands of dollars and to rent a building for a year cost hundreds of thousands of dollars too. I wondered why Dad had not bought a building here, to show off, since the Wales lived here. But he could have a property—no one could tell with Dad. I made a mental note to ask Aunty Agii when I got home.

'I am excited.'

'About what?'

'Taking you home.' Bob Marley's 'Redemption Song' played on the stereo. 'If Mum doesn't approve; then, I am dead.'

'Approve of what?'

He beamed at me and sped up.

'Please, slow down. Approve of what? I thought you said your dad wanted to see me; that he had something to tell me?'

For days he had disturbed me, telling me his dad wanted to meet with me, and now I suspected he wanted to show me to his parents and if they did not approve of me, he would change his mind about marrying him.

'What's it? Talk, Akin.'

'Nothing. You see, truth is, Mum is aware that Dad wants us to be married. She has heard about you and seen your photos on the papers, and she wants to see you in person.'

'What for?'

'Calm down, Darling. She is aware that Dad wants us together. And she wants to see you before knowing whether to join him in pressurising me.'

'Oh, I see. So, if she says that I am not worth becoming a Wale and you should back off, then?'

I wondered if I sounded childish. I did not want this guy, yet I was worried his mother was not going to approve of me. I wondered if he noticed.

'See, Leo.' He braked and cleared by the kerb. 'I love you. I cherish you. I want you to be my friend, forever. If my mum doesn't like you, which I doubt, it doesn't change anything. Even if my dad doesn't like you after all, it still won't change a thing.'

Then, I tried to sound strong. 'I pray they don't like me.'

'Why?' He bent towards me.

'So that you can back off, finally.'

He whistled and nodded to the music playing on the stereo. The car began to move slowly.

Then, he said, 'I have even consulted my village oracle and asked that she turn the odds in my favour.'

'You are dreaming, boy.'

The building was indescribable; it was surrounded by a dwarf fence, finished with beautifully wrought iron-designed balustrades. The mansion was visible from the streets, and the lawn before it stretched towards the back to what appeared to be a large expanse of land downwards a sloppy area towards the sea. I wondered if there was a fence somewhere down there too. When we drove into the compound, three Alsatian dogs ran out from the back, barking and jumping over three feet up, their tails wagging.

'They like you,' Akinola said. 'What?'

'The dogs, they like you.'

'They haven't even seen me yet.'

'Dogs have strong spirits.' He parked beside a Toyota Sequoia and while the car was idling, he said, 'Please, do not make this difficult for me.'

I gazed at him. 'I am scared of the dogs.'

'Don't worry, I am with you. Okay? My dad isn't well. He had a stroke and is still recovering. Each time he talks about you, I see some light in his eyes. I don't know why, but he seems to want to have you as a daughter-in-law with so much desperation. I don't know why. At first, I didn't know why he wanted to recommend a wife for me, and this wife is Igbo and we are Yoruba, until I saw you. Then, I became the one pressurising him to speak with your dad.' We saw a heavy man being wheeled out the front door. Two hefty men who were dressed casually stood by the entrance door, while another stood behind the wheelchair. The dogs ran back to join the man, waiting. I sighted a garden by the far left. 'Let's not keep the old man waiting.' As we stepped out of the car, my heart began to beat, and my blood turned to bile. Rage filled my being and made my eyes swoon. The green lawn turned to the colour of hate, and everywhere turned reddish, even the white-coloured mansion was red. I stood transfixed. 'Are you alright, Darling?' Akinola was walking towards my side of the car.

I was hyperventilating, and I could not see clearly. My hands trembled and curled into a fist, and saliva was draining from my mouth. I could feel its dryness. I thought I was fidgeting, and I wondered if he noticed. I saw Dad and me in front of Doctor Malik Al-Jazrula's house in Omdurman and Grandpa on the ground, blood everywhere, and the man with the empty socket saying, 'I do not kill someone who does not look for my trouble.'

Now, Akinola was with me, holding me by the shoulder, talking to me, but my mind was far away, in Omdurman.

I do not kill someone who does not look for my trouble.

I do not kill someone who does not look for my trouble.

I do not kill someone who does not look for my trouble.

THIRTY-FIVE

'Sweet, are you okay?' he called. He nudged me, and I came to. I blinked several times and looked away from his father.

'What's the matter, babe?'

'No... nothing.'

'You are shaking. What's it?'

'Your dad,' I lied. 'I am surprised to see him like this. I've heard so much about him, this powerful billionaire—'

'Come on.' He threw up his hands.

'I didn't imagine he would be this helpless.' I turned to look at him, praying he did not take me too seriously. My eyes twinkled, and he beamed at me.

'Do not worry, Leo. The illness doesn't make him any less powerful.' He nudged me forward, holding me by the elbow, and I found my feet moving. 'I am happy you show concern, makes it all good.'

I did not say anything. Two of the dogs came running, jumping all over Akinola, sniffing me.

'Don't be scared. They like you, I told you. First hurdle, crossed.'

I smiled at him.

'Billy! Don!' his father called his dogs. 'Out!' and they scampered off.

We climbed the wide stairs of the front threshold.

'Dad, good afternoon.'

'Akin, my man.' The tone showed they were close pals, more of friends than father and son. 'You brought her, boy?'

'Yes, Dad.'

'Good boy.' He smiled broadly. 'Now, my heart is settled.'

'Meet Leona, Dad.'

'Good day, Chief.'

'Come. Come.'

My body shook. Akinola noticed. He removed his hand and looked at me. I was sure he must be wondering if I was scared of his dad. I stood still, staring at him. The old man's hair was all shaved off and his skull was oiled. He wore an overflowing dress, which reached the ground and an over-powering cologne. He was heavily pot-bellied and choco-late complexioned. His hands were on the armrest of the wheelchair, and I could see the curly hair on his arms. He was wearing a silver chain watch with diamond studs around its face; his neck was thick, and he wore a tiny necklace that sparkled to the evening light. When he smiled, I noticed that his teeth were well flossed and shiny, and his eyes looked indecipherable—brown and cold, but he was smiling at me.

'Come, my child.'

Akinola pushed me lightly, and I went to him.

'Good day, Chief,' I repeated, genuflecting.

Just then, an elegant woman of average height but also heavily built walked out. 'What are you men doing there, standing and keeping the guest outside? Come in! Come in!' she beamed.

'Now, let's go inside,' Chief Wale said.

The man behind him, a bodyguard I guessed, turned the wheelchair, but Akinola took it from him, and I followed. When he got to the door, his mother offered her cheek, and he kissed it. She waited for me.

'Look at you, girl. You're more beautiful in the flesh. Wow!'

'Good day, ma.' I genuflected again.

'Good day, my daughter.'

She smiled at me.

'Come in. Come in.'

She took my hand and led me into the most amazing home, ever.

There were chandeliers everywhere. The stucco-covered wall reflected off the gold-coated balustrades of the stairs, the wall panels, the ceiling fittings, and the ceiling roses; and the heavily embroidered curtains matched the massive couches in the expansive sitting room. The floor was slippery, and I had to tread carefully. It was as if the large television was built into the wall. The room smelled of roses or vanilla ice cream, I could not tell. I could see the dining room somewhere a bit far away. Its table looked magnificent, surrounded by about ten chairs. On the wall hung paintings and other artworks that I was sure were worth millions. There were flowerpots by the corners, at the back.

'Sit, my child. Sit,' Akinola's mother pointed at the cushion.

I sat and made sure not to look around too much; so, they would not think me foolish. If not for the bile in me, I would have been so happy. I was in the most lavishly furnished house I had ever been in, but it was the house of the man whose only son I was to kill, after I became his wife.

Akinola helped his father sit on a long cushion. Aside from the soft, feathery padding of the cushion, every other thing, including the footings, were covered in gold. There were phones on the cushion and the day's newspapers and other documents. The bodyguards were not in the sitting room. I later found out that there was another room adjacent where they stayed and watched whatever was happening in the room, ready to burst in if a visitor was no longer welcome.

'What do we get for you? We have ewedu and Amala. I prepared it myself. And the cook prepared pounded yam and onugbu soup, if you want that.'

I smiled at her.

'Don't rush the young lady, Beatrice. Let's offer her a drink. Akinola, bring wine.' Akinola made to leave and his father said, 'The best of the best.'

Akinola turned and winked at him.

So Akinola's mother's name is Beatrice? I nodded at the thought.

'I had a friend at the university whose name was Beatrice.'

'Oh, you did?' she sat down on the sofa beside the chair where I was seated, beaming at me.

'Yes, ma. She studied Medicine. I haven't seen her in a while. It is such a nice name. People who bear it are nice.'

She threw her head back and said, 'Oh, I am nice!' She beamed at her husband.

'You? Nice?' the chief said some things in Yoruba, and they both laughed.

Akinola returned and an elegant tall lady, dressed like a professional steward, came in with a tray of wine and glasses. She brought out stools and placed the glasses in front of everyone. Akinola sat beside his dad as she opened the wine and poured. While that was going on, Beatrice asked about my job, and if it was tedious. Did I get many proposals from men? She said she could imagine that. She asked about the agency and how lucrative the business was. Did I travel often? How many times in a month? I would later find out she wanted to know if I would have time to take care of the babies that would come after I got married to her son. If only she knew my plans.

'Now, we shall toast to Leona and Akinola, that their friendship be like that of oil and salt.'

'Asee!' Akinola and Beatrice concurred in Yoruba, smiling.

We stood and went to Chief Fegun Wale and clicked our glasses. The wine tasted like watered-down honey, but it was intoxicating. The smell was overpowering and fresh.

'My child, your name, Leona, is special.'

'Thank you, sir.'

The chief cleared his throat. 'Your father and I have come a long way. I must admit that there was a time we did not see eye to eye. We were young and over-ambitious.'

The word struck me. I recalled when Mum yelled at Dad and accused him of being too ambitious.

'Today, we are friends. We came to realise that, after all, there is nothing to gain if only one person owns the world. It would be akin to living in a rural village, and you are the only one who has a car. If a woman is in labour and you are about to pray, they would come and ask you to drive her to the clinic; if a neighbour's son falls from the mango tree, you'd leave your business to take him to the clinic; if someone is getting married, you would chauffeur the couple about. So, there is no gain holding one another at the jugular.' His hand went to his neck. He shook his head, 'None at all. So now, your mother—' He stopped and cleared his throat.

'Do you want water?' Beatrice was at alert.

'No. I am not a child, woman.' He coughed twice and fell back against the cushion. Beatrice rolled her eyes.

'I am getting old, my daughter.' He sat up again, now with great difficulty. 'I am getting old. I have seen things, good and bad. I have done things, good things, bad things. Sometimes, I wonder which is greater. I have seen places, far and near; I tell you. But there is nothing as joyful as seeing your son marry... seeing your grandchildren, right Beatrice?'

'You're right, dear.'

'I visit my friends and see their grandchildren play, dirty their clothes, and pull down things,' he was smiling to himself now. 'And I say to myself, I want to see my grandchildren before I join my ancestors. I tell you, there is nothing greater than that. No fortune is greater than that of having a child. I will tell you another thing that is great. It is reparation. When you make amends, you ease your soul and release your heart from troubles and worries. I wronged your people. But today I can call your father and tell him this or that stock is good, invest in it, and he does, and it works. And today, I see my son,' he stretched to touch Akinola. 'I see this boy here bring you to my home as a friend. I know it is going to move from friendship, by the grace of God. I am happy. I wish your mother was alive to see this.' He did not hold my gaze.

I gambled, 'Would she have approved?'

Then, he seemed lost for words.

'Why? Why wouldn't she approve, my daughter?' Beatrice asked. Then, she looked at her husband and at me. 'Come. Come. All of you, let's go to the dining room.'

When we were saying our goodbyes to them, Beatrice busy with packing me a gift and Akinola talking with one of the guards about a football match; Chief Wale said to me, 'Your mother was a great woman. And when she was alive, I never stopped telling her what I am about to tell you now,' his voice was low, wheezy. 'I am sorry. I am old and I want to die in peace.'

I wanted to ask him what he was sorry for, but something

got caught in my throat, and I fought back tears. I hated him.
He killed my mother, one way or the other, I was certain.

THIRTY-SIX

As we drove into town, Akinola kept asking, 'What's the matter, dear? Why are you crying?'

I did not say anything. I had been fighting against the tears, but they were running down, ruining my makeup. I was filled with raging emotions, pondering on what decision to take, wondering why this had to happen. I was sure it was Chief Fegun Wale who first reached out to Dad, extending a hand of friendship. I wondered what Dad's reaction was when he did, and if it was after Dad found out what he did with Mum. Was he the one who confessed to Dad? I was not sure. I could not ask Dad. If I did, I do not know if he would be strong enough to tell me. I wondered if Chief Fegun Wale was truly dying and had gone to confess his sins to Dad so his soul would be at rest; if offering that his son married me was part of the reconciliation, his penance.

'I will offer my son to you as an in-law.' Was that what he said to Dad?

Did he say it in a way that Dad would understand that he was offering his wealth too to our family for blocking our businesses, our source of fortune, for taking Dad's wife to himself while Dad was away in prison—the jail sentence he orchestrated?

I cried because Akin's mother was a good woman. I liked her. In many ways, she was like Aunty Agii, elegant and wide-hipped and happy. Those characteristics, the smiles, and the heart that screamed of kindness and friendship. She had a good heart. She joked easily. She loved her son and was happy with his choice. She was devoted to her husband. Could I afford to break this woman's heart? If I refused to marry her son, I would break her heart; but that was nothing compared to marrying Akinola and killing him afterwards, making her childless. When Akinola told me about his sister, I had imagined the sadness they felt when she died. What if he died too? But this man killed my mother, and I cherished my mother. And Dad wanted me to avenge her death. I could not go against that.

'Did Mum do anything wrong? Did Dad say something to you that you do not like?'

I cleaned my eyes with a handkerchief.

'I will see you,' I said.

We were in front of my house now.

'Let me drive in and be sure you are fine, Leo.'

'I am home. Thank you.' I opened the door and hurried to the gate. He was by my side.

'I am sorry if I hurt you, but I don't know what I did. Please, you break my heart. What did Dad say to you?'

'Nothing. I am just overwhelmed.'

'Oh! That shouldn't make you cry, Babe.'

I knocked at the gate. It opened. 'I must go.'

'I don't want your step-mum to see you this way.'

'I am fine. She won't see me.'

'Wait.' He hurried to the car and brought the gift bag. 'You forgot this.'

I took it. 'Thank you.' I pushed open the gate and got in.

If I said 'no' to Akinola Wale, he would never be happy; but marrying him meant I would have to kill him. How could I kill someone who did no wrong to me? How would I look his mother in the eye afterwards? I could stand his wicked father, but not Beatrice.

Aunty Agii pushed open the door to my room and entered.

'Okwudili told me he saw you crying. What is it, Nne? O gini?'

'I am not crying.'

I had taken a shower and was trying to concentrate on the book, *The Kite Runner*. The cover was all dirty now, yet I had not finished reading it because I rarely had time to pick it up. She took the book from my hands, tossed it away from me, and sat on the bed.

'Did they say anything to you? I don't understand these wealthy Yoruba people.'

'No. No.'

'Was his mother welcoming?'

'Yes.'

'And the billionaire?'

'He did nothing to me.'

'Then, o gini? What happened?'

I was folding and unfolding the helm of my shirt, twisting it until she removed my hands.

'Look at me, Leona and stop behaving like a toddler. What is it?'

'Aunty?'

'Yes.'

'His father did some terrible things to my family.'

She looked at me for some time and took my face into her hands. 'I won't ask you about the things he did, but I will ask you this; has he made up with your father?'

'Yes.'

'O siri gini? Did he say anything to make you sad, to belittle you?'

'No. He was all remorseful but wasn't straight to the point. He kept on apologising but didn't say what he did. He didn't go into specifics.'

I heard Chinwe singing loudly downstairs and the boys urging her on.

'And do you know what he did? The things he did?'

'I think I know.'

She paused.

'Then, he knows that you know and finds it difficult to say them. You see, my dear, men have ego. They find it difficult to say they are sorry. If one brings himself to say he is sorry for the things he did, I want you to know that he went extra miles to do that. I want you to know that it is more difficult to ask for forgiveness than accepting to forgive. That is why some would rather die than ask for forgiveness. True. Now, this man wronged you and he is sorry about it, and he tells you he is. Gee nti, if you do not want to forgive him, there is no bad in it, there is no shame in it. You are at liberty to choose to forgive or not, but that shouldn't stop you from loving his son. His son is not him. Mbanu.' I looked up at her. She nodded. 'Unless you find the son is like his father. Then, you can tell them goodbye, but if his son is different, why deprive yourself of love because of the sins of your lover's parents?'

'I don't know. I don't want to end up being with the son and hurting the father.'

'What?! Is it that serious?'

'I don't know.'

'Do you want to tell me what it is?' I shook my head. She paused. 'Think about it, Nne. No one will make the decision for you. But do not be in a rush to accept him. Inugo? The good thing is his father likes you, and his mother likes you; just that you can't love his father back. But you are not going to be married to his father, I tell you. Haa! I can't remember the last time I was at your father's village o. I can't remember the last time my mother-in-law, your grandmother, came to this house. You know, not that we are not on good terms, but we have our boundaries. I established it as soon as I came in. I send her gifts and stuff and money but that is that. I do not hate her, but she has her home, and I have mine, shikena.' She placed her two hands on my arms. 'If you like your man, marry him and live with him and establish a boundary between your family and his other family, his father's family.' I nodded. 'Never ever allow anyone make you sad, not even a man, Nne. No man is worth crying for, not even an old, weak billionaire.' Her words reminded me of Grandpa. How I still missed him. She ruffled my hair. 'So, come on, let's go prepare ukwa.'

THIRTY-SEVEN

Aunty Agii invited me to hang out with her friends. They belonged to the Beach Samaritans Club dedicated to cleaning up the beaches in Lagos, and they had just finished one of their projects and were hanging out to chat. There were about seven of them, all members of this club that had over a hundred members, including children and teenagers.

The venue was the Bogobiri House, a quiet and reserved artistic building, comprising of restaurants and some guest rooms on the island where folks hung out to chat and drink. It was purely traditional and had benches, sofas, and stools carved out of trunks with rustic sculptures and patterns. There were African masks, rocks, and fabrics interwoven with the walls of the building; and cocktails were served by young women dressed in traditional outfits looking sharp and elegant.

The women gossiped about various things. One of them, Maria, a Lebanese, was arguing with Aunty Agii about how Lebanon helped develop Nigeria's economy and infrastructure, but Aunty Agii kept saying that the first set of Lebanese that came into Nigeria were rogues and fraudsters out to dupe people. Maria was laughing even when I expected her to be sad. Then, the dark, tall woman, the tallest among them said that the only thing the Lebanese brought into the country was AIDS.

'They were pimps,' she claimed.

Her name kept evading me. She was a development worker and carried herself with the air of someone who had lots of money. She insisted she was taking care of the bills right from the start. When she talked, her bangles jingled and ran to the joint of her elbow when she raised her arm to make a point.

'Aww! That's too harsh, biko,' Aunty Agii interjected.

'Too harsh? Spare me. When you were the first who started this story about how my countrymen were criminals and all what-not?'

'Well, Lebanese are known for their hard work,' Madam Kufre informed. She was the founder and director of the club and was good friends with Aunty Agii. 'My father had some business dealings with them. He was into construction and they had some good engineers.'

'I bet your father used them to launder money.'

'Agnes! Haba. My father would do no such thing.'

'How do you know he wouldn't? He was a politician and the easiest way for them to launder money is through these contracts to foreign companies. They inflate the contract sum and pay the money to the company and the foreign company launders their share of the loot for them in accounts domiciled in their foreign country,' Aunty Agii explained. 'I work with the Federal Airport Authority, so I know what I am saying, girl.'

Madam Kufre was in her late fifties, and her father had been a governor in one of the western states, decades back. She looked sad now, but no one noticed, or they pretended they did not notice.

'Agnes could be right you know,' the tall development worker said. 'But who cares anyway. Nigeria's money has always been available for looting since time immemorial.'

'My father wasn't such a man. And who brought him into this discussion anyway?' She swallowed her wine and beckoned on the waiter.

'You did. You were trying to defend the Lebanese.'

Everyone laughed.

After they all left, Aunty Agii ordered coffee. 'Black, please. Let me see if it will push down this alcohol I've been having all night,' she said to the attendant.

'You are still sipping your wine, Leo?' she asked me.

I nodded. Then, I took a draft and rested the glass noisily on the wooden table. I leaned back against the cushioned bench, resting my legs on the free one beside me.

'You look tired. O gini?'

'I don't know.'

She pushed her coffee aside and faced me.

'Gwam, is there anything in the world that you cannot forgive? Answer me.' I stared at her. I did not want to hear her talk to me. Increasingly, she was becoming an expert in reading my mind and offering words that were disarming.

'You see, gee nti, forgiveness is the key to happiness. It frees your heart and makes you whole. See it as having a huge rock wedged against your chest, or say a truck fell on top of you, and a Superman, out of nowhere, comes and with one hand lifts the burden away. Forgiveness is that Superman, Leona.' She flipped a strand from her hair extension off her face and tilted her head. Her deep red coloured blouse melted into the earth colour of the surrounding. 'When you forgive, you gain yourself some relief; and relief comes with less head-ache, less heart attack, and buys you time.'

'I can't see myself marrying someone whose father did horrible things to my family.'

'Whatever this man did to your family that you are not telling me, is not worth killing yourself over.'

'I am not going to kill myself.'

'But when you deny yourself the gift of love, you kill yourself. No? Look at it well. Nee ya anya ofuma, Nne.'

'I don't know how I am going to look him in the eye every day as my father-in-law.'

'You are going to be married to his son, not him.'

I looked down on the table.

'Unless you want to deny yourself the gift of love, other-wise, don't hurt yourself because someone hurt you. You don't pay back evil with evil, my girl.' She reached for her car keys. More people had left the café now. 'You don't. What are you going to do? Leave Akinola? Marry him and never allow his father into your home? Marry him and never visit his family house? Or kill his dad?'

I looked up at her.

She rolled her eyes. 'Yeah. Kill him?'

'I could kill him.'

'Jeez! Is it this serious?' I was mute. 'It is serious then. Don't ever do anything you'd live to regret o. Killing is easy. What is most difficult, what is unbearable, is living with the knowledge that someone's blood is on your hands. I tell you, you might not be able to sleep a wink again ever, in your entire life. I know what I am saying.' Our eyes met and locked. After a minute she said, 'You see those men who have killed? They live a terrible life, if only you could take a peep into their minds, their heads. They are dead; they have deteriorated. You'd never know, my girl, unless you are a different person, someone whose heart is now stone, someone like... Never mind! Now, when that thought comes into your head, say to it 'Be gone!' and never ever think about it anymore. Ka m gwa gi, the worst punishment you give to someone you hate this much is to get them to know that you hate them.' She was standing over me, now. 'Get them to know why you hate them and never show that you intend to punish them. That way, they wait for the punishment, expecting it, dying for the punishment is atonement for the sin they committed against you, but it doesn't come. That is the worst punishment to someone who has wronged you. Inugo? So, I tell you, whatever this man has done to you, to your father, or Mary, let him know that you know. Then, do not seek vengeance. I tell you, when you do this, you'd make him your slave in perpetuity. Now, I must go. Apuo m.

Are you coming along or you want to sit here at Bogobiri thinking about the hatred in your heart?'

When we got home, I called Kosi, and we talked for close to an hour discussing the planned marriage. He said as long as I was happy he had no objections, since he was going to become a priest soon and there was no way he was going to marry me.

That night, I could not sleep. I cried all through. I was going to miss Kosi so much. I wondered if he would no longer want to have anything intimate to do with me when ordained a Catholic priest. I could not ask him because I did not want him to question why I would like to be intimate with him when I would be married while he was a priest. What was I going to do? How would I avenge my mother? She meant the world to me, and someone took her life or contributed immensely to killing her; and I was expected to live the rest of my life with the son of the person who did this? How could I survive this? These questions and more raged in my heart, colouring my heart black, red, and hundreds of thousands of shades of these colours… until Dad brought the poison that would do the work.

THIRTY-EIGHT

FEBRUARY 2006
LAGOS, SOUTHWESTERN NIGERIA

The euphoria of Ellen Johnson-Sirleaf becoming the first female president of an African country was still in the air, and each time we visited Chief Fegun Wale, he did not stop talking about how he played some role in making that possible. He always beat his chest and told his son, 'Make your mark in the world, boy. Make your mark.'

And Akinola would respond, 'Well, let's see how she handles it.'

'Oh, she is a great woman, believe me.'

It was February and the fifty-sixth Berlin International Film Festival just happened and my favourite movie, *Grbavica: Land of My Dreams* won the Golden Bear. When Akinola learnt that it was nominated, and that I loved the film, he gave me a gift—that we attend the festival. I was excited and my joy knew no bounds when the film won. Akinola said that I was drawn to the film because of the story of Esma—a single mother who lived with her twelve-year-old daughter, Sara, and the sacrifices Esma had to make to save up money for her daughter to go on a field trip, and how this threw up discoveries that bound them stronger.

But Akinola did not know that I was mostly attracted to the movie because it was about war, what people lost, and how it affected them. It was based on the history of Bosnia & Herzegovina and set in post-war Sarajevo. In the movie, Sara thought she lost her father in the war but unbeknownst to her, she was a result of rape, and when she got to know this, she drew closer to her mother. The film made me remember how Mum and I became closer after our experience in Sudan.

The trip was also part of our after-wedding tour. Our wedding took place a few weeks before the Berlin Film Festival. First, we travelled to Peru and Azerbaijan, and after the festival, Akinola took me to Paris before we went to London and stayed a few days with his friend. When we came back to Nigeria, I was looking plump and fresh.

Our wedding was tagged the 'Wedding of the Decade'. People speculated that Akinola and I met when I went to his company to finalise the modelling contract; others said that he liked me and only used the contract as bait. Only a few people, mostly family members, knew better.

For the guest list, Chief Fegun Wale had drawn a long one, mostly of Forbes world wealthiest men, inviting them all to Lagos where I preferred that the wedding take place, while Dad pulled the president and his business partners. Parties ran for three consecutive days after our wedding.

Just as it was the month of the film festival, it was also the month of love, and when we returned on the last day of February, everything had changed. My things had been moved from Enugu and from Aunty Agii's house to the family house in Banana Island. Beatrice had insisted she wanted to live with her new daughter-in-law for a year and enjoy her to the fullest before we moved to Akinola's house in the centre of Ikoyi. Akinola had objected to this, arguing that he would not have enough room and freedom to enjoy his new wife, but his mother had been adamant.

'Look, son. Leona and I need to learn each other's likes and dislikes,' she argued. 'We are women. I need to teach her a few things like how to make Yoruba meals. I know you like your ewedu, and unless you want a cook, I need to teach her. I don't advise you start eating out or employ a cook this early? Besides, we need to catch up on a lot of things. We need to gossip.' She had rolled her eyes.

'Mum, my wife doesn't gossip.'

'I will teach her. Show me a woman who doesn't gossip, eh?'

Later on, Akinola told me that his mother was mostly lonely in the house and needed company. He warned that if we moved in with her, she would not allow us to leave, ever.

'When we announce we're ready to leave, she would ask us to stay until the babies begin to come. And when the babies come, she would suggest that we stay so she takes care of them, and on and on.' Beatrice persisted and with her husband on her side, she won. We stayed.

I was not used to being waited on, but here, everything was done for me. I was not allowed to cook. The only time I was allowed into the kitchen was when my mother-in-law was in the mood to cook.

'Come, let me teach you how to make this...' She usually asked when she wanted me in the kitchen, while the chef scampered about, getting this or that.

A chauffeur was instructed to never allow me behind the wheels of a car; two bodyguards followed me about as if I was about to vanish into thin air—this was the part I hated the most; and there were parties almost every other week. When there were no parties, we hosted friends and business associates to dinner or to lunch and sometimes to breakfast.

Akinola was a lovely gentleman. Though I still nursed the idea of killing him, I needed to get angry enough to do so, but he gave me no reasons to. How do you kill a man who foregoes pursuing a billion dollar business deal to take you on a date or leaves work early enough to drive you to see the family physician, insisting that it was his responsibility? He also urged me to accept modelling contracts and encouraged me to follow the news on Sudan.

'You love Sudan. It is as much your country as Nigeria is. Don't turn your back on her. Your mother did, but at some point, she had to go back. Have you ever considered travelling there? For fun? Can I take you, Sweet?'

'I don't think I am ready yet.'

'You are ready. If you ever want to go, I will be there for you.'

'I don't know.'

'You are not scared, are you?'

'I don't know.'

'You know, the crisis is mostly in Darfur, and even if you decide to visit Darfur, the government of Sudan will provide you with so much security that not even the rebels will bat an eyelid.'

He smiled at me. 'You are a powerful lady, you know.' He kissed me lavishly. 'You are my lady.'

'I know.'

'You are the most beautiful woman in the world.'

'In your eyes.'

His hands smooched my backside before he drew me to himself. 'Not just in my eyes. You got that South African contract because of your beauty. The papers say you are one of the most beautiful black women alive.'

'You are tuning me. You want my head to burst, Darling,' I laughed.

'But it is true, I am not flattering you.' I grinned, as he counted off on his fingers the jobs I was signed on: Mary Kay Black Beauty products, Luxury Soap, Dragons Investments, LG, MTN, and the biggest of all, Coca-Cola. 'And many are on the way. Let's toast to that.'

It was at my new home that I acquired a rich taste for expensive wines; and it was while there, few months after the wedding, in mid-May, that my dad had a stroke, and I learnt that all I held to be true were not, and everything changed.

THIRTY-NINE

Chinwe visited with Okwudili and Johnson. Their mother was away in Canada on a six weeks' course. While in the house, Chinwe never stopped talking about how beautiful everything was, how easy life was, and how unlucky she was to have been married to 'that low-life of a husband who thought he owned the world and used me as his punching bag—kai! Atago m afufu'.

I tried to steer the discussion to neutral grounds but not long after I introduced a topic or mentioned this or that, she would chirp again, 'Very wealthy people don't have bad hearts but when you are not close to them, you think they are evil. See how rich they are, yet they are this humble.'

Other times, she threw her hands up in surrender and stared about.

'See the man, coming to play with Okwy and Johnson. See gentleman! He is such a good man. He is sure to have a room in heaven.' I laughed. We heard the boys throwing ball with Chief outside. 'Biko, Nne, take care of your husband always. His kind of man is rare to find.'

My phone rang. It was Smart, crying and screaming at the same time.

'Chief is sick. He fell in the bathroom and has been rushed to the hospital. For God's sake, hurry home. Leona? Leona?'

The phone fell from my hand and Chinwe, alert, swooped like a cat to grab me.

'What happened? Who was that?' she pinned me to the cushion.

'Smart—'

'What? Who?'

'Smart is… Dad's housekeeper.'

'Oh, Smart! What about her? What happened?'

'She said Dad fell down.'

'Oh my God! Oh my God!' she stood up, frightened. 'When did this happen?'

'I don't know. I didn't ask. She was frantic.'

'God! I hope my sister hasn't heard. I hope she didn't hear it this way. The shock may kill her.'

I ran out to the porch.

'Baba!' I called.

My father-in-law was in his wheelchair, catching the ball and laughing heartily as the boys threw it to him. He wheeled around and saw the fear all over my face.

'What? Kilode?'

'It's Dad. I just got a call. He fell in the bathroom.'

The ball fell from his hands and rolled to the green lawn.

'Damian! Chuks!' he yelled instantly, and four hefty men came running out. 'Take me in. Now!' he commanded, and they did as he instructed.

Chuks was already looking around the compound. Alert. I heard Damian already dialling a number by the time we got to the sitting room.

'Get the cars ready.' I heard him mutter on the phone to someone,

'What happened? Come here. Come and sit beside me,' Chief Fegun Wale beckoned to me.

I was hyperventilating. It was as if someone had tied a string around my throat. I could not breathe.

'I can't breathe, Baba.'

Chinwe hurried to me and helped me to the cushion where Akinola's father was sitting.

He held my shoulder, but I shivered and recoiled. The more he tried to show me love, the more the colour red got deeper and darker.

'It's all right.' He picked up one of the phones on the cushion. 'Which hospital was he taken to?'

'It should be the National Hospital.'

He nodded and dialled a number, talking to someone whom I presumed worked there. The person said he had not heard anything. He asked him to check. Then, he called Elizabeth, and she answered the phone instantly.

'Where are you?' he asked straight away. I was surprised he had her number. 'It's Otunba Fegun Wale.' He paused and grimaced. 'The National Hospital? We thought as much. Call me when you get there. I will be with you in a few hours. Have one of his assistants call me as soon as you are there.' He ended the call.

'Your father's wife said she is on her way to the hospital, that she just heard. I have asked that she tells one of his personal assistants to call me as soon as she gets to the hospital.'

He also called Akinola, and he said he would get on his way immediately.

While he was on the phone with Beatrice, Akinola called me.

'Hey baby, I am so sorry.' I began to sob. Chief Fegun Wale rubbed my shoulder, while he talked with his wife. 'I am on my way. Hang in there,' He said.

The boys were all around me now, with tears in their eyes too. I wondered if they had heard or they were crying because I was.

'Take the boys to the other sitting room, Chuks.'

Chinwe followed them. 'Oya, bia nu. Come, the two of you.'

'I spoke with Chief Egbufor a few days back, I didn't hear he's sick.'

'I didn't hear a thing.' I shook my head. 'Does he have a case of high blood pressure?'

'None that I know of, no. I know he has an ulcer... picked it up from detention.' I raised my head to look at him, he looked away.

'It's alright,' he said.

Akinola got in before his mother, and as soon as I saw him enter the sitting room, I ran into his arms, my tears soaking his white shirt, my face rumpling his tie.

'There, there,' he said. 'Take it easy. He is not dead. It is stress, I am sure.'

Then, Chief Fegun's phone rang and he talked briefly.

'His PA said your dad is being taken care of. He said he's had a stroke, it seems.'

'Ahh!' I screamed.

Akinola held me tightly, dragging me up so that I would not fall to the ground. He led me to the couch.

'Please, don't act like this.'

Chinwe came out and took me from him.

'Hey! Leona, no behave like baby. He will be fine.' She was sobbing too.

I wondered why Dad would suffer a stroke. Why was the world so unfair to me? I was afraid he was going to be like Chief Fegun Wale who never recovered the use of his legs since his stroke and was confined to a wheelchair. Was their fate entwined? Would Dad forgive me for not avenging Mum? Was that what was bothering him that made him have a stroke? I sobbed some more.

Beatrice came back, hurrying inside with her handbag on the crook of her arm. Her stilettos sounding like the steel gong boys played while chasing after masquerades during the Christmas that I visited Dad's village, the first year we got back from Sudan.

'My lovely girl! Look at you. You look terrible. Come here. Come.'

She embraced me and sat beside me, engulfing me in a bear hug, her perfume filling up my nostrils, calming me.

'My darling. It's all right.' She wiped my tears. 'How bad is it?'

'The minister had a stroke, but they are reviving him. I just got off the phone with a consultant there at the hospital. He said it's partial.'

'Oh! Thank God.'

'Agnes called me,' Beatrice said. She made my head rest on her shoulder. 'Said Elizabeth called her. That Elizabeth is so unintelligent.' She made a face. 'She shouldn't have rushed to call someone who isn't in the country. Nothing is clear yet. Now, she has made Agnes panic.'

'Ah! Women!' Chief Fegun Wale sighed.

Akinola loosened his tie and sat up on the edge of the chair; then, his personal assistant came in and handed him his phone. He excused himself and went into the room to join the boys.

'I asked Agnes not to bother coming back until we are sure of the situation.'

'Exactly. Thank you, Dear.'

'So, what do we do?' Beatrice addressed her husband.

'I want to be on the next flight to Abuja. Where is my phone?' I said instantly.

'Why do you want your phone? What is it?' Beatrice asked.

'I… to call the agency to book a flight for me.'

Chief Fegun Wale smiled. 'Don't worry. You can't get a flight to Abuja today. It's already evening, four.'

'Oh, yeah.' I fell back on the couch. 'If it means driving to Abuja—'

'Relax, dear.' He raised his right hand in a gesture for me to calm down. 'I will call up the jet.'

'Please do,' Beatrice said.

'Chuks?'

'Yes, Chief.' His men were hanging around the sitting room, waiting for instructions.

'Tell Chapman to get the jet ready to fly in an hour.'

'Yes, Chief.' He hurried away.

'Thank you, Baba.'

'Don't mention, Leona.'

'But I don't think Leona should go to Abuja,' Akinola said as he walked back. He stood behind the cushion, his hand massaging my shoulder.

'No, no. Please, I want to go to my dad. He needs me.'

'Your dad is an old lion,' Akinola said lightly, and every-one smiled. I found myself smiling too. 'He can take care of himself.' He came around and sat beside his mother. 'You shouldn't go to Abuja, not in this condition.'

'What condition?'

'I think Leona is—'

'What?' Beatrice shouted in joy, smiling, 'How? I never noticed.'

'Oh, Akinola. Don't be silly. How did you know?'

'But you were vomiting the other day?'

'Oh! When a woman vomits, it means she is pregnant?' Chief Fegun Wale laughed heartily.

'I was going to call the doctor to come check you.'

'But I am not pregnant.'

Beatrice face changed instantly, disappointed. 'Oh!' She sighed.

'I am not pregnant,' I repeated.

'Still, I insist she stays. She will crash if she sees her father. I will go in her place.'

'You have a business to take care of, Akin.'

'No, Darling. Don't worry.'

'But I want to go.'

'Aren't you busy?' his father asked. 'I have reliable staff, Dad.'

Shrugging he said, 'Okay, if you say so.'

'I agree with Akin. Let Leona stay.' Beatrice looked at me, at my stomach. She was not yet convinced that I was not pregnant. 'I can go with Akinola. Since Agnes isn't here and that Elizabeth behaves like a mad woman. Who knows where she is at the moment?'

'I rang her. She must be at the hospital now,' Chief Wale informed.

'I don't trust Elizabeth.'

'Let me go with her. Leona, please stay back and take care of Baba.'

'Oooh! I can't stay—'

'Hey, hey, girl,' Akinola stooped before me and took my

313

face in his hands. 'Not today, please. Let's get there first and access the situation. Mum and I can handle it, whatever it is. And I bet by now your dad must have the best medical facility and personnel at his service. Besides, Mum has experience in situations like this. Mum, right? We've been here, you know. You can join us tomorrow or next. Our jet or Dad's can pick you up. Hang in there, Babe. All right?'

My chest heaved up and down. I placed my hands on my head and closed my eyes. Memories of the information Dad fed me about Akinola's family flooded my brain. Staying back would be a great opportunity to be alone for the first time with my father in-law. I sat up and wiped at my eyes with the back of my arm, nodding to myself.

FORTY

That night, Chief Fegun Wale and I ate alone, seated at the dining table and not talking. I wondered if he had noticed that when we were together, I made no attempts to talk to him. If only he knew how I hated him. Now that Dad was sick, I could not stop heaping the entire blame on him.

He made attempts at light talk, but I just nodded or shook my head to his comments. He was a meticulous man, and it showed with how he ate his meals, the way he balanced the cutleries in his hands, the way he scooped the food and chewed with ease as if the world could wait while he ate. I wondered if this was because he had a stroke or just how he always ate his meals. Could it be that when he was still actively running his business he rushed his meals so as to meet up with appointments? Did he even have the time to eat at all? And the anger in me was eating me up, forcing out breath from me.

When he was done eating, he said, smiling, 'A kobo for your thoughts.'

I looked away, my eyes descending on a miniature glass flowerpot filled with coloured stones standing on the centre of the long dining table. The stones reminded me of the night in Omdurman, the night before the day Grandpa was killed and we were driven to Omdurman to meet him. How the streets were busy, lights flickering from shops and stores, and dancing in the air, mesmerising me with their brilliance and aura; how they were different from the lights I used to count every night in Khartoum.

'You remind me so much of your mother. You so look like her, just that she was less beautiful than you are.' He smiled widely. 'But she sure had a sharper tongue.' He was grinning at me, holding a glass of water, looking happy. I stared at him, thinking about why he brought up the issue of Mum. 'Your mother was a hardworking woman, Leona. James is lucky to have had such a woman as a wife.'

'Thank you, Baba.'

'You know, we had some business deals together, your mum and I, and we had our disagreements. We were rivals then... the ways of the world. No one can tell what the wind would throw up.' He wiped his hands on his napkin. 'She was a good woman.'

'Do you know how she died?' I asked.

The napkin nearly fell from his hands.

'Oh. I don't. I don't know. I heard she wasn't sick,' he managed to respond.

'She must have been sick, but no one noticed.'

'Possibly. It could be stress. She never took a minute for

herself. Now, if you must excuse me, I have to go take my drugs.'

He wheeled himself backwards and reversed, moving towards the lobby. Akinola told me that before he returned from the hospital after he first suffered the stroke, his things were moved to the large room downstairs that served as the visitors' room. It was easier than getting him to the rooms upstairs. I stared at the door after he left and thought about what he was hiding. Definitely, he was hiding some things from me. I choked and had to open my mouth to let in air. I hated this man.

I called Akinola for the ninth time since he left, and he said Dad was stable. He was on his way to the hotel. Elizabeth was in the hospital with Beatrice and Smart. I was already missing him. Now that Dad was sick, I thought about the possibilities of not having to kill Akinola, and I felt some relief. I missed Akinola every time we were not together, and I wondered what would become of me if he died, died for what he knew nothing of. Dad must be up to some mischief for putting me up to this kind of misery. For what agony is greater than being coerced and manipulated to kill someone you love in vengeance for a sin he knows nothing about? Sure, his father killed Mum but that was not enough reason to kill his son. I thought about the sacrifices he made for me like leaving whatever he was doing to go make sure my dad was being taken care of—the same man that he was not aware wanted him dead. I wondered if he would still feel the same way for my dad if he found out his plans for him—that he wanted him killed by his own wife, the wife he cherished so much. I stared at the coloured stone-filled-pot for a while as tears welled up my eyes, fogging my thoughts.

Finally, I made it to my room. There were new towels and nightrobes laid out for me by the maids. I folded the ones I would not be needing for the night into the wardrobe drawers and prepared to freshen up, thinking about what to do and how best to avenge my mother that would not leave me in perpetual agony. And the most logical, the less sinful way was to leave my husband alone—no matter what Dad said—and go after the one who did kill Mum—Chief Fegun Wale; and I had already started.

FORTY-ONE

There is no burden stronger than harbouring the plot for murder. Could it be this load that was squeezing life out of my heart or Dad's illness was taking its toll on me? I sat on the floor of the toilet, my head in my hands, my mouth dry. I wiped my nose with the back of my left palm and stood, but it came again. I heaved, and turned to the toilet, kneeling before it as I got sick again. Then, I remembered that I had a pregnancy test kit in my bag. While I rummaged for the kit, it occurred to me that there was not going to be a better opportunity than the one I had this night. Beatrice was away with Akinola. Chief Fegun Wale and I were alone, all alone in the house. This was my opportunity to get to him—to get him to confess to the sins he committed. I changed into a pair of shorts and a singlet and hurried to the kitchen. The house was empty and the servants had retired to their quarters. I pulled out one of the six kitchen knives pinned to the wall and hurried to the first room close to the lounge, where my enemy was sleeping, helpless.

The door was obviously bulletproof. I prayed it was not locked. My heart was beating fast as I turned the knob and the heavy door pushed open gently, noiselessly. I had been in the room several times but this time, it looked larger. Only a coloured light bulb was lit and it made the grey wall paint appear dim. I could see the figure on the bed and the wheel-chair by the side. I fell back against the wall, breathing hard. There were lamps by either side of the bed but they were not lit. The floor was covered with a heavy but soft rug, which swallowed the sound of my feet as I crossed to the bed, my heart doing over two hundred kilometres per hour. This was what my mother wanted. This would make my dad happy. The revenge, though it would not be that of someone he loved who was going to pay for his sins. He would pay for it himself.

He had not woken up, not knowing that someone had entered the room. His disturbing loud snores disgusted me. I turned on the silver-coloured lamp by the left side of the bed. He was startled; he coughed, and rubbed at his eyes before adjusting to look at me. For an instant, the light blinded him, causing him to frown tightly.

Then, he jolted up, 'Leona mi?'

I stood, staring at him. Obviously, he had not seen the knife.

'Leona? Are you all right? So wa pa?' He sat up, dragging his useless legs. 'Is there any news about your…' I raised the knife and his eyes flicked to it and widened in surprise more than fear. 'What?'

I yanked off the thick duvet covering him, exposing his legs. He was dressed in boxer shorts and wore nothing on his upper body. His massive stomach drooped and wrinkled. I stared him down. I recalled the day Mum and I were driven to the Calabar seaport and ferried to Limbe, how scared Mum had been, and how she had kept praying silently. I recalled the day Grandpa was killed, how she had run out of the house with Doctor Malik and the other men, screaming and throwing herself on Grandpa's lifeless body; and Doctor Malik's older wife screaming, 'Wahyooo Allah! Bismillahi! Bismillahi!' I remembered that Mum wanted to build a foundation that would provide aid in Southern Sudan. Now, she was dead. She never enjoyed her life because of this man, who was now helpless before me.

'You thought no one can get to you, right?' I scoffed.

'What is this?' he barked.

'You built this mansion in one of the safest places in this country, surrounded by your dogs and bodyguards.' I sneered, pointing the knife at him. 'So, you thought no one can get to you, eh? I have come to tell you that this will be your last night on earth; believe it or not.'

'What did I do to you?' He struggled to sit up, his hands on the bed at his back, gawking at me. I had never seen so much fear in one person's eyes before. 'Please. Jo. Please.' He looked confused. 'Please. Whoever sent you. Whatever it is. Tell me. Whatever you need, so fun mi. I will pay you. I will—'

'Shut up!'

'Jo, omo mi. Please don't do this. What's this?'

'I am going to stab you on the throat and stab your body multiple times so that when they discover your body in the morning, you'd be unrecognisable.'

His eyes widened. 'You'd never get away—' The steady tick of the clock could be heard. A distance away, his dogs barked.

'Oh, I will.' I laughed a little. 'They'll never find the knife, and they will never think it was me.'

'It is easier said. It might take time but they will find you. Don't do this, my girl. Leona mi.'

'Your girl? Don't ever say that to me.'

I struck. It took him by surprise. He ducked a second or two too late and the knife connected with his shoulder blade, cutting an inch. I fell on the bed and his scream jolted me up. I grabbed him by the collar and pinned him down. Then the dogs began to bark again, this time louder.

'Please... don't... do... this...'

I held him by the throat. I had not realised how weak the sickness had made him. He did not put up much fight. The knife was on his face.

'Sshh... sshh. Shush. I will feed your eyes to you.' I was breathing hard. 'Why? Why did you kill my mum?'

'Eh?'

His eyes flickered as if a torchlight had been shone into his face.

'Answer me,' I spat on his face. Slapping him hard on the mouth.

'I didn't… did not… kill your mother.'

'Why did you kill my mum?'

'Listen. Your mother did.'

'What! You're an idiot.' I slapped him hard.

Tears and shame mixed in his eyes. 'Believe me. Your mother did. She killed herself. You are strangling me, Leona. Please believe me. I. Did. Not. I swear on my son's life.' My hand relaxed. I was weak. He was coughing now, spittle coming out of his mouth 'The signs were there. She talked to me about it.'

'She talked to you? What did she tell you?' I ruffled him. 'You blackmailed her. I saw what you sent to her.' His eyes widened again, this time in shame. 'Will you not talk now?'

'I blackmailed her into sleeping with me. I frustrated her business. But she was a strong woman. So, we… you are strangling me… jo.'

I eased up and came off the bed, dragging a chair. I sat down, facing him. He backed away until he hit the bedpost. I wiped my sweaty face with the back of my palm.

'I was pompous and full of pride. I was wealthy and famous and had my way. I got whatever I wanted. I ruled this country until your father came in and built his business and, in two years, became wealthy. He invested in everything I did, bought stocks in markets where I had interest, and bid for the same contracts that I did. I became fearful. He made friends with the military, those who wanted to oust the government. James was moving so fast. So, I had to act to make sure I stifled his business, and the best way to do that was to put him away. I did.' He coughed. The blood from his shoulder was tickling down his stomach, entering his boxers. He looked down at his stomach and winced. 'I had him put in jail, but I didn't know his wife, your mother, was going to be as good in business, even more tenacious and shrewd than your father. And she was, pardon me, Leona, she was a beautiful woman.' He looked away, shamefaced. 'I had to… I had to blackmail her. You probably know the story. But your mum had other plans. She did not succumb out of fear. She succumbed because she wanted to be close to me, but I didn't know this at the time.' He coughed again and again. 'The first time I got her to do it was out of blackmail. Then, she came again, the second time, on her own. I was excited. I thought she liked me. We became friends. It was shortly before she died that I discovered it was because she wanted to be close to me, to steal from me. Your mum stole from me, stole my business ideas.'

'Come on, what nonsense are you talking about?'

'I usually talk in my sleep about the things I am passion-ate about. Beatrice knows this. This was also how she got to know about your mother; because I talked about her.' He looked up at me and blinked several times and looked down at his hands. 'She stole my business ideas and grew hers. She was an intelligent and sharp woman. She turned from being naïve to being strong and independent, but she was inse-cure.' He coughed again, then wiped spittle from his mouth. 'She… your mother had psychological issues.'

'God punish you for saying that—' I nearly rose to attack him again.

'She thought people were out to hunt and kill her. She sought the help of witchdoctors. She got charms. She practised voodoo. She would visit this native doctor for a charm, then another, and another, and another. She was confused. She didn't know what this or that charm was meant for, how to sacrifice to it, how to keep their rules, and all. I warned her against all that. She didn't listen.'

'As if you aren't diabolical yourself,' I accused him.

He shook his head. 'Your mother was into so many of them; at some point she was confused.'

'You killed her because she stole the idea of the steel factory from you.'

'Which steel factory? What are you saying?'

'The steel factory the government took.'

His face twitched. 'Oh! Your father told you this? I thought as much. Is he the one who asked you to kill me? So fun mi. Was it James who told you that I killed your mother?'

'Did you kill her because of the factory?'

'When your mother stole the documents, I didn't pursue her. It was an idea that wasn't going to work. My team had found out, so I never told anyone. While she pushed to gain certification for it, I pretended I didn't know. But I knew she wasn't acting with her right senses; it was as if she was sick or something. If I told her, it would spur her to prove me wrong. Mary was dabbling into everything like a mad person.' I gawked at him. 'Trust me I did not... kill your mother.' Tears ran down my face. 'Leona, I believe strongly that your mother killed herself.' He leant forward. 'Do not cry.'

I believed him. The way he said those words made me cry. I was killing a man who was innocent.

'Look, I forgive you for what you did tonight.' He made to reach out to me. 'Do not cry. I do not blame you, child.' He dropped his hands when he saw the shock on my face. I was not crying because of what I did. I was crying because he was already dying and did not know it. He held my gaze. 'You don't believe me? Wait. I will show you something. Come. Help me to my wheelchair.'

FORTY-TWO

When I did not budge, he said, 'Your mother and I became close friends. It was your mother's idea that you and Akinola should meet.' My head rose up instantly. He was staring at me, nodding several times. Was he lying to me? He was a cunning man, dangerous and shrewd. Was he trying to throw me off my guard to alert his security men? Was there some remote or button somewhere that would summon them, and he was going to get to it? 'Mary.' His face relaxed. He was trying to hide the pain from the injury I had inflicted on him. 'Mary was a good woman caught in the midst of a war so strong and powerful that she had to fight dirty. She told me everything that happened in Omdurman. Every time we met...' he looked away.

I understood what he meant.

'She told me the story. I learnt by heart the details, the names of everyone involved in her life there: her sister, Yaya, Doctor Malik Al-Jazrula, Pa Thomas, Sheikh Abdula Keyeb, Edward Kofuo, and the rest. She told me how the general, your grandfather, was murdered before your eyes, how she forgot a jewellery box, rushed back into the estate to get it, and had just closed the door leading into the sitting room where the men sat drinking tea when the first gunshot sounded.

'Leona, your mother was affected deeply by what happened that morning, many years ago. It was the cause of her mental challenges. More—'

'You liar!'

'You didn't know?'

'You fucking liar.' I stood. My hand was fidgety and sweaty. I could not hold the knife steady.

'Your mother was seeing a psychiatrist.' He stared at me in the eyes. 'I need to show you things. I still have your mother's things with me.'

He was sitting on the bed, his useless legs before him. Helpless. I was standing, facing forward and on the tip of my toes, ready to pounce, but I was becoming weak.

'Your mother travelled to Sudan to recuperate. The aid and good works for people in Sudan, building the pharmaceutical company and living there most of the time were all part of the health plan to get her back to normal. Leona, your mother was not stable. She had mental challenges, but not many people knew. Many times, she was admitted at the hospital, a private clinic. I can prove these things to you.'

'Show me,' I muttered.

His eyes lit up. He beamed at me, then winced. 'Is there a way you could get me upstairs? To my main room. I need to show you some things.'

I stood for some seconds transfixed, hyperventilating.

Then, slowly, like a robot, approached him, grabbing him by the armpit and dragged his heavy body to the side of the bed. I brought his wheelchair close and helped him into it. He began to cough uncontrollably, I feared he was going into a seizure. When he calmed, he asked. 'How do you get me up the stairs?'

I did not say anything. I wheeled him out and went through the lounge to the lobby and the bottom of the staircase. He was panting, muttering to himself incoherently. I did not pay attention; so, I did not follow what he was saying.

'Here we are. How do we get upstairs? I am sure if you can get me to my room, you will get to know more about your mother, and you'll believe me.'

The dogs were still barking loudly.

I grabbed him by the armpit and began to drag him upstairs. He was wincing, nearly crying out in pain, his legs were hitting the stairs. I was sure those were not painful to him but his waist and the shoulder where I had stabbed him were tugging at his heart. My height was my leverage but by the time I got to the first landing, I was breathless. We fell on the floor, heaving, while he apologised repeatedly. *Why was he apologising if he was not wrong?* I was filled with rage. I dragged him up again through the rest of the staircase.

The room was larger than the one downstairs, and it had a massive bed at the centre. There was a silver-coated cupboard behind the bed, all with drawers, locked and safe. There were paintings on the wall and a thick curtain blinding the large window.

'Take me to the shelves.' I dragged him to them. 'Go to the bed. On the right front leg of the bed cabinet, there is an in-built compartment. Run your hand on the leg and when you feel a joint, push at it.' I did as he instructed. The pop sound surprised me. A bunch of keys was the only thing in the small compartment. I handed it to him. He shook his head. 'Inside these drawers are my private files and documents.' He pointed at the four drawers at the bottom of the shelf. 'With the wrong key inserted in any of the keyholes, they will lock permanently, releasing chemicals from small holes inside the drawers that would render the documents useless. If you insert the right key, do not turn it. Just wait for some seconds.' He seemed to force out a smile. I looked down at the keys in my hand. They were numbered one to four discreetly. 'Open the third drawer.' I inserted the key number three into the third drawer and without turning it, something clicked. A light I had not noticed earlier blinked twice on the front of the drawer and it pulled open. There were four thick files inside. 'They belonged to your mother.' I pulled them out, set them on the tiled floor, and opened the first one. There were documents containing account information, bank notes, bills of quantities and estimates, business plans and studies, so many of them. It was more like what I found in Enugu. 'Check the second file.'

They contained documents from one Harper Veins Specialist Hospital.

'Where is this based?'

'Chicago. I own it, partly.'

'Oh.' My voice was low now, subdued. Now that I had seen what he was saying, I began to calm down.

'I asked your mum to go there. I made sure she had the best medical attention, but she was beyond repair.'

I looked sharply at him. 'How come I did not know this?' Tears welled up in my eyes.

He dragged himself to the wall and propped himself against it. 'It was one thing she feared the most. She didn't want you or your father to find out. Ever. But it is possible your father knew... he is very wily. When your father left prison and took over the business, she was tired of everything, and she refused to go back.'

'For checks?'

'Yes. I tried everything.'

'You were still seeing her?'

He looked away. 'Yes.'

'Even after my dad got out?'

'We met, yes. She saw me a few days before she died. She flew back to Enugu. Then, I heard that she was dead. It devastated me. It caused my stroke.'

'Jesus!'

'We were... in love. I loved her. I am sure she loved me too,' he muttered.

Then, he looked down to the floor and like a child, tears ran down his face.

CHAPTER FORTY-THREE

'You? My mum?' I pointed at him.

'I was... in love with your mother, Leona.'

I fell back on my buttocks and my tears wet the documents in my hands. He crawled to me, held my shoulder, and took me to his chest.

'James, your dad, he didn't deserve your mother, Leona. He is such a bastard. When I heard he had a stroke, I was nearly elated, but I cautioned myself. I admit he wasn't good to your mother, but I wasn't good to her either, at least at the beginning. I blackmailed her and got her into my... bed using my powers and influence. But then, if not for that, we would not have known each other the way we did. I am sorry. I am not proud of it, but there is a reason for everything.' Our eyes met briefly, and he looked down. 'I am sorry you are learning all these this way. It was never meant to be this way. She didn't want you to know. She didn't. She was ashamed.'

'There is no shame in it. There is nothing to be ashamed of,' I sobbed. 'She should have told me. I am her daughter.'

'It was going to devastate you.'

'She said I could be her friend. She asked that I call her by her name.'

'It was going to kill you.'

'Which? That she was having an affair? Come on!' I left him and sat back, looking at him. 'Dad had multiple affairs. He betrayed her trust and her love,' I choked. 'She deserved some happiness. She should have filed for a divorce.'

'And then what? Come live with me? Marry me?'

I gawked at him.

'Come on, you know who we are. It would have been the worst news of the century. Imagine what that would have done to our reputation.' We were silent. 'Go on. Don't you want to read the files? Go through them.' The wall clock chimed. I looked up. It was past two in the morning. I shook my head. 'Take them. They are yours. Study them.'

I took the next file. It contained information on the blackmail. The video cassette, the photos, and documents about the ship.

'You kept this?'

'I didn't keep them to use them against Mary. I was going to sift through and shred those that weren't important when I had the stroke, and I couldn't access this room anymore. I couldn't ask them to bring me here. I guess I wasn't yet ready. Seeing you marry Akinola was the healing drug for me. I was finally going to face my demons. My God!' He raised his hands in surrender.

'I am sorry, sir.'

'Did anyone put you up to this?'

I said nothing.

'Please tell me, Leona mi.'

I stared at the huge clock on the wall before me.

'Do you love my son? Did you agree to marry him to get to us, to get to me?'

I was silent.

'Oh my! Please tell me you do love my son.'

'I am sorry.'

I was not sorry because I did not love his son. I was in love with Akinola. I loved him so much, more than anything else in the world. I was sorry because I had poisoned Chief's food the previous night; before I got impatient and went into his room to confront him, and like Dad had informed when he gave me the substance for my husband's meal, he would die in a few months, less than six, and no autopsy would detect a thing. It was irreversible.

Akinola and Beatrice returned the next day, in the afternoon, looking all tired out. I cooked spaghetti in fresh tomato and pepper sauce. While we all ate in the dining room, they told us about my dad's condition.

Akinola said that I did not need to worry about him, 'It's partial. He still has the use of his hands and legs. Good thing Smart got to him fast. That lady is a strong woman.'

'The maid?' Chief Fegun Wale asked.

'Our housekeeper,' I answered.

'I heard she has been in the family since you were a child,' Beatrice said.

'Oh, yes. Since we go back from Sudan. You talked with her?'

'Oh, yeah. We clicked. She brought food for us and insisted we didn't eat out.'

'Is she married now?' Chief Fegun Wale asked.

I shook my head.

'What's wrong, Darling? You are acting all moody,' Akinola observed.

'It's because of her father. You don't blame her,' Chief Wale replied Akinola, giving me the side eye.

I shovelled food into my mouth.

'Your father is fine, Leona dear,' Beatrice assured me. After a brief silence, Beatrice said, 'I spoke with Smart. She is getting married this year.'

'What!' I looked up. 'Oh! There was this man who used to visit the house while I was in Abuja, but she didn't tell me anything.'

Beatrice shrugged.

Later that evening, Beatrice hurried out of her husband's room screaming. 'Akinola! Leona!' she called hysterically. 'Akinola!' she was almost running. She pushed open the door. My husband and I had disengaged and were sitting awkwardly on the bed.

'What, Mum?

'Your dad has an injury. A plaster on his shoulder blade.'

'What? What happened?'

She was frantic. Almost hysterical. 'He isn't talking.'

Akinola was already climbing out of the bed.

'Leona? What happened while we were away? Was he taken to the hospital?'

I shook my head, pretending to look confused. She turned back, and we hurried after her.

Chief Fegun Wale had made me get the First Aid kit from Beatrice's room and dress his wound that night. He had made me promise not to discuss the incident with anyone. He said he had forgiven me.

'You are right to act the way you did. This is atonement for the way I treated your mum in the beginning.'

The next morning, he had dressed up, covering himself so no one would notice. I was sure he had taken some pain-killers. Now, his wife and son were asking him about his injury and he was mute. Beatrice had seen the wound while she helped him take his bath. Akinola stomped out, obviously to have a word with the guards. When he came back, confusion was written all over his face.

FORTY-FOUR

Akinola encouraged me to follow the news on the Sudanese crisis. He said he wanted me to start a foundation that provided aid to war-torn zones around the world. Chief Fegun Wale readily agreed. It was an idea Mum had toyed with and was already working on, he told me. Everyone was surprised that Chief was all in on the idea, suggesting a suitable name, telling us how to go about the registration, calling up the family lawyer, and promising to speak with President Al-Bashir and some notable Sudanese about it.

Around that time, we only discussed Sudan and my foundation in the house. I followed Sudanese news on the internet and on television, and I watched as skinny women and malnourished children walked in straight rural paths, their little belongings tied into bundles as they trekked hundreds of kilometres looking for the next refugee camp to rest or the next settlement that had not been bombed. I felt so heartbroken that the country I had played with its sands and danced with its donkeys had grown so dangerous. I usually sat for long hours, my eyes glued to the television screen tuned to CNN, watching the Darfur report. Akinola loved it each time I tuned to CNN; he was tired of watching fashion and entertainment channels with me and getting rebuked each time he changed the channel for news updates. I still thought about Kosi most often. I dreamt of him as well and sometimes, if Akinola and I were making love, I pictured Kosi on top of me. But he rarely took my calls now—it was as if he was building a barrier between us to protect us from crossing the line, now that I was married.

The first day Chief Fegun Wale slumped, he was giving a keynote address at a convention. That same day, it was confirmed that I was pregnant. It was just twilight and I found Akinola in the orchard, sitting under the canopy formed by flower plants and fruit trees, listening to the birds tweet and sing. He once told me that when he was younger and lived in New York with his aunt, he often went to the state park to listen to the sounds of pigeons. It was his aunt's favourite pastime, which rubbed off on him. A newspaper was spread across his laps and some documents were on another chair.

I leaned on him and began to caress his back.

His lips quivered, 'Doctor Yetunde called.' My heart skipped. I sat facing him. He smiled, looking all handsome. 'Sugar, you are with my child.'

'Wow! Are you serious?!'

'Oh yeah.'

'Wow!' We stood at the same time and hugged each other. He swept me off my feet and began to run. I clenched my two hands around his neck. I was sure he was taking me inside to celebrate, but his phone rang in his pocket. It was then that he got the news. Chief had slumped in his wheel-chair and was being taken to the hospital. I had been expecting it but praying fervently that the poison did not work. After what happened that night that Akinola and Beatrice were away in Abuja, I had developed some affinity for Chief Fegun Wale, but each time I was in the same room with him, I feared to look him in the eyes, I was afraid of what I would see.

Akinola barked at the guards and his driver, and as they reversed the vehicle, he yelled that I get into the house and not tell his mother until he was sure of the situation. He ran into the car and they zoomed off. I did not get into the house. As soon as the car left the gate, my knees became weak, and I fell on the ground. This was difficult. I hated my father for talking me into doing this. How did I ever agree to do this? Where did I get the strength to do it? To even put a knife to a man's shoulder? How did I ever think the poison would not work? Dad worked with a pharmaceutical company in Sudan for years as a pharmacist, experimenting with gum-Arabic and great many other products—whatever poison he gave me that I used on my father in-law was sure to be deadly. I felt my heart being crushed into pieces. Chief Wale was a good man; at least he was good to my mother. He had helped her a lot, and I was killing him. I was going to deprive him of the joy of holding his grandchild. How did I get the strength to poison him? When did I become so evil? The knowledge was devastating. I was sure it was not his blood pressure or anything, it was the poison. Dad had said it would kill slowly and the doctors would not detect a thing. I wondered what was happening to him.

Since Dad suffered a stroke and Akinola and his mother returned from visiting him, I had not gone to Abuja. I had not even taken his calls or called him unless the few times he got Akinola when we were together, and he gave me the phone. Dad was mad that I had not come to see him. He was cross at me for abandoning him, and that I had not done as he instructed. Akinola gave long sermons about how it was good for me to visit my father, but I gave excuses, using new modelling contracts and the Mary-Darfur Humanitarian Foundation as reasons. The truth was that after the incident with Chief Fegun Wale, I came to view my dad differently. He had always had a strong heart but now I knew that his hatred for people was as big as Mount Kilimanjaro. I was beginning to think he knew that it was not Chief Fegun Wale who killed Mum, yet he wanted to use me to take revenge on the man who put him in jail and took his wife. I was sure he knew that Mum and Chief Fegun Wale had a long-lasting affair and that Mum was in love with him. I wondered how much Dad knew about them and if he ever spoke to Mum about it.

FORTY-FIVE

Chief Fegun Wale's illness was a blow to the tranquillity in the house. Everyone was on edge; the maids and house-keepers and the guards, including Akinola. Beatrice never stopped yelling at everyone, and when the plates gave out sounds as they clinked in the dishwasher she rushed into the kitchen and slapped Satan out of the person in the kitchen.

'Common plates you can't wash!' she would scream. 'Why can't we hear ourselves because you are washing plates?'

Beatrice used to be so lovely and so motherly to the servants but now they feared every of her words, even to walk past her in the lounge or to serve the meal if she was at the table. Nothing Akinola did was right too. None of the doctors he brought or the hospitals he took his father to seemed perfect and good enough in her eyes. And this was worsened by the fact that no one could seem to detect what the problem with the old man was. A hospital in the UK detected some toxins in his blood and bone marrow, but nothing they did seemed to be working. Now, the man was tired of moving about from one doctor to another specialist, to this and that hospital, so he returned home. There were several specialists on standby in the case he relapsed; and he did relapse so very often. This minute he would be all jovial and talkative and the next minute, blood would slowly ooze out of his nostrils; he would not even notice unless it dropped on his cloth or someone saw it and alerted him. In the evenings, he would have this piercing headache that came with a fever that shook his entire body.

Chief never let go of me. He wanted me by his side always, more than he wanted his wife. He told me stories about how he grew up in Abeokuta and how he came to Lagos and became a newspaper vendor before travelling to the USA on scholarship to study Business Development and Administration. While he told me these stories, tears trickled down my face. I could not face him, I tried to avoid him as much as I could, but it was impossible. I was his only happiness, and if that was the case, if making him happy was atonement for my sins, I readily accepted to be beside him. It was better, less painful than confessing what I had done. That would be the end of me.

I was the only one Beatrice cared about, the one she seemed to give attention and love because I was always with Chief Fegun Wale. I was his happiness. Chief Fegun Wale and I had developed a strong bond. Beatrice reduced her travels to take care of her husband. She had refused to take in a nurse since he had his stroke, bathing and caring for him herself; and now the added burden was taking a great toll on her. She did everything for him, cutting out her friends and most of her social gatherings. She rarely visited her office and when she did, she came back complaining to me about this or that staff, and how she believed they were stealing her money. The three of us, Chief, Beatrice, and I often sat in the orchard, listening to the radio or analysing the news and arguing. Then, I would look at him and remember how he was Mum's friend in the years of her solitude, and the pain and tears would come.

Beatrice would swoop on me saying, 'Oh dear, don't be a baby. Baba will be fine. If you are like this when we are together, what do you expect of me, hmm?' She would wipe my tears with her large palm and caress my hands and shoulders.

Chief Fegun Wale would try to laugh but spasm in fits of cough, 'Remember your… condition, please.' Then, he would add, 'Do not worry about me, Leona mi… I am an old man.'

'She is a baby, of course. My baby.'

He would wheel himself towards me. 'If you cry like this, you break my heart and hasten my death.'

His wife and I would look at him and cry in unison, and he would call on the guards to come take him away from 'these crying babies.'

Aunty Agii came to the house one Saturday evening, all moody and worked up, and while I saw her off to her car she said, 'Your father is enraged, Leona. It is now over three months since he fell sick.'

'I know.'

'Why don't you go to see him, Leona? Biko.'

'But he's recovered. He has resumed his duties.'

Dad had resumed work but rarely made any public appearances. It was rumoured that if not that he was close to the presidency, he would have been compulsorily asked to resign.

'He has recovered but not fully. He doesn't seem to have full use of his right side, but the physiotherapists are good.' She placed her purse on the roof of the car. 'Go and see him, biko. You will lighten his heart. Inugo?'

'I will try.' The way I said it, she knew I did not mean it.

'He said to tell you that you both have some unfinished business, and he needs an update.' She eyed me suspiciously.

I snorted. 'Tell him I don't have any business with him.'

Aunty Agii took my hands. 'Bia, why are you so caring of your father-in-law, working on him, getting him to heal, but your father is left to die?'

'Perhaps he deserves death, Aunty?'

'What?' She stared at me, her jaw dropping.

I looked away, my arms folded against my chest. 'Dad still has so much hatred in his heart. I thought that with what happened he would be a changed person.'

'And I must tell you, young woman; you inherited the same traits from him. The hatred in your own heart is so heavy it can pull down a storey-building. Why?'

She tried to find my face, but I looked far away. If only I could undo what I had done.

'Leona, please. Go see your father and lift up the burden in his heart.'

'No.'

'Then, I have nothing more to say to you, cha-cha. If you want him dead, I do not. He is my husband, and I can't be friends with someone who doesn't mean well for the father of my children.'

She entered her car and slammed the door. She forgot that her purse was on the rooftop and I did not care to alert her. She zoomed off.

Adulike called the next day. She had gone to Dad's office to see him and he had given her some money.

'Babes, he is still such a sweetheart even though he is sick. He told me you haven't come to see him. Why, Leo?'

'I don't know.'

'Why don't you know?'

We said nothing for some seconds.

'I guess I am scared. I used to see him as this powerful Dad and now... I think I am not yet ready to see him weak,' I lied.

'Well, I think I understand your point, girl, but try.'

I did not.

Adulike visited my dad almost every other day, calling to tell me how he was doing, helping Smart to prepare his food, and clean the house. I wondered if Dad was going to take another wife. I knew that if he asked Adulike to marry him, she would not refuse.

Onyinye agreed that Adulike would jump at the proposal. 'She'd always loved men with wives. Just as some of us like women, some like older people. There are people who like to date married people. I do not hold it against them.' I snorted and she laughed at me. 'You are too backwards-minded, Leona. And you are a celebrated model? Do you know how many of my friends here in Leeds talk about your beauty and want to have your skin and be like you? If only they know that you are still so backward.'

'I don't understand it when civilised girls want to marry men who are already married. Dad has two wives, Onyinye.'

'I know. Is it not better than getting him to divorce his wives and having him all to yourself? If a woman is ready to share a man and co-exist with his other women, it is better. Makes the world a more peaceful place to live in and helps to make sure we don't have bastards and helpless, hopeless children who don't know about their father or mother.'

'Abegi, leave this matter, Nne. In fact, when are you coming back?'

'In a few months. My convocation is on September twenty-three.'

'I can't wait to see you, darling,' I cooed. 'I miss you like hell.'

'And you couldn't spare a few hours for me when you were in the UK.'

'I came with my father-in-law.'

'No. When you came for the modelling thing.'

'Haba! I only spent two days, girl!'

FORTY-SIX

AUGUST 2006
LAGOS, WESTERN NIGERIA

I was now five months pregnant and my tummy was protruding. There were already plans in the agency to book me for modelling jobs with a few baby products company—Pampers was already interested. Emily and I were in my office at the agency, discussing the Darbur Fashion Week when the phone rang.

'He is gone.' Akinola sobbed into the phone. My phone slipped from my hands and crashed on the floor, scattering into pieces. Emily was fast. She held me and asked what the problem was. Tears ran down my eyes before I let out a loud cry.

They buried him in September. Onyinye was in the country. She flew back a day after her convocation and attended the funeral on the twenty-ninth of September. Dad came with the government delegation and stayed a few days in Lagos. Aside seeing him at the funeral, I refused to go to Aunty Agii's house. Akinola and Aunty Agii were mad. Akinola did not talk to me for a day, and Aunty Agii called me a witch.

Two days after the funeral, Aunty Agii came to cause some uproar in my office. Onyinye had escorted me to shop for baby stuff; she said she was paying for them, predicting jokingly that the baby would be a boy so she would marry him.

'But you are lesbian,' I'd said.

'If it's a boy, I would turn bisexual.' She laughed heartily.

'Impossible.'

After shopping, we dropped by at the office to pick up a few documents when Aunty Agii burst in, yelling at me, 'So you want to kill your father too, abi?'

I bet everyone in the office who heard her stopped in their tracks.

I was speechless. 'What? Aunty?'

'Your father cried before me this morning. For the first time, I saw him cry like a child. You are tormenting him.'

'Please. Leave me alone. You said you don't want my friendship, right? What are you doing here in my office?'

'I have come to warn you. If you kill my husband, I will hurt you.'

She was not holding any purse or phone. She was dressed in blue jeans and a tank top, her wig in shiny curls.

'Wait! Hold it there,' Onyinye stood, facing her, approaching her.

She was of average height and they were the same size as if someone had used a measuring tape to get a certain measurement and cut off the rest of their height.

'I heard the word "too". You allege my friend killed

her father-in-law?' Onyinye approached her, this time their noses were almost brushing. My heart was pounding steadily. 'And you say you will hurt her?' She threw up her hands; then, she sidestepped the speechless Aunty Agii and locked the door. 'You have some explanations to make, old stinky lady.'

'What?!' Aunty Agii shouted.

'Oh, yeah. You heard me.' Onyinye pinched her nostrils together, briefly. 'What's wrong if she refused to visit her father, even if he is dying? She is an adult, isn't she? This is 2006 and not 1846, right?'

'Get out of my way. I have said what I said.'

'Fuck you!' Onyinye surprised all of us. She slapped Aunty Agii so hard, so hard that I was sure her hand hurt. Aunty Agii's surprise knew no bounds. Her hands held her cheek as if it would fall off, and she backed away until she hit the closed door.

'My God,' was all she said.

Someone banged on the door. It was Emily.

'Open this door now! Leona! Leona! I know you are in there,' her American accent almost sounded gibberish.

Akinola heard about the fight and when we got back home, he dragged me to the room.

'I don't expect you fighting when you are this heavy.'

I thought when he was dragging me upstairs that he was going to yell at me for being disrespectful to my step-mum.

'Onyinye did the fighting, not me.'

'I see. So, what happened?'

I sat down and narrated the incident to him. He sighed and sighed again. I could see a few strands of grey on his hair.

'You are greying, darling.'

'I noticed.'

I laughed, 'You are too young to grey.'

'There is no age limit.' He stood and headed towards the bathroom. 'What's for dinner?'

'Asaro.'

'What? Haa!'

I laughed at him.

In the month of August that Chief Fegun Wale died, the Mary-Darfur Humanitarian Foundation sent our first relief package to Sudan. My only sadness was that Chief was not alive to see it come to pass. He had thrown his weight behind the entire project, talking to a few of his friends to come on board and declining to sit at the head of the board. Even when others suggested they would only serve if he was there, he maintained that he was a dying man. It had broken my heart when he said that.

Chief Fegun Wale had organised a fundraising dinner for the Mary-Darfur Humanitarian Foundation in the first week of August. He had seemed a happy man, finally confessing formerly the relationship he had with Mum to Beatrice, the day after the fundraising. Beatrice, who had always suspected, had run out of the room, refusing to see him for days. When Mum was still alive, Beatrice had heard him talk about her in his sleep and confronted him, but he had denied it; now, she was devastated that he lied to her all the while. Akinola pleaded with his mum.

'Who am I to judge you? Who am I? Now we have Leona, and she is such a wonderful gift to this family,' Beatrice said in tears.

It was so disheartening to see them both together, happy as if Beatrice knew her husband was already almost dead and would not want to burden him these last days of his existence. If she had not forgiven him, she told me, she would not have forgiven herself when he died not long afterwards. But how do I confess what I had done? How do I forgive myself talk more of asking another to forgive me if they found out what I did?

FORTY-SEVEN

My son is dark, like my mum. And immediately he was born, there was a problem about what was going to be his name. Beatrice wanted him named Fegun after his grandfather, but I refused. I would find it difficult looking my son in the eye and calling him the name of the man I killed, the man who loved my mother and me so unconditionally.

We settled for Osinachi, meaning, 'It came from God'. Akinola liked the name because of the meaning. And to make him and Beatrice happier, I agreed that our son should also be called Fegun, after his grandfather, knowing that what he would be called mostly was Osinachi.

Onyinye was all over the baby like she was obsessed with him. She bought him stuff more than Akinola and I did. The only person she could not outdo was Beatrice, and together they fought for the baby's attention. Whenever we were together, she talked and talked a lot, about the UK and all the other countries she had visited.

'Do you know that white people envy you? They say

you are beautiful?' she would laugh. 'In my school, some girls would do anything just to be like you, if it is possible for them to change their skin to black, they would do that just to be like you.'

'But I am an old woman now. See how big I look.'

'You are okay, just added a little flesh, that's all. Nothing a little exercise won't take care of.'

'Sure?'

'Of course! You are from Sudan; you guys don't get fat.'

'Haba, Onyinye. Don't generalise like that.' She laughed. 'I am a Nigerian oh!'

'Remember long ago in primary school, when I told your secret to everyone?' she grinned.

'You said I wasn't a Nigerian.'

She waved me off, 'We were children, but wait, are you a Nigerian?'

'Gerrout!'

She dressed elegantly now and looked sharp, more than before she left the country. She told me that with our childhood pictures, she had won herself lots of friends; and once when she was broke, she had sold my photograph to one of her friends who always admired it. I was amazed when she said the girl enlarged it and hung it on the wall of her room.

The agency was working well and fine-tuning some details about a contract with Dimples, a baby products company. I was to model with Osinachi, and Onyinye was excited about the idea. She planned to go to the photo sessions with me to take snapshots herself and help carry Osinachi.

While Onyinye and I were chatting, Aunty Agii called. She wanted us to bring Osinachi to the house and reminded us she was the baby's grandma of sorts and deserved to see him, making Onyinye and I roll our eyes. I told Akinola later, and he said I could do whatever made me happy.

Osinachi had started to crawl, but Aunty Agii and Dad had not seen him. Elizabeth flew in to Lagos to spend two days with us, three weeks after the baby was born; and Aunty Agii was not happy that she was not allowed to see him. After the incident at my office where she threatened to hurt me if anything happened to my dad, Elizabeth and I were now sort of close. Elizabeth had heard from Onyinye and used the opportunity to call me up to talk about this and that. Eventually, she switched the discussion to Aunty Agii.

'That Agnes is a witch, you must believe me. She is a wolf in sheep clothing.'

'We are not friends any more, but I know her so well. I lived with her. She is no witch.'

'She has a hard heart, I must tell you, Leona. I can't lie to you. She is a witch. You won't believe this, but someone told me that she is trying to kill my boys so that her children will inherit Chief's wealth when he is no longer with us.'

'Haba, Elizabeth! Now, I don't like such talk.'

'This is no false talk, Leo.'

'Who told you?'

'A prophet. My pastor, in fact.'

'Oh! You see? You believe those scallywags? I thought you should know they are only out there to jam people's heads together. They kill and go.'

'Just be careful is all I tell you.'

When I told Akinola, he dropped his tie on the floor and stared at me. Then, he picked it up and said, 'Women say anything. Don't pay heed to such talks.' Later, he stretched and said, 'I saw your photo and that of our son on a billboard, a new board on the Third Mainland Bridge.' He came to me, taking me in his arms, 'I drive past those billboards with photos of you and Osinachi; and they are so beautiful that I wonder if some women who are yet to have babies might begin to look for handsome men to make them single mothers.'

'Osinachi is handsome because you are his father?' I shook my head.

'Of course.' He brought out his tongue in playful mockery.

'But everyone says he looks like me.' I stuck out my tongue too.

He smiled. 'But he now looks more like me every day. You will see; boys look like their fathers.'

'Where did you get that from?'

He kissed me, his tongue doing wonders in my mouth. His hands reached my backside and he squeezed.

After we visited Aunty Agii, I began to have nightmares, terrible nightmares. They were usually long and confusing, and I woke up sweating, my head banging. Sometimes, I woke up screaming. In the nightmares, I saw a cup over-flowing with blood; sometimes, the blood was being poured all over my body, and some of it entered my mouth and my ears, soaking my eyes and colouring my dark body. At first, I thought my mind was playing tricks on me because of what Elizabeth said about Aunty Agii being a witch, but the nightmares persisted. Sometimes, I was afraid, but I did not know what made me so uneasy because the visit to Aunty Agii's house was uneventful. We drank wine, ate lunch, and chatted about nothing in particular. She was so jovial and lovely, and I was sure she had forgotten about all that happened in my office. When I got back home, I had called Onyinye and asked her to ring or visit Aunty Agii and apologise, but she had said she would only do that over her 'dead body'.

Once, I had a nightmare and awoke in my husband's arms. He had returned late and creep-crawled into my bedroom to lie by my side. When I screamed and woke up, I was lucky he was there to hold me in his arms.

'Hey, shush, baby. It was just a nightmare.'

'It was scary.'

'Do you want to talk about it?' I was silent. He did not push. He held me. I held him tight. 'You were talking in your sleep, agitated.'

'And you didn't wake me?'

'It was spontaneous.' He wiped the sweat on my forehead. 'Are you okay?' I nodded. 'Do not worry about it. I bet you won't remember what it was all about in the morning.' He held me tighter and kissed my forehead. After a while, he said, 'You should go to the bank tomorrow to discuss with our account officer about the trust fund.'

'Tomorrow?'

'Yes.'

'Okay. I will.'

'And who is Kosi or Kose?'

My heart skipped. 'What? Who? What do you mean?'

'You mentioned the name before you woke up.'

'I don't know. Can't remember.'

I could not sleep anymore. Does it mean he did not know about him?

A few days later, Kosi came to the agency to see the baby, but he left before Onyinye came. She had wanted to see him, but he was in a hurry to catch the night bus back to Enugu, refusing to take my offer of money for a plane ticket. It seemed he was heartbroken, but we had no future together. He made his decision the day he said he was going to become a Catholic priest, married to the Virgin Mary.

'You talk about class. Class, to me, is a word that has no base. No foundation.' I had argued, 'It's like a mud house with the mud blocks laid on the bare ground. If a slight wind comes, it carries the house away. Class is like that, if you believe so much in it, when the scale tips, you go down with it. Kosi, wealth and fame are easy to acquire, but the problem is maintaining them. If you achieve wealth or fame or both and neglect your old friends and make some new ones, then you shall be, like they say, an old woman who exhausted her firewood in the dry season and when the rainy season came, she died of cold. That's why I don't like it when you talk like this. I still want your friendship. I want you to be the baby's godfather.'

'Will your husband approve?'

'I will talk to him... tell him about you.'

'What?' his eyes opened wide as he gawked at me.

'What?'

'How can you tell him we were doing...' He broke off.

'I will just tell him we were friends from primary school and now you are a priest.'

'I don't want troubles, please. Don't tell your billionaire husband that I was doing *you* before him.'

I laughed out loud. 'You see, Akinola is a good man.'

'Good man? No man is good when it comes to women, especially one as beautiful as you are. Don't just tell him, please.'

'You fear he'll come after you?' I took his hand. 'He is a good man, Kosi.' I was looking into his eyes. I wished I could kiss him.

'That isn't what I hear.'

'I am his wife, and I tell you he is.'

He stared at me all the while that we talked. He took his glass of wine and gulped the content. 'Talk with him. Let's hear his opinion.'

'Thank you.'

'Don't just tell him about the other—'

'Okay. But he isn't going to suspect. He didn't marry me a virgin.'

'You don't seem happy.'

I flushed. 'But I am happy.'

He bent his head sideways. He knew me well.

'Just this terrible nightmare that's been tormenting me.'

'Tell me about it.' He leaned towards me like a priest in the confessionary.

'Never mind.'

When he stood to leave, after blessing the baby and holding him for some time, he took me in his arms and hugged me so tight, refusing to let go.

I cleared my throat. 'You are going to be a priest, next year February, Kosi.'

He sighed. 'And you are someone else's wife now.' He released me reluctantly.

FORTY-EIGHT

Akinola thought it would be best for the family if we spent the summer holiday touring a few cities. Beatrice did not think she would survive two weeks without the baby; so, she insisted she must tag along. She promised not to serve as a hindrance to our romantic adventures, and we agreed reluctantly.

'This is why I didn't want my wife and me to come live here,' he joked.

'But I've been feeding the both of you fat. See your stomach.'

Things were brightening up in the house now, with Beatrice humming some old Yoruba songs and the maids singing along, forcing her to laugh. Once, I caught them betting on whose tenor was the coolest, and the gateman was the judge. It was fun. I usually sat outside, looking about the massive compound, and it felt like the meadow on the lawn were growing new flowers for my happiness. The colours of love were replacing the hatred in my heart, filling the heart-break and the guilt, though that was difficult. I wondered if I would grow strong enough to one day tell Akinola and Beatrice what I did.

Then, darkness came.

It came the morning I visited the agency to catch up on mails and read contracts that were overdue since we were on vacation. Like Chief Fegun Wale, I slumped. Everyone joked that I had obviously overdone it during the vacation. Akinola thought it was jetlag. Beatrice wondered if I was pregnant again, to everyone's consternation. But I did not think it was due to anything until a few weeks later when rashes appeared all over my body, followed by a constant drumming head-ache and fever. It was the same symptoms Chief Fegun Wale had suffered. Beatrice knew so too and was fearful. Akinola invited specialists. It was the same. There was an unidentifi-able toxin in my blood. This time, Akinola vowed to get to the root of it.

I was the most fearful. What was the problem? I did not know what was wrong. I had thrown away the bottle that contained the poison in the dumpster outside in the street. So, how was it that I was now having the same symptoms Chief Fegun Wale had, suffering as he did? Could it be that my sins had come to haunt me; that the dead had resurrected to pay me back? It was a devastating thought, so strong that it made me weak. The thought and fear of how the poison got into me killed me more than what the disease inside me was doing.

One Sunday, several weeks after, Akinola brought some eggs and fried plantain to my room and found out that I was breathing hard. My eyes could not open well and my head ached. My temperature was high. Panic hit him and he knelt, begging me not to die.

'I won't die, baby,' I promised him.

Onyinye, who now practically lived in the house—just like I heard Adulike lived in the house in Abuja with Dad—came in and helped feed me the eggs, while Akinola hurried away to Dragon Investments' annual general meeting. Rosa visited in the afternoon and together with Onyinye, they sat on either side of me on the bed, while we watched Osinachi play in the room with his toys, and listened to Onyinye complain about how men would not allow her to rest.

Rosa had just returned from Angola where she went to visit her husband. He was an engineer working with an agricultural firm, and though she was married with children, she looked so slim and elegant that one would mistake her for a girl in her early twenties. When we came to the story about Kosi, Rosa said I was stupid if I still thought about him or communicated with him, and that all the women in the world would die to have Akinola as their husband.

'Osinachi! Osi baby! Come here!' Onyinye cooed. My baby turned, smiled, and drooled. She swooped him off the floor to her body. 'My own husband.'

'Leona, I will marry your baby. In fact, when he grows up, I will be waiting to marry him,' she said, kissing and throwing him up and catching him mid-air.

'If you like stay single, your mates are all getting married. See Leona living happily,' Rosa teased. 'My baby girl will marry Osinachi. You cannot marry him because you're already an old woman, too old for him.'

'Me? Old woman? Kai, damn it! I don finish.' We laughed.

'No, my baby is Onyinye's husband. Onyinye is ready to wait for him o!' I jokingly supported Onyinye who came to the bed and shook my hands. 'Before he was born Onyinye booked him to be her husband.'

My joints ached. I groaned.

'What kind of illness is this?'

'I wonder,' Onyinye replied her sister. She patted my legs. 'Ndo, dear.'

'See Leona looking like something the wind can carry off any moment.'

'You need to travel out to see a specialist abroad.'

Rosa agreed with Onyinye.

'If all Nigerians travel out when they are sick, it means we have all lost hope in the Nigerian state entirely,' I said.

'I know, but this one is different. You have taken all the medications, yet it persists.'

'We have an appointment to go back to the Indian hospital we visited two weeks ago.'

'Good.'

'Good?' Onyinye questioned Rosa, turning to Leona, she said, 'You've been taking their medications and nothing seems to be working.'

'I feel empty.'

'Do you say you feel empty? That one is a sign of malaria.'

'Malaria? This is no malaria… well, at first I took malaria drugs.

Then, my doctors ran some tests. They said no malaria. Now, we are waiting for some more results.'

'Many people living in this country will resort to herbal medicine when they feel the way you do.'

'My illness is not a matter for jokes,' I sighed. They beamed at me, coming to sit by my sides. 'The poor will always bear the burden of poverty even though they are uncomfortable, just like the rich will always be afraid and struggle with their conscience. Do you think it is easy to be rich? It is a curse. Once you are rich, you cease to have a conscience, and even peace of mind becomes your enemy.' I sighed again.

'So, would you have chosen poverty?'

'Poverty is an affliction. It is like an epidemic.' I yawned. 'I feel dry.'

Onyinye got some water from the refrigerator, but I shook my head.

'Sometimes, I wish I was never rich, sometimes I wish I am richer. It's dependent on what I am passing through, but I must tell you something,' my voice was low. 'A rich man has no friends; a famous man has no friends. People are attracted to your wealth or fame. It's just like beauty. People do not like you because of what you are inside of you, they like you because of your beauty. Even if you are evil but beautiful or rich, they flock to you like moths to the flame.'

Later, I woke Akinola up in the middle of the night. He looked at my face and drew me to him.

'You look pale, darling.'

He sat up. 'Is everything okay?'

'Yeah. I just feel so empty.'

He drew me to him. 'I am so sorry.' His eyes became misty. 'My beauty. My angel. You are too beautiful, darling. I don't want anything to happen to you, please. Leona? Chizorom Egbufor-Wale?'

'Nothing is going to happen to me.' There were tears in my eyes.

'How do you feel now?'

'Just tired.'

'Should I call your doctor?' he asked in concern.

I sat on the bed, caressing his tummy. The room was large, the sofa, the beanbag in a corner, the television, and the artworks that sat on a long table beside the lamp stand all stared at me. If only they could talk, they would have told my husband what I had done, what I had taken away from him; and what I now feared was haunting me.

'Your father called, dear.'

'Oh?'

'He is doing well.'

'Adulike is trying then.'

'Adulike? Your friend who is helping him?'

'Fucking him.'

He shook his head at me. 'They are grown up, Leona.'

'Adulike is twenty-eight.'

'She is old enough to be married. You are not older, and you are married.'

'But not to a man old enough to be my dad.'

'She isn't planning on marrying Chief.'

'Who knows?'

'The most important thing is he is getting better, Adulike or not.'

I said nothing. He held me to himself. 'You don't seem to care, do you?'

I was silent. He shrugged.

'Well, let's not tire you out.' He closed his eyes and kissed my neck. While I was drifting to sleep, my body burning in fever, my husband said, 'I don't want to lose you. I don't know what would become of me.'

I had never heard him sound so desperate before.

Two months later, I returned from a German hospital, worse than I was when I was admitted. Just like Chief Fegun Wale, there was no cure for my malady. Beatrice set a camp bed for me in the garden, and while I slept, she would hold my hand and talk to herself about how the world was so unfair to her; then, when she was sure I had slept off, she would cry until her sobs woke me.

Now that I was too weak to stop anyone from visiting, Aunty Agii came. She came with Chinwe. Chinwe was all tears when she saw how I looked, but Aunty Agii's face was set straight. I wondered if she felt any pity for me or if she had come to laugh at me. My greatest fear was that either Chief Fegun Wale had cursed whoever poisoned him and the curse had brought the same illness he suffered on me; or that someone—possibly Dad—who had access to the poison had put it in my food or drink or had somehow got it into me, and I was suffering the same way my father-in-law did. But how was this possible? I had not seen Dad. Then, I remembered how powerful he was; he could have paid anyone to do it—one of the staff in the mansion, a staff at the agency or even at the restaurant I frequented. But why would Dad poison me? Why? And if I had been poisoned, then I had less than three months to live. I had never been so scared in my life.

I got one of the servants to help me upstairs to my room. My head was banging, and I was shivering. Okwudili and Johnson were all gloomy, seeing me skinny and tired, so Aunty Agii asked Chinwe to take them home.

She came to me on the bed where I lay and took my hands. 'You have to be strong, my girl.'

Tears came to my eyes.

'You have always been a strong woman, like your mother.'

But she was grinning. Why was Aunty Agii grinning? My temperature was picking up now that I was in the room, and the windows and the door were closed.

'You should see your father now; he is recovering so fast.'

I did not know what she was getting at; so, I stared at her. My body was so hot now that I wondered if it did not hurt her hand. She held my hand tighter.

'You see, Leona.' She dropped my hand and clenched hers together. 'Your family is full of evil people, your mother, your father,' she lowered her voice and it sounded fiendish, 'And you.'

I forced my eyes open. I had no strength to say anything to her.

'Your mother was bad, but you... gi nwa... you are the worst.'

She pointed at me. 'Yes. You.'

She had this grin on her face. 'You accepted poison from your father to kill your husband.' She smiled now and broke out in spurts of laughter. I took my hand away but she grabbed it, squeezing and hurting me.

'You are definitely the worst of all the Satans in the Egbufor family. You think I did not know? I saw him give it to you, at my house. I heard him tell you to kill Akinola.'

My heart fell into my stomach, and I could swear I heard the sound it made. It took several seconds for me to force down the saliva that had gathered in my mouth.

'But I... but I talked to you at Bogobiri. You told me how wrong it was to have a bitter heart.'

'And only succeeded in melting your heart enough not to continue with the plan of killing your husband.' She laughed. 'You decided to poison your father-in-law instead, hmm?'

I looked away. So, she knew all this while. Agnes is a witch. Why did I not listen to Elizabeth? Now I remembered those days in Sudan when Mum and her friends talked about witches and how she always said there were lots of them in Nigeria, and how I had been so afraid of our visiting Dad's country because of it.

Tears ran down my cheeks. I was shaking and sweaty. Aunty Agii brought her head close to my ear. I would have moved my head if I had the strength.

'Are you surprised that you now suffer the same ailment that killed Chief Wale?' She laughed. It was not the laughter that I knew. She had changed.

'You shouldn't be surprised, beauty queen.'

Then, she stood.

'When do you plan to tell them of your sins?' She swept her hands around. 'This family that loves you so much. These people that make your head grow. Tell them, go ahead. Tell them you killed their father. The entire world would love to know.'

'It is… it is… a sin. I am not… proud of. I am… ashamed.'

'Oh, you are?' She laughed gleefully. 'Look at you, o, beauty queen, look at you, all bony and skinny and dying.' She approached me and I flinched, scared. 'Do you still excite him?' She held my shoulder and shook me hard. It ached. 'Do you still make his thing,' she demonstrated with her left hand, 'Stand hard?'

I sobbed. My head was pounding like a pestle against a mortar. I could feel the blood ooze out of my right nostril.

She smiled. 'Your face is on all billboards in Lagos, on all TV ads. I can't stand you. Your father was talking about you, even in bed after making love to me, as if you're the only woman on earth.' Then, she shouted the last one, 'As if you were his wife!'

'Why... did... you... do... this... to me, Aunty?' She grinned wickedly.

'Why did you do this to me, Aunty,' she mimicked in mockery. She looked sideways as if watching for anyone's approach. 'Because I hate you. I couldn't stand your beauty. I couldn't stand all the attention you were getting. Yes, and because of everything. Yes, everything is wrong with you.'

'I... never... hurt you. I... never... hurt the... boys.'

'You would have if your father left everything for you like he was planning to do.'

My eyes widened. I had just written a will behind Akinola's back and was going to leave most of my things and what I inherited from Mum to Osinachi, Okwudili, Johnson, and Elizabeth's boys. She did not know that. Thank God she mentioned this when there was still time.

'Do not cry, Leona. You're just getting what you gave to another.'

'Please... tell... me. When... when... did you... do... this to—'

'Oh. You want to know?' she laughed and backed away until she was almost at the door.

I reached out to her, stretching out my hand. 'Please, tell me.'

'I will tell you when we meet, someday, in heaven. Bon voyage, little beauty queen,' she laughed heartily.

I was sure that people downstairs could hear her for she had now opened the door, and she was still laughing. It was a laughter that carried her entire heavy body and rocked her back and forth, back and forth. I could hear her laughter and the *koi-koi-koi* sounds her stilettos made as she walked down the tiled stairs to the ground floor.

FORTY-NINE

AUGUST 2007
ENUGU, SOUTHEASTERN NIGERIA

'Father, I ask for mercy from this heinous crime that is ripping my soul apart.'

The priest sat up, stretched his back, and yawned. He blinked several times and looked down at me. I was lying on Mum's bed in the house at Enugu. I had been sick for over five months, going on six and was now as tiny and lean as a pencil. My rib bones could be counted if I removed my cloth. They were like those of an ekuke dog, my neck was long and multiple veins zigzagged across it, and my once beautiful dimpled cheeks were now hollow, and they could swallow a finger if it was stuck into them.

The priest shook his head. 'There is no doubt you were once a pretty woman.'

I sighed. 'I have come to realise, Father, that beauty is like fire, no matter how much it blazes, it dies down eventually.'

'Like every other thing God created.'

There was a long silence.

The young priest looked at me for a long time, and we just stared at each other. Occasionally, he would look down.

The distant sound of water trickling down from a tap in the bathroom could be heard. The sound of the hand of the wall clock that hung directly opposite me could be heard too, and apart from those two sounds, the quietness of the sitting room was not defiled.

The priest tried to say something more but could not. It was as if his lips were gummed with glue. He was not so tall, and his cassock made him look as splendid as angels seen on paintings. He had a well-shaved moustache. His eyes were like those of an eagle, darting from one side to the other.

After the silence, he raised his head, looked at me straight in the face, and said with lots of authority in his voice, 'I have no power to forgive your sins.'

'Why?' I was surprised. I thought it was said that even though your sins were as red as the scarlet that it would be made as pure and as white as the snow. Only what you had to do was to confess them. 'Why, Father?'

He saw the disappointment on my face. He heard the fear in my voice.

'Hmm.' He shifted in his seat. The leather seat made some noise as he did. 'Young woman, I do not have the powers to forgive sins. Only one person does, and His name is God. My work is to intercede for you and through me, your sins would be forgiven, but only if you have truly repented of them with all your heart.'

His mouth was tiny and when he talked, the lips moved a little and you would have to clearly pay attention to hear him.

'I am so sorry for my sins. I pray that I am forgiven.'

'You have done a good confession, Missus Leona, but before your sins are truly forgiven, you must do something; and when you do, you achieve not just freedom but purity. You have to atone for this sin of yours, and there is no other way of doing that than going to the one you have wronged to ask for forgiveness.'

'What!' I made to sit up. Tears ran down my cheeks into the hollow of my neck. I tried to shift but could not.

'Do you want to sit, Missus?'

'No. I am fine, thank you.' Throughout the confession, he had helped me sit or lie intermittently.

'We can also see the Bishop if you like.' Then, he looked at me, remembering my condition, 'I can see him on your behalf, but I am sure he would say the same thing.'

'The Bishop?' I asked in surprise.

'Yes, young lady. I am frightened by the long story you narrated to me, from morning until evening. The most grievous is the sin of murder, Missus.'

'Father, I am deeply sorry for my sins.'

'You have to confess to the ones you've wronged, else you'd leave me wondering if you are truly sorry or you are only showing remorse because you are dying.'

'My sins weigh me down, Father. They kill me more than this affliction.'

'It is your conscience, Missus.'

I nodded, 'I know.'

'You thought deeply about killing this man before you

did. There were many reasons why you shouldn't have done it, but you chose the easier path to destruction.' I said nothing. 'Do you have regrets?'

'I regret everything I did. My regrets began the same night I poisoned my father-in-law, before he told me about Mum.'

'You have regrets because you discovered you poisoned him for no reason at all, that you'd allowed your father manipulate you. If you'd found out he was the one who killed your mother truly, would you have had regrets for poisoning your father-in-law?'

I did not know what to answer. I looked away.

'You are right, Father.'

The hand of the clock continued to break the silence, the noise of the running water in the bathroom too. We heard the squawking of chickens passing by the backyard.

'Do you not know that no human is allowed to take another's life, no matter what?'

'I was not a religious person, Father.'

'What is your own definition of religion or being religious? The way you understand it?' he asked.

'I understand religion as an institution that adheres to the principles of God and promotes God's work. I define someone being religious as someone who adheres to the principles of God and the stipulations of the religious bodies to whom the person is affiliated. If someone is a Muslim and adheres to the principles of Islam; then, I believe that person is religious. And these are the things that I lack. So, it implies that I was never religious. Father, I've harboured this shame for long, and it's killing me. I can't bear it any longer. That's why I invited you to hear my confession. I want to prepare myself for death. You can't see it, but I can. The process of viaticum—confessions and communion—that is what I want. This is my last confession as a living being. I will die soon. Don't deny me viaticum.'

'Do you contemplate suicide?'

'I don't know.' I coughed.

'The church frowns against that. Your life is not yours to take.'

'But the spirits that haunt me are strong. If the church can do anything at all to stop them, won't they? If my being religious can help me regain peace of mind; then, I would become religious even to the extent of becoming a fanatic.'

'That is why you need to let your husband know what you did.' He took my hands. 'Please.'

FIFTY

My illness turned the world upside down, especially Akinola's world. It was like he was hit by a moving train at a crossroad. For months, he rarely visited his office, travelling with me for this or that surgery for the poison had attacked my lungs and was eating them up. At some point, I needed assistance to pass urine and defecate. I was always in a diaper, with a catheter inserted into my body. Akinola would change the diaper himself and help throw away the urine bag when it was filled. He weakened with me, refusing to eat most of the times.

Akinola always found Beatrice in her room, sobbing. Sometimes, he whispered to me that he caught her crying in the kitchen, especially while preparing my meals. Most times, if she was with Osinachi, rocking and singing to him, he would catch her shedding tears but pretending to be strong. Beatrice loved me so much and when it was obvious that I was dying, she began to transfer the love to my son.

What was more difficult was that I was suffering from what killed her husband. She wondered if I got infected while caring for Chief Fegun Wale.

Sometimes she spoke out aloud, while shaking her head. 'My enemies have woken up before the cock to plan evil for me. Ah!'

Other times, she seemed lost for a moment, staring into oblivion with tears running down her eyes. She began to look odd most times, and on some mornings, she came out dressed in a purple headscarf on green polo, and a red long skirt. She was clearly losing touch with reality. While she poured herbal tea for me or served my meals, she soliloquised to herself, muttering as if she was going insane and talking about how unfair the world had become.

It was the sight of Beatrice—more than any other—that forced me to go to Enugu. I wanted to be alone, with only Madam Imo and Smart for comfort in my last days. I was not sure I was going to see Osinachi again. I was scared that if he saw me like this, the image would stick as he grew up.

The priest was waiting for me to make up my mind. When tears continued to run down my eyes without me saying anything, he shook his head.

'I will come back tomorrow, Missus. Can you tell them tonight about what you did? Call them on the phone and tell them what you did. You can do them a letter or email, but I want them to know that you did this thing; only then would

I know that you have prepared yourself for viaticum. I assure you, you will gain greater forgiveness.'

I shook my head with great difficulty. 'No, Father, I cannot. Please, can't you see this is difficult for me?' I turned the other way, covering my ears.

'Please.'

I could still hear him faintly.

'No.'

I heard the chair shuffle back and knew he was standing. I turned to face him.

'Please, don't go. Please.'

'I will come back in the morning, Missus.' He bent down towards me and rested his palm on my forehead. 'I want you to atone for this sin the best way. Only then will you be granted forgiveness.'

'Even if they don't forgive me?'

'Even if they don't. The most important thing is that you make them aware.'

I nodded.

He sneezed. 'Excuse me,' he said. 'You can ask your husband to come down, that you want to see him. Will he come?'

'He will… yes.'

'But you don't even need to. You can just tell him on the phone or send him a text message.'

I wondered what that would do to the love they had for me. They would hate me forever. Their memory of me would be an insult to them; my name would become the evillest they had ever heard. What of my dad? If they learnt that he put me up to it, Akinola could kill him. I had caused enough damage as it was already. I sneezed.

'I can come as well. I can be here to make the burden less for you.' He smiled at me reassuringly.

'I don't know if I can do it.'

He touched my head, staring at me, his eyes full of pity. He had now removed his confessional stole and folded it on top the small chalice box containing the communion.

'I want to tell you a story, Father.' He hesitated.

'Please, sit.'

He sat, reluctantly.

'Once, Grandpa and I visited his friend's village. It was late afternoon but the sun still blazed with intensity. I can still remember.' My eyes twinkled in happiness. It was nostalgic, these thoughts and memories about my beloved Sudan. 'On our way back to Khartoum, we bumped into some local rebels—there were a lot of small franchised rebel groups in Southern Sudan then. Most of them engaged in criminal activities, including kidnapping to survive. They jumped out from the road as we negotiated one pothole and another. They stopped the vehicle. They were carrying long machetes and clubs. It was near a bushy area where one could hide in the rocks without being seen. The weather was hot so Grandpa was wearing only his singlet. I wore my little top and combat trousers. On my neck was a golden necklace that Dad had given me. It glittered in the sun.

The criminals were about seven. All of them young boys between fifteen to their late twenties, their clothes almost rags. Only one of them had a gun. The one carrying a gun stood in front of the car, pointing the gun at Grandpa. The rest pulled us out and searched the car. They took all the clothes and the money we had. They took the biscuits and snacks in the pigeon-hole. They even collected his watch and his shoes. All the while he was talking with them calmly, trying to explain who he was. But they did not pay attention. "We are rebels. Everyone is our enemy, Mister!" the guy with the gun shouted at him.'

I coughed ceaselessly.

'Do you want me to get you help?' the priest asked.

I coughed some more and wiped the blood that had spurted out with a piece of scarf on the bed. It was already well-stained. Then, I continued.

'The rebels looked lean and hungry, but with strong arms. One of them approached me and looked me in the eyes. I was frightened as I stood by Grandpa, crying—stories of what they did to women and girls were in every mouth in Sudan. So, this rebel began to unhook my necklace, and I wailed. Grandpa shouted at him to stop. He stepped in between us and placed his hand on the rebel's chest.

"Leave her alone."

"Out!" the boy screamed.

"Leave her alone," Grandpa's words were more assertive now. "She is your sister, you know. She is one of you. She is but a child."

Grandpa turned to the others and asked that they tell the boy to stop. They laughed aloud, whistling and cajoling him. The boy pushed past him and pushed me to the ground and bent over me to unhook the necklace.

"Stop!" Grandpa screamed. I could hear his voice boom so loud. "Please."

"Fuck off, old man!" One of them pushed him.

Then, I heard two gunshots. I could still remember that I buried my face on the ground and for some time, thinking I was dead. The shot deafened my ears. I was in shock. Moments later, Grandpa took my trembling body into his arms and got me into the car and locked the door. I turned to look at the sides and saw two of the criminals sprawled on the soil, dead. One of them had a gun beside him and the other was the boy who was trying to collect my necklace. I touched my neck; the necklace was there.

Grandpa forced a smile. "Your necklace is safe, my princess."

I touched my neck again, while he cleaned my eyes with his handkerchief.

"Stop crying, my princess."

I nodded.

"I took care of them, my damsel. Be happy; they did not collect your... what's precious to you."

I touched my neck again. Then, I took it off and put it inside the pocket of my trousers. He drove off. There was blood on his singlet and on the left side of his face.'

The priest took a deep breath.

'He killed them because of a common necklace?'

'It wasn't a common necklace, Father.'

'Did he think they were going to rape you?'

'I don't think that was their intention.'

'Father, I have never told anyone of this incident, not even my mother. I would have told her back then, when we came to live in Nigeria and I began to have constant dreams and nightmares, but I couldn't.'

'Why couldn't you tell her? Because you promised your Grandpa not to?'

'No,' I shook my head. 'She'd always wondered if I was spending too much time with Grandpa and if it was a good thing. Telling her would have made her have regrets.'

FIFTY-ONE

'Thanks for telling me this, Missus.' He sat back. 'It explains a lot.' He nodded two, three times. 'It explains a lot.' He paused for a little while then asked, 'Did you ever see a psychologist, since you returned from Sudan?'

'A psychologist? No. Why?'

He scratched his head and was uncomfortable, 'Have you heard of post-traumatic stress disorder before? You know, I think that the things you experienced in Sudan affected you somewhat.'

I shook my head, 'No. No.'

The priest inhaled deeply. 'Leona, do you not know that if you die this night without confessing your sin to the ones you've hurt, even your soul will not have freedom?'

He drew nearer and held my two shoulders with his hands, squeezing gently. If he tried harder, he could break my bones.

'Please, do as I have instructed, tell them what you'd done. Please.'

'What of Agnes?'

'Do you forgive her?'

I remained silent. *Do I forgive her? How does one begin to forgive like that?*

The priest shook his head. 'Do you forgive her for poisoning you?'

Tears ran down my face, and I began to sob.

He looked confused, but after some time, he stood. 'I must leave, Missus, but I will be here tomorrow morning, and I expect to hear the great news. And you must forgive Agnes too. You can't expect to receive forgiveness when you can't forgive, yourself. May the Spirit of the Lord Jesus be with you, heal you, and bless your path, in the name of the Father and of the Son and of the Holy Spirit.'

I said nothing. I was sobbing. I was ruined, whichever way.

The priest said, 'Amen.' And after taking one last glance at me, he walked out the door.

I stared after him, at the door. It was wooden, painted chocolate colour, and had a basket affixed to it where Mum used to keep notes for me and Smart. The clock ticked. My heart was beating fast now, faster than the hand of the clock. The sound of my heart pounding was stronger and louder than that of the clock—at least to my ears. I raised my arms and stared at them, at the dark patches, the bluish veins and all. I was a waste. Life was a waste.

My son. I wished I could see my son. I wished I could see him now.

There was a gentle knock on the door. Smart walked in.

'Leona? Dear?'

I opened my eyes, and she rushed to me.

'My God, it was so long a meeting, and you must be drained now.' She sat on the bed. 'You've been with this priest since morning.'

I forced out a smile.

'Do you want your food now? Please, say yes. Eat something.'

She sat at the foot of the bed.

'Smart, I want to see my son.'

She looked surprised. I had warned her against allowing anyone to see me, including Akinola and Osinachi. It had hit Akinola so bad, and I knew he must be suffering so much.

'I will go down now and call Lagos.' She was sobbing but smiling at me.

'Thanks.'

She smiled at me. 'Oh, look at you. You look so beautiful, my girl.' She patted my forehead. 'Let me go now and make the call, then bring food.'

I nodded.

When I took the decision to relocate to Enugu, I called to inform Smart, and she jumped at the idea. She travelled to Lagos by night bus that same day I called her so she could help me move my things the next day. I had refused Akinola or Beatrice from accompanying me. I knew it was going to be the final journey and that it was easier I walked down the path alone. For how do you look at your loved ones in the eyes, knowing you would leave them soon? How do you be with them, eat with them, and talk with them, knowing you took someone special from them? How?

At the door, Smart turned, 'Leona, I want to tell you something.'

I beamed at her.

She said, 'You have always been beautiful. Even now. Just… just like your mother… just like Madam.'

I looked away. What is beauty if not fire? No matter how fierce it blazes, it dies down eventually. It was the first time in the over fifteen years I had known Smart that she would say something like this.

'Leona, in God's name, tell me please, will you see the priest tomorrow?'

I was surprised to hear that. Had he talked with her, telling her he was coming back?

'Please.'

'It is not… Smart, it is not if I will see him tomorrow. It is if I will be here.' I smiled broadly.

She walked back quickly and knelt by the bed. 'You will be here. I am certain of that.'

Now, instead of leaving, she sprawled on the ground and wept.

ACKNOWLEDGEMENTS

I began work on *Colours of Hatred* in 2009, while living alone in a flat in Enugu. Many people helped midwife its birth and many more worked to groom it into what it has become.

The lead character in this novel, Leona, is named in honour of my long time friend, Leona Taylor-Moore of Liberia.

I would like to thank the first readers; Nwamaka Okpo, Adaora Udenwe-Achi, Nnediuto Janice Okpo, Paul Liam and Davingson Onwuakpa for pointing out places that needed tightening.

I acknowledge and appreciate the editors who encouraged me to rework the story and made invaluable suggestions, especially Jazzmine Breary of Jacaranda Books UK, Amara Chimeka of Purple Shelves—you rock!—Tayo Keyede of Krosdot Consult and most specially, Lemya Shammat—Assistant Professor at King Saud University, Saudi Arabia, for many expert information beneficial to this work, especially with parts of the story set in Sudan.

I am grateful for the friendship of Jamie Nelson of Red Telescope Global, Chika Unigwe, Temitayo Olofinlua and C.N.C Asomugha—for encouraging me to never give up.

I appreciate you, Zukiswa Wanner for always giving me your time, no matter the hour, James Murua for being there always, Ikhide Ikheloa for the advice you give without knowing it—we share a lot in common, you know.

Thank you, Wale Okediran for providing me space at the Ebedi International Writers Residency in 2014 where this story became what it is now.

Thank you most specially, Nwamaka Okpo for your love, Osemome Ndebbio for your kindness, and Karen Jennings for always checking up on me from far away Brazil. Thanks to Kgauhelo Dube, queen of South Africa.

Thanks to the team at Parresia Publishing especially Azafi Omoluabi-Ogosi and Femi Ayodele.

Thanks to my colleagues and editors at The Village Square Journal for what we do together, Osemome Ndebbio, Amara Chimeka, Ngum Ngafor and Noma Sibanda.

Finally, I have been blessed with the gift of a wonderful family—my anchor. I say thank you to Chief Michael & Felicia Udenwe, Ifunanya, Ujunwa, Akudo, Oforbuike and Anna Udenwe, and to Ikenna Mbam, Chief Fabian Muoneke, Nduka Nwode, Ifeyinwa Nzeadi-Bello, Ngozi Obichukwu, Iquo DianaAbasi, Richard Inya, Chioma Iwunze-Ibiam, and Fr. Anacletus Ogbunkwu.

To everyone listed here, I pray that the good odds always be in your favour.

ABOUT THE AUTHOR

Obinna Udenwe is a Nigerian novelist and short story writer. He is the winner of the first edition of The Chinua Achebe Prize for Literature in 2021 for *Colours of Hatred* which was also a finalist for the 2021 NLNG Nigeria Prize for Literature. His first book, *Satans & Shaitans* won the ANA Prize for Prose Fiction 2015.

His short stories have won *The Prairie Schooner—Glenna Luschei Prize* 2020, *The Short Story is Dead Prize* 2016 and was a finalist in the *Prairie Schooner-Raz Shumaker Prize* 2020. His story, 'It Has to do with Emilia', was acquired for film & television in 2020 by Bridget Pickering at Bump films, shot in Yeoville, South Africa in 2021 and released in March 2022. His stories have appeared in *Gutter Magazine, Prairie*

Schooner, Munyori Literary Journal, The Village Square Journal, Fiction 365, Brittle Paper, ANA Review, Ake Review, Expound Magazine, The Kalahari Review, The Short Story is Dead anthology Vol., 1 & 2, and many more. He is the author of a short stories collection, The Widow Who Died With Flowers in Her Mouth, a chapbook, The Brief Story of the New Love Software, and the novella, *Holy Sex.*

He lives in Abakaliki in southern Nigeria where he works as a writer, engineer and farmer, and is very active in local politics.